MOL

THE CASE OF SIR ADAM BRAID

MARY 'MOLLY' THYNNE was born in 1881, a member of the aristocracy, and related, on her mother's side, to the painter James McNeil Whistler. She grew up in Kensington and at a young age met literary figures like Rudyard Kipling and Henry James.

Her first novel, *An Uncertain Glory*, was published in 1914, but she did not turn to crime fiction until *The Draycott Murder Mystery*, the first of six golden age mysteries she wrote and published in as many years, between 1928 and 1933. The last three of these featured Dr. Constantine, chess master and amateur sleuth *par excellence*.

Molly Thynne never married. She enjoyed travelling abroad, but spent most of her life in the village of Bovey Tracey, Devon, where she was finally laid to rest in 1950.

BY MOLLY THYNNE

MOLLY THYNNE

THE CASE OF SIR ADAM BRAID

With an introduction by
Curtis Evans

DEAN STREET PRESS

INTRODUCTION

ALTHOUGH British Golden Age detective novels are known for their depictions of between-the-wars aristocratic life, few British mystery writers of the era could have claimed (had they been so inclined) aristocratic lineage. There is no doubt, however, about the gilded ancestry of Mary "Molly" Harriet Thynne (1881-1950), author of a half-dozen detective novels published between 1928 and 1933. Through her father Molly Thynne was descended from a panoply of titled ancestors, including Thomas Thynne, 2nd Marquess of Bath; William Bagot, 1st Baron Bagot; George Villiers, 4th Earl of Jersey; and William Bentinck, 2nd Duke of Portland. In 1923, five years before Molly Thynne published her first detective novel, the future crime writer's lovely second cousin (once removed), Lady Mary Thynne, a daughter of the fifth Marquess of Bath and habitué of society pages in both the United Kingdom and the United States, served as one of the bridesmaids at the wedding of the Duke of York and his bride (the future King George VI and Queen Elizabeth). Longleat, the grand ancestral estate of the marquesses of Bath, remains under the ownership of the Thynne family today, although the estate has long been open to the public, complete with its famed safari park, which likely was the inspiration for the setting of *A Pride of Heroes* (1969) (in the US, *The Old English Peep-Show*), an acclaimed, whimsical detective novel by the late British author Peter Dickinson.

Molly Thynne's matrilineal descent is of note as well, for through her mother, Anne "Annie" Harriet Haden, she possessed blood ties to the English etcher Sir Francis Seymour Haden (1818-1910), her maternal grandfather, and the American artist James McNeill Whistler (1834-1903), a great-uncle, who is still renowned today for his enduringly evocative *Arrangement in Grey and Black no. 1* (aka "Whistler's Mother"). As a child Annie Haden, fourteen years younger than her brilliant Uncle James, was the subject of some of the artist's earliest etchings. Whistler's relationship with the Hadens later ruptured when his brother-in-law Seymour Haden became critical of what he deemed the younger artist's dissolute lifestyle. (Among other things Whistler had taken an artists' model as his mistress.) The conflict between the two men culminated in Whistler knocking Haden through a plate glass window during an altercation in Paris, after which the two men never spoke to one another again.

Molly Thynne grew up in privileged circumstances in Kensington, London, where her father, Charles Edward Thynne, a grandson of the second Marquess of Bath, held the position of Assistant Solicitor to His Majesty's Customs. According to the 1901 English census the needs of the Thynne family of four--consisting of Molly, her parents and her younger brother, Roger--were attended to by a staff of five domestics: a cook, parlourmaid, housemaid, under-housemaid and lady's maid. As an adolescent Molly spent much of her time visiting her Grandfather Haden's workroom, where she met a menagerie of artistic and literary lions, including authors Rudyard Kipling and Henry James.

Molly Thynne--the current Marquess has dropped the "e" from the surname to emphasize that it is pronounced "thin"--exhibited literary leanings of her own, publishing journal articles in her twenties and a novel, *The Uncertain Glory* (1914), when she was 33. *Glory*, described in one notice as concerning the "vicissitudes and love affairs of a young artist" in London and Munich, clearly must have drawn on Molly's family background, though one reviewer reassured potentially censorious middle-class readers that the author had "not over-accentuated Bohemian atmosphere" and in fact had "very cleverly diverted" sympathy away from "the brilliant-hued coquette who holds the stage at the commencement" of the novel toward "the plain-featured girl of noble character."

Despite good reviews for *The Uncertain Glory*, Molly Thynne appears not to have published another novel until she commenced her brief crime fiction career fourteen years later in 1928. Then for a short time she followed in the footsteps of such earlier heralded British women crime writers as Agatha Christie, Dorothy L. Sayers, Margaret Cole, Annie Haynes (also reprinted by Dean Street Press), Anthony Gilbert and A. Fielding. Between 1928 and 1933 there appeared from Thynne's hand six detective novels: *The Red Dwarf* (1928: in the US, *The Draycott Murder Mystery*), *The Murder on the "Enriqueta"* (1929: in the US, *The Strangler*), *The Case of Sir Adam Braid* (1930), *The Crime at the "Noah's Ark"* (1931), *Murder in the Dentist's Chair* (1932: in the US, *Murder in the Dentist Chair*) and *He Dies and Makes No Sign* (1933).

Three of Thynne's half-dozen mystery novels were published in the United States as well as in the United Kingdom, but none of them were reprinted in paperback in either country and the books rapidly fell out of public memory after Thynne ceased writing detective fiction in 1933, despite the fact that a 1930 notice speculated that "[Molly Thynne] is perhaps the best woman-writer of detective stories we know." The highly discerning author and crime fiction reviewer Charles Williams, a friend of C.S. Lewis and J.R.R. Tolkien and editor of Oxford University Press, also held Thynne in high regard, opining that Dr. Constantine, the "chess-playing amateur detective" in the author's *Murder in the Dentist's Chair,* "deserves to be known with the Frenches and the Fortunes" (this a reference to the series detectives of two of the then most highly-esteemed British mystery writers, Freeman Wills Crofts and H.C. Bailey). For its part the magazine *Punch* drolly cast its praise for Thynne's *The Murder on the "Enriqueta"* in poetic form.

> *The Murder on the "Enriqueta"* is a recent
> thriller by Miss Molly Thynne,
> A book I don't advise you, if you're busy, to begin.

It opens very nicely with a strangling on a liner
Of a shady sort of passenger, an out-bound
    Argentiner.
And, unless I'm much mistaken, you will find
    yourself unwilling
To lay aside a yarn so crammed with situations
    thrilling.
(To say nothing of a villain with a gruesome taste
    in killing.)

There are seven more lines, but readers will get the amusing gist of the piece from the quoted excerpt. More prosaic yet no less praiseful was a review of *Enriqueta* in *The Outlook*, an American journal, which promised "excitement for the reader in this very well written detective story … with an unusual twist to the plot which adds to the thrills."

Despite such praise, the independently wealthy Molly Thynne in 1933 published her last known detective novel (the third of three consecutive novels concerning the cases of Dr. Constantine) and appears thereupon to have retired from authorship. Having proudly dubbed herself a "spinster" in print as early as 1905, when she was but 24, Thynne never married. When not traveling in Europe (she seems to have particularly enjoyed Rome, where her brother for two decades after the First World War served as Secretary of His Majesty's Legation to the Holy See), Thynne resided at Crewys House, located in the small Devon town of Bovey Tracey, the so-called "Gateway to the Moor." She passed away in 1950 at the age of 68 and was laid to rest after services at Bovey Tracey's Catholic Church of the Holy Spirit. Now, over sixty-five years later, Molly Thynne's literary legacy happily can be enjoyed by a new generation of vintage mystery fans.

Curtis Evans

CHAPTER I

Sir Adam Braid rose stiffly from his comfortable seat by the fire and hobbled across the room to the massive bureau which stood against the opposite wall, well outside the radius of the heat from the glowing, heaped-up coals. And, on his way, he gave vent to his opinion of the weather, importunate relatives, his man Johnson, and life in general with the venomous gusto of an ill-tempered old gentleman who has just discovered a new, and perfectly legitimate, grievance.

As he let himself down carefully into his swivel chair and picked up the letter which had served to disturb both his physical and mental serenity, he noted, with a certain bitter satisfaction, that the draught that played on the nape of his neck was even more piercing than he had expected—a sure sign that Johnson, as usual, had omitted to shut the door into the kitchen.

He drew the letter from its envelope and glanced through it, in a mood that augured ill for the innocent writer, who was, even then, waiting in suspense for an answer. And as he read, his eyes gleaming maliciously under the heavy grey eyebrows and the ill-tempered lines at the corners of his thin lips cutting deeper and deeper into the thick, sallow skin, he was already, at the back of his mind, composing the letter to his solicitor which should put an end, irrevocably, to the hopes of the one relative he possessed who did not actively dislike him.

"Damned impertinence!" he muttered, framing his thoughts aloud, after the manner of the old and self-centred. "Thinks I'm made of money, eh? Might have known it. You give an inch and they take an ell! All alike, the whole lock, stock, and barrel of them. Well, she had her chance and she's lost it! 'Advance the money you are leaving me,' eh? And what if there is no money, miss?"

He drew a sheet of paper towards him and began to write, the venom in his eyes deepening as he saw the words take form in his small, neat script, the writing of a man to whom a pen or pencil is the most natural form of expression. He had reached the bottom of the page and was about to turn it when the draught from the door smote him cruelly on that part of his scalp where the hair grew thinnest.

He raised his head and bellowed, a surprisingly robust sound to come from so old and shrunken a figure.

His voice had barely died away before he heard the soft click of a latch, followed by a discreet tap at the study door.

"Come in, confound you!" roared the old man.

The door opened and Johnson appeared.

"Did you call, sir?"

His voice was smooth and his manner perfectly respectful, but beneath the surface lurked a veiled insolence that suggested that he both disliked and despised his master.

Sir Adam swung his chair round and faced him. If Johnson had had imagination he might have compared him to an old, ill-conditioned, shaggy terrier, his few remaining teeth bared to bite; but Johnson's mind was intent on ending the interview as soon as possible and getting out of sight and sound of his master into the congenial atmosphere of the bar of "The Nag's Head."

"Of course I called! What did you think I was doing? Shut that kitchen door! This room's like an ice-house!"

"It is shut, Sir Adam," answered the man blandly.

"Exactly. I heard you shut it a second ago. God knows how long it's been open. See that it stays shut."

"Yes, Sir Adam."

Johnson waited, his long-suffering gaze fixed on the pattern of the wall-paper over the bureau.

"Hum. Make up the fire and give me the *Times*. The *Times*, you fool, not the *Mail*."

The old man literally snatched the paper from him and ran his eye down the page. It was his boast that he could still read without spectacles.

"I thought so," he muttered. "Switch on the wireless and bring me the earphones."

He heaved himself on to his feet, limped back to his big armchair by the fire, and settled himself comfortably.

Johnson turned on the valves of the wireless and brought the earphones across the room. Sir Adam adjusted them carefully and sat listening, his face, for the first time, exhibiting an expression of comparative tranquillity.

Johnson bent once more over the fire, then straightened himself and stood waiting.

With a look of intense annoyance, Sir Adam removed the earphones.

"What is it?" he snapped.

"Any letters for post, Sir Adam?" asked the man imperturbably.

Sir Adam glanced uncertainly at the bureau on which lay his half-finished letter. For a second he hesitated, then the faint sound of music came from the earphones he had dropped across the arm of his chair. He readjusted them hastily over his ears.

"No," he mumbled. "Finish it later. And see that you leave the kitchen door shut when you go out."

Johnson departed, and stretching out his feet to the warm blaze of the fire, Sir Adam gave himself up to the enjoyment of Schubert's "Unfinished" Symphony.

A few minutes later a far more human Johnson, clad in a heavy overcoat, and unlighted cigarette between his lips and exasperation plainly written on his face, emerged from his bedroom. He went into the kitchen, picked up a beer jug from the dresser, and came out again, shutting the door audibly behind him. Then he made his way out of the flat, pausing for a moment on the landing to light his cigarette, and ran down the stone staircase and out into the dank November night.

As he passed through the main door of Romney Chambers the clock of the church that stood at the end of the street chimed the half-hour. Six-thirty. He glanced involuntarily up at the windows of the flat he had just left. It was in darkness save for a knife-edge of light where the heavy curtains in the study did not quite meet. For a moment he pictured the old man sitting there, alone with his music, in the otherwise empty flat, and, for the first time since he had entered Sir Adam's service three years before, felt an inclination to turn back and forgo the pleasantest half-hour of his working day. The impulse passed, and he hurried on in the direction of "The Nag's Head," stopping for a moment to buy an evening paper at the little shop at the corner of the road.

Mr. Ling, the proprietor, glanced up with a friendly nod, as he picked up his paper and threw a penny on the counter.

"Easy to see where he's goin' to," he remarked facetiously to his only other customer, a labouring man who, both elbows on the counter, was spelling out the winners in the stop-press news with the aid of a grimy forefinger.

The man grinned.

"I'll lay 'e'll 'ave a couple afore gettin' 'is little jug filled," he said; "and then a pint with 'is supper after 'e gets 'ome. Some people don't 'alf 'ave luck. You wait till you've got a wife and 'alf a dozen kids, my son!"

Johnson's mouth twitched, then closed stubbornly, as if he had had a mind to answer and had then thought better of it.

With a nod to the proprietor he left the shop, and less than ten minutes later was deep in the discussion of that most absorbing and unfruitful of all topics, racing, with the barman of "The Nag's Head."

He had hardly disappeared round the corner when a woman who had been standing in the doorway of a block of flats opposite to that which he had just left, emerged on to the pavement. Carefully avoiding the circle of light thrown by the street lamp, she stood in the shadow, scanning the windows of the flats above that of Sir Adam Braid. They were both in darkness, and with a little sigh of exasperation she turned to re-enter the friendly shelter of the doorway. As she did so, her attention was caught by the movements of a man, who, like herself, had been lurking in the shadows between the lamps. She had noticed him more than once during her vigil, and now she watched him, with the casual interest generated by boredom, as he slipped furtively across the road and into the doorway of Romney Chambers. Driven out of her shelter by the return of the porter in whose doorway she had been standing, she moved farther up the street, still idly watching Romney Chambers, in the upper windows of which she seemed to take so keen an interest. Thus it was that though she saw a second man enter the flats and actually noted the fact that the two men had gone in within five minutes of each other, she was not standing close enough to distinguish either their faces or the clothes they were wearing. Neither could she tell which of the two men it was that came out some two minutes later and almost ran down the street and round the corner. After that nearly ten minutes elapsed before the other man appeared, and mechanically her brain registered the fact that his gait was less hurried, suggesting that of a man who has been about a more legitimate business.

It was owing partly, no doubt, to the fact that she was tired and bored with waiting and that she welcomed any incident, no matter how puerile, which might serve to divert her attention, that the movements of these shadowy figures remained so clearly in her mind. Also her own desire to remain unobserved would render her specially sensitive to anything furtive in the actions of others. The fact remains that, later, she was able to give a fairly accurate account of the times at which these people, whose appearance she could not even describe, had gone in and out of Romney Chambers between the hours of six-thirty and seven-five. The entrance of one, the third and last, she was able to place to a minute, for the church clock had just struck seven when she saw the figure of a woman—a girl, judging by the lithe freedom with which she moved—turn the corner, pass down the street, and enter Romney Chambers.

From then onwards, any one who went into the building did so without her knowledge. For, tired of waiting, she strolled to the end of the street, still taking pains not to linger within the radius of the light of the street lamps.

It was close on half-past seven when one of the two people for whom she had been waiting swung round the corner and passed her, walking so quickly that she almost failed to recognize him.

With a low cry that brought him to a standstill she hurried up to him and gripped his arm.

CHAPTER II

ROMNEY CHAMBERS was a less imposing edifice than its name suggested, and, in fact, cut a poor figure compared with the row of majestic "mansions" which faced it on the other side of the road. These, equipped with lifts and uniformed hall porters, were the real thing, as their rents testified, whereas the origin of Romney Chambers was written all over its unassuming frontage. Originally one of those unwieldy large houses which spring up sometimes in unfashionable neighbourhoods, it had stood unlet for several years after the war. Then an enterprising builder had seen its possibilities, bought it from its relieved owner at a price which, only a few years before, would have been considered exorbitant, and converted its four stories into four passably convenient flats. In the basement he had installed a caretaker and his wife, the former acting as a sort of agent and rent-collector for this and other property he had acquired in the neighbourhood, while his wife "did for" such of the tenants as cared to avail themselves of her services. The rents were moderate, as rents go, and the position not inconvenient, King's Road, Chelsea, running across one end of the street and Fulham Road across the other. The erection of the row of mansions opposite Romney Chambers had served to lift Shorncliffe Street out of its original squalor, and for a road lying between two main thoroughfares, it was very little troubled with traffic.

On the whole the house provided comfortable and sufficiently reasonable quarters for people who were willing to forgo the conveniences of lifts and elaborately-appointed bathrooms, with the result that the Romney Chambers flats seldom changed hands, and their tenants were perhaps on more friendly terms and knew more about each other's movements than would have been the case in a more pretentious type of building.

Thus it was that when Everard Webb, the tenant of the ground-floor flat, having addressed and stuck down the last of a neat pile of envelopes, discovered that he had run out of stamps, his thoughts naturally turned to Johnson, old Sir Adam Braid's man, who invariably left the flats punctually at six-thirty to fetch his supper beer. If he could catch him on his way out, Johnson, he knew, would be willing to drop into the post office and see to the stamping and posting of the letters.

He looked at his watch and realized, to his annoyance, that he was too late. Johnson must have left five minutes ago.

Gathering his letters together he rose from his chair.

"Bella!" he called.

A plump, middle-aged lady appeared in the doorway. She also carried a pile of letters in her hand.

"You might put these with yours," she began, "and, if you've got a stamp, I'll write to Ellen. I've just used my last."

Her brother groaned.

"I was going to ask if you'd got any," he said. "I've missed Johnson. Now I suppose I shall have to go all the way to the post office."

"Not with that throat of yours," she answered decisively. "You ought not to have gone to the office at all to-day. Surely somebody in the building has got some stamps."

Webb considered the matter.

"Dr. Gilroy won't be back for some time yet, and I don't particularly want to ask a favour of the Smiths. A pity they ever came here. Not the sort of people we've been accustomed to in the Chambers at all."

She nodded eagerly. They were born gossips, these two.

"There have been one or two little things I've noticed about her," she said vaguely. "Mrs. Adams tells me that Adams isn't very satisfied about them either. I shouldn't wonder if he spoke to the landlord. After all, as caretaker, he's responsible, in a way."

"That leaves Sir Adam," said her brother thoughtfully. "Unless I wait till Johnson comes back. And the worst of Sir Adam is that you never know where you are with him. Last time I saw him he was positively affable; but he's capable—quite capable—of biting my head off if he's in the mood."

Miss Webb glanced apprehensively at her brother's small, tidy features. It seemed almost as if she were taking Sir Adam's cannibalistic propensities literally.

"Then wait till Johnson comes back," she suggested. "He's never more than half an hour."

Webb hesitated. The brother and sister seldom made any move, even of the most trivial importance, without giving it what they called "due consideration."

"On the other hand," he said, "if Johnson hasn't got any stamps he may have to go out for them, and apart from the fact that I very much dislike making use of another man's servant, the post office may be shut by then."

"Then I should just run up and ask Sir Adam. After all, he may be in one of his pleasanter moods."

Webb rose.

"I think I'll risk it," he decided. "Yes, I think I'll risk it."

He went out, leaving his own flat door open behind him, and trotted up the stairs to the next landing.

Outside Sir Adam Braid's flat he hesitated. A timid, peace-loving little man, he particularly disliked what he called "unpleasantnesses," and there was no doubt that Sir Adam could be extremely unpleasant when he chose.

Then his ear caught the sound of a man's voice, Sir Adam's presumably, judging by its acerbity, coming from the other side of the door of the flat.

He was on the point of retreat, reflecting that it would be awkward to break in on the old man if he were entertaining a guest. Then his native curiosity overcame his prudence. After all, it would be interesting to see Sir Adam's visitor, and it would give him something to impart to his sister on his return to his own flat.

He pushed the bell tentatively and waited.

No notice was taken of his summons. Instead, Sir Adam continued to entertain his guest in a voice that increased in volume each moment. Evidently he was working himself into one of his frequent rages, and Webb's hand, raised to ring again, fell to his side. This was no moment in which to disturb the old man. He was about to turn away and descend the stairs when his curiosity was further aroused by the sound of a second voice, as violent in its way as that which had preceded it, but pitched on a higher note. Apparently Sir Adam, for once, was getting as good as he gave. Webb listened eagerly. Here was a situation after Bella's own heart, for Sir Adam's visitor, with whom he was apparently having an appalling row, was a woman!

Webb waited, entranced. He could not distinguish what the woman was saying, and concluded that the disputants were in Braid's study, probably with the door open. He waited until the woman's voice faltered and dissolved into hysterical sobbing, then, becoming suddenly aware of his own undignified position, turned and made his way hastily downstairs.

As he entered his own flat he looked at his watch. It was just on six-fifty-five, and Johnson, he knew, usually returned punctually on the stroke of seven.

He was standing in the window of his sitting-room, listening to his sister's interested comments on the little drama he had surprised, when he saw Sir Adam's man coming down the road. He consulted his watch again.

"Johnson's late," he said. "It's close on ten past seven. The post office will be shut."

"Not the one in Fulham Road," his sister reminded him. "I daresay he won't mind running round there, if you ask him. I wonder if he knows who the lady is with Sir Adam? She may have come before he left. You might try, delicately, to find out, but don't let him think we're asking out of curiosity."

Webb nodded as he hurried to the door. He had every intention of pumping Johnson on his own account.

He caught him in the hall just as he entered the main door. It stood open, as usual, and Webb shivered as the cold air struck him. He proffered his request. Johnson proved only too ready to oblige.

"I've a couple of shillings worth upstairs, sir," he said—"if you'll wait a moment."

But Webb was not going to miss the opportunity of a word with Sir Adam's man.

"I'll go with you," he volunteered. "It'll save your coming down again. I'd better wait on the landing, though. Your master seems to have a visitor."

Johnson, who had reached the foot of the stairs, stopped dead and stared at him.

"A visitor, sir? He was alone when I went out."

"He's got a lady with him now, at any rate. I went up just now to ask if he could oblige me with a stamp and I could hear him, ah, talking to her, so I decided not to disturb him."

Johnson stood gazing at him, the light from the hall lamp overhead shining full on his face. It struck Webb, for the first time, what a pasty, unhealthy colour the man had. No doubt his life with the cantankerous old man was not a bed of roses.

"As a matter of fact," he explained, his voice sinking to a significant whisper, "I could not help hearing. I'm afraid they were having something of an argument and their voices were a good deal raised. I think the lady must have said something to upset Sir Adam."

Johnson's hand jerked suddenly, and the beer he was carrying slopped over the edge of the jug and ran down the side on to his coat. His astonished gaze was on Webb's face.

"There was no lady there when I went out," he said incredulously. "Are you sure you weren't mistaken, sir?"

"Certain. It was a lady's voice, and she seemed, well, considerably upset. Knowing that Sir Adam can be a little hasty at times, I thought it better to come away."

Without another word Johnson turned and mounted the stairs, Webb following close on his heels. Outside the door of Sir Adam's flat they paused and listened, but they could hear nothing.

"She may have left while I was downstairs waiting for you," suggested Webb.

Johnson took a latchkey from his pocket and let himself into the flat.

"If you'll wait a minute, sir, I'll fetch the stamps," he said—"unless you'll step in and see Sir Adam?"

Webb declined hastily. After what he had heard through the door he had no desire to meet the old man.

He watched Johnson go down the passage to his room. Except for the sound of his discreet movements the flat was silent as the grave. Evidently the visitor had departed. From where Webb stood he had a view of the entire length of the passage, which ran through the centre of the flat, and could see Johnson emerge from his room with the stamps in his hand. To reach Webb he had to pass his master's bedroom, and the little man, waiting rather nervously on the threshold, saw him turn his head and glance casually in at the open door as he went by.

After that things happened so swiftly that Webb was never quite sure of their exact sequence.

It began with a startled cry from Johnson, who swung round and darted into the bedroom, only to reappear immediately. Whether Johnson called him, or whether his own movement was instinctive, Webb could never afterwards remember, but, a second later, he found himself standing in the doorway of Sir Adam's bedroom, his heart beating sickeningly somewhere in the region of his throat and his eyes riveted on the ghastly face of the old man, who lay on the floor, half-way between the bed and the fireplace.

Johnson was already kneeling by his master, staring stupidly at his own hand, which, a second before, had lain on the old man's shoulder. It was wet and sticky with blood.

Webb made an effort to speak, but no sound came. He cleared his throat and tried again.

"Is—is he dead?" he whispered, though instinct told him the question was futile.

Johnson nodded. He was trying to get his handkerchief out of his pocket with his left hand, the right, with its horrible red stain, held stiffly in front of him.

Webb, in spite of his curiosity, was seized with an intense desire to get away from this room.

"I—I'd better fetch some one—" he began uncertainly, turning towards the front door.

Johnson rose and came towards him. He had found his handkerchief and was wiping his fingers. Webb's eyes fell on the handkerchief and he felt suddenly sick. He turned away so as not to see it, fixing his gaze resolutely on the front door. As he did so a woman appeared in the opening, having, apparently, come from the staircase leading to the floor above. She paused irresolutely in the doorway, and Webb stared at her, dimly aware that Johnson was speaking.

"We ought to search the flat," he was saying. "Some one may have got in——"

"There's a lady there," broke in Webb. "She mustn't come in here."

He heard an exclamation from Johnson, who brushed past him and hurried towards the waiting figure in the doorway.

The name, "Miss Braid," reached Webb's ears, and he stood, hesitating, his eyes steadily averted from the bedroom, while Johnson engaged in a low conversation with the lady. Then, followed by her, he approached Webb.

"This is Sir Adam's granddaughter, Miss Braid," he explained. "If you'll stay with her, I'll just run through the flat. Perhaps you'll keep guard in the passage, sir, in case any one tries to get out."

Webb would have infinitely preferred to get out himself; but he was a chivalrous little man, and it was plainly his duty to stand by the lady.

He tried to interpose his body between her and the sight that awaited her inside the bedroom, but he was too late. She was already in the doorway, her hand on the jamb, staring at the dead man. Then, as the full force of Johnson's last words came home to him, he swung round to meet the possible onslaught of a desperate man intent on escape, and as he did so he realized with a tremor that he was not cast in a heroic mould.

But there was to be no further call upon his courage, and his tightened muscles relaxed as he saw Johnson emerge from the kitchen. The man's face was livid, and he did not look as if he had relished his job.

"If there was any one here, he's gone, sir," he said "I've been through every room in the flat."

"He must have slipped out while I was downstairs," suggested Webb. "There was certainly some one here when I rang the bell."

He paused, puzzled.

"But it was a woman's voice that I heard," he cried. "A woman couldn't have—"

His voice died away.

"It may have been a fit," said Johnson shakily. "The blood's coming from his mouth."

"It's on the carpet too, under his head."

The two men turned sharply at the sound of Miss Braid's voice, and Webb found himself observing her intelligently for the first time.

She was kneeling by her grandfather's side, her right hand on his forehead, and he could see that the cuff of her sleeve was soaked with blood. He realized, for the first time, that she was quite young and very good to look at, in spite of the lack of colour in her cheeks and the distress in her eyes. But, shocked though she was, she had her nerves well in hand, and her voice, when she spoke again, was even, though, so low that she had to repeat the sentence before the two men realized that she was calling them.

"Can you help me?" she said. "I want to lift his head."

Johnson hurried to her side and bent over the body. Webb noticed that, of the two, Miss Braid's hands were the steadier as, together, they lifted the dead man's head gently, and tried to ascertain if it had been injured in the fall.

Webb cleared his throat.

"As a matter of fact," he volunteered, rather pompously, "I fancy we ought not to touch anything until the police have been. Perhaps it would be wiser—"

He realized that he was speaking to deaf ears. Sir Adam Braid was once more lying as he had first seen him, and his granddaughter was staring across his body at Johnson with horror in her eyes.

"The blood's coming from a cut at the back of his neck," she said slowly. "He couldn't have done that in falling. Some one must have—"

Then, as she realized the full force of her own argument, her eyes became fixed, and for a moment her body swayed ominously.

Johnson, who seemed incapable of speech, sprang to his feet and went to her side. He slipped his arm under hers and helped her to rise.

Supported by Johnson she stood looking down at her grandfather. The dead man's features had relaxed into a serenity that gave a value to the intellectual forehead and sensitive, well-cut mouth, which even the bloodstain that ran from the lips and over the chin could not mar. Adam Braid was nobler in death than he had ever been in life, and for the moment all that she and hers had suffered at the dead man's hands was wiped out, and she remembered only her kinship to the man lying murdered at her feet.

"That he should have died like that!" she cried passionately. "An old man who couldn't even defend himself!"

Johnson drew her gently towards the door.

"Come away, miss," he said. "There's nothing you can do here."

Webb made another effort to assert himself.

"We really ought to send for the police, you know," he insisted nervously, "and a doctor. I can telephone—"

Miss Braid seemed to notice him for the first time. Her indignation at the mode of her grandfather's death had steadied her nerves and she caught eagerly at his suggestion.

"There's a man at Scotland Yard, an old friend of my father's," she cried. "I know he'd come if I could get hold of him."

"I think we ought to notify the local police first," said Webb, as he led the way down the passage. Now that he was out of sight of the bedroom he was experiencing a distinct thrill at the thought of being, as it were, in the heart of the drama. "I'll ring up the police station, and then, if you'd care to call up your friend, Miss Braid, the telephone is at your service."

He bustled her downstairs to his flat, introduced her to his sister, and leaving her to a cross-fire of questions from that voluble and deeply interested lady, glued himself to the telephone. Though he was a little hurt at the calmness with which the inspector in charge received his news, and never quite forgave him for hanging up the receiver just as his recital was getting into full swing, he had the satisfaction of knowing that his evidence was bound to be called for sooner or later.

Johnson, left alone in the flat overhead, stood in the doorway of Sir Adam's bedroom, staring blankly after the departing figures of Webb and Miss Braid. He seemed too stunned to be capable of any definite action. Every now and then his nervous gaze would travel over his shoulder into the room behind him, and once he took a step in the direction of the still open front door as though to shut it, only to abandon the idea and fall back into his old position.

He had been standing thus for perhaps five minutes when the thing happened that made him clutch, in momentary panic, at the door to save himself from falling.

For the silence which had begun to weigh like lead on his tortured nerves was broken with an abruptness that would have startled even the most phlegmatic hearer.

The sound came from the study, the room which, only a short time before, he had declared to be empty, and, his first consternation over, it seemed almost as if the voice that spoke was one he recognized and might even have expected to hear.

With a furtive glance in the direction of the front door he hurried across the passage and into the study.

CHAPTER III

WHILE MISS BRAID was telephoning to New Scotland Yard, Webb, standing in the bow window of his flat, watching for the arrival of the police, gave his sister an account of what had happened. She was essentially a kind-hearted woman, and her first feeling was one of genuine pity for the old man, whom she had disliked heartily during his lifetime, and sympathy for his granddaughter. Then her practical mind reasserted itself.

"Does his money go to her, do you think?" she whispered, with a backward glance at the girl. "Though he lived so quietly, he must have been a rich man for an artist. His drawings used to fetch big prices."

"I don't know. He seemed to have no relations, and certainly never spoke of any. I don't remember ever to have seen her before—do you?"

His sister shook her head decisively.

"If she'd been here often I should have seen her," she declared, and she spoke nothing but the truth. Very little that took place in Romney Chambers escaped her eye. "There's Dr. Gilroy, Everard, a little earlier than usual too! Don't you think you'd better run and meet him? After all, he is a doctor."

But Everard was already on his way. He had reached the stage when his whole being cried out for an audience.

He caught Dr. Gilroy as he was swinging up the stairs, two steps at a time. At the sound of Webb's agitated summons he stopped and peered down at him through the thick lenses of his glasses with kindly grey eyes that held a twinkle of amusement in their depths. He had always regarded Webb as one of Nature's more humorous efforts, and had, more than once, amused himself quietly by baffling the little man's insatiable curiosity.

"Anything wrong?" he asked pleasantly.

The laughter died out of his eyes as Webb imparted his news.

"I'd better have a look at the poor old chap," he said. "But it doesn't sound as if there was anything I could do. Johnson's there, you say?"

He found Johnson standing in the doorway of the flat and ran a professional eye over him.

"Sorry to hear this, Johnson," he said. "Nasty shock, eh? Which way? The bedroom? Right. Don't you come if you don't feel like it."

Johnson gulped. He was evidently badly shaken.

"You'll—you'll find him in there, sir," he muttered.

He hesitated; then, as though his feet carried him involuntarily in the direction in which he least wished to go, followed slowly in the wake of the doctor, and stood watching him while he made his examination.

It did not last long.

"Must have died almost at once," said Gilroy, as he rose to his feet. "From the look of it, that stab went clean through the artery. Mr. Webb tells me that he's sent for the police. Anything missing?"

"I haven't looked, sir. What with the shock of finding him—"

Gilroy nodded sympathetically.

"Don't blame you. Got any whisky handy?"

Johnson led him into the study and produced a bottle and glass from the cupboard. Gilroy poured out a stiff dose and handed it to him.

"Drink this," he said. "You look as if you needed it, and you'll have a busy quarter of an hour when the police arrive. I shall be upstairs if they want to see me."

He turned to leave the flat, only to be met in the doorway by Webb and the local inspector of police.

"I hear you've examined the body, sir," said the latter. "The police surgeon will be here in a moment, but I'd like to hear if you've come to any conclusion."

Gilroy shook his head.

"I only made a very cursory examination," he answered. "Sir Adam was stabbed in the back of the neck, and probably died within two minutes. From the look of things, I should say that the carotid artery has been severed. But your own man will be able to tell you more."

Gilroy gave the inspector his name and qualifications, adding the information that he had given up his practice, and was engaged in research work at the Lister Institute in Chelsea.

"By the way," he said, as he turned to leave, "that man of Sir Adam's has had a nasty jar. I understand that he was the first to find the body. I've given him a dose of his master's whisky, and he should be all right, but you might go easy with him."

"I shan't trouble him much," said the inspector, "except to find out if anything's missing. He'll have to see the detective-inspector, though, when he comes."

Gilroy halted.

"Who's that?" he asked. "I know some of the people at the Yard."

"I understand that Chief Detective-Inspector Fenn is coming down with the superintendent," answered the inspector, rather stiffly. "He will probably be in charge of the case."

People with friends at the Yard were apt to be a nuisance, hanging about and asking questions, instead of answering them. Gilroy's reception of the news only served to increase his gloom.

"Fenn? I'm glad he's on it. Tell him from me that there's cold supper and as much beer as he can drink waiting for him upstairs as soon as he's through with his job here, will you?"

He peered at the other, and catching the look in his eye, gave a low chuckle.

"Cheer up, inspector," he said blithely. "I'm not going to make your life a burden. My own job keeps me too busy! Bacteria hunting's my line. I'd like to see old Fenn, though, if he's not too busy running after his murderer."

He strolled up to his flat, gave a glance into his little dining-room to make sure that his charwoman had laid a large enough cold supper for two, and then spread out his papers and settled down to work.

Within five minutes he had completely forgotten, not only his invitation to Fenn, but the tragedy that had occasioned it. Life was full of interest for him just then. For the past year he had been doing work he really liked, which in itself was pure bliss after the drudgery of a poor and certainly not re-munerative practice; and now at last it seemed as though the experiments on which he had been engaged for the last six months were about to bear fruit. So absorbed was he that he did not stir from his table until the sound of the front door bell brought him to the realization of his own hunger and the fact that it was past eleven o'clock.

He opened the door. On the other side he found a thickset, stolid-looking individual, who held a hard felt hat in one hand and thoughtfully stroked a grizzled moustache with the other.

"Am I too late?" he asked.

Gilroy stared at him.

"Good lord, it's Fenn!" he exclaimed. "And I asked you to supper! My good chap, you've come just in time."

Fenn's good-natured smile broadened into a grin at the sight of the untouched food on the table.

"Thanks," he said, "but I fed a couple of hours ago. If I didn't know you so well I might be afraid you had waited for me, but I'm willing to bet that the thought of food had simply clean gone out of your mind. I'll watch you eat, though."

"Then you'll watch something worth seeing," announced Gilroy, pouring out a couple of glasses of beer. "I'm starving. Good thing you came when you did. You'll hardly believe it, but I'd completely forgotten that poor old fellow downstairs and everything to do with him. And I liked the old chap, too, in spite of his infernal bad temper. He was a distinguished man, you know, in his own line. And he was still doing un-commonly good work."

He fumbled for his tobacco pouch, and threw it across the table to Fenn before settling down to his supper.

Fenn took a good pull at his beer and began filling his pipe.

"That's the sort of thing I want to hear," he said. "It's a bit of luck for me that you should be living here, Robert. Who are the people who live in these flats and what do they do?"

Gilroy glanced at him with a twinkle in his eye.

"You'll get all that, with frills on, from little Webb downstairs," he suggested.

Fenn laughed.

"I've had it, thanks. It's the frills I object to. And the worst of it is, that those incurably inquisitive people very often do have information of real importance, only it's so swamped by their own observations and theories that one's apt to miss it. I know exactly what Webb and his sister think of all the people in this house, including the caretaker and most of his relations. What I want is a little first-hand information about them."

"I'll give you what I can; but I'm out a lot, you know, and neighbourliness is not one of my vices. There are the Smiths, on the top floor, just above this. He's a quiet sort of fellow with a delicate-looking little wife. Then there's Webb and his sister. You've seen him, and that should be enough. Works in an architect's office. Most harmless little chap that ever lived. Even that infernal curiosity of his is largely due to genuine kind-heartedness. The same applies to the sister. What did they tell you about me, by the way?"

Fenn chuckled.

"Quite a lot that you don't know yourself. You keep very late hours, but there's no reason to believe that you're anything but sober when you come in, among other interesting items. I'll let you have the rest some day. Give me any points you can on Sir Adam."

Gilroy considered.

"I can't help you much there. You can get all I know from the newspapers. He was about the best known black-and-white man in England. Moved out of his studio about ten years ago and came here. He used to do a lot of book illustration and that sort of thing, but I fancy he'd given that up.

I know he exhibited a series of drawings of London about a year ago, and sold the lot in the first two days of the show, so he was still working. Sort of old chap to work till he dropped, I should imagine. He had a kind of studio in the flat, and he took me in once and showed me a lot of his stuff. He lived very simply, and the caretaker's wife and that chap Johnson looked after him between them."

Fenn looked up sharply.

"What do you make of Johnson, by the way?"

"Never thought much about him. He's an obliging enough fellow. Ready to take in a parcel for one or anything of that sort. I should say he led a dog's life with the old man; but he looked after him well, I believe, and he certainly never complained to me: a quiet, secretive sort of fellow."

"His nerves are badly on the hop now," commented Fenn.

"Small blame to him. He's not a cold-blooded policeman. You may be accustomed to clearing up the mess after a murder; it's probably a new sensation to him."

"All the same, I don't understand his manner. I've got an impression the man's more frightened than shocked. Was he fond of his master, do you suppose?"

"Speaking dispassionately, I should say it was very difficult to be fond of Sir Adam for long. He once told me he had outlived most of his relations, and he spoke so bitterly about the few that remained that I concluded he had broken with them. I fancy the trouble was that they thought him a rich man and behaved accordingly, and, for some reason, he considered himself a poor one. As a matter of fact, he must have made a lot of money in his day. You don't suspect Johnson, surely?"

Fenn shook his head.

"Johnson's cleared all right. He left Sir Adam alone in the flat at six-thirty and went straight to his favourite house of call, 'The Nag's Head.' He was there, gossiping in the bar, till about five to seven, when he went back to the flat. I sent one of my men up to 'The Nag's Head.' His story holds good. He's got a dozen witnesses."

"But you don't like the fellow. Fenn, I'm ashamed of you! Is this the official attitude? And you had the face, not so long ago, to sit at this very table, uttering words of wisdom. 'What we want, my dear Gilroy, is facts, not fancies. Remember, private impressions, however strong they may be, cut no ice with a jury.' Rather pedantic, perhaps, but quite sound, from the point of view of a scientist. Pull yourself together, man."

Fenn laughed, but his colour deepened under Gilroy's gibing. He placed his pipe on one side and leaned forward, his elbows on the table.

"I've got facts," he said slowly—"plenty of them. And, for the first time since I entered the force, I don't want to use them. Look here, Robert. I've given you inside information more than once when I've been on a job; in fact, from the official point of view, I've been thoroughly indiscreet: but I think I've been justified. I know that what I tell you in this room goes no farther. And you've got, as you say, a scientific mind. More than once you've helped to sort my ideas for me. Feel inclined to exercise your wits on this Braid business?"

Gilroy pushed away his plate and tossed down the last of his beer.

"Come into the other room," he suggested, "and we'll have it out over the fire."

Fenn waited till Gilroy had made up the fire and propped a battered coffee-pot on the hob; then, from the depths of a roomy armchair, proceeded to unbosom himself.

"I'll give you the facts first," he began. "Sir Adam Braid was undoubtedly alive at five minutes to seven. Webb heard his voice and that of a woman through the door when he called at the flat at about a quarter to seven. According to him, Sir Adam was shouting at the top of his voice and the lady was in tears."

"And friend Webb naturally stopped to listen," put in Gilroy dryly.

Fenn nodded.

"He admits it. He stood outside for ten minutes or so, and the row was still going on when he left. That's not all. If Miss Braid is to be believed, Sir Adam was alive at seven, still talking, but to a man this time. That is the last we know of him until his body was found by Johnson at ten minutes past seven."

"The inference being that he was killed between seven and ten past. From the little I saw, that fits in with the state of the body when I reached it. Why do you cast a doubt on Miss Braid's evidence?"

"Because her account of her own movements between seven and ten past is not very satisfactory. She claims to have arrived at Romney Chambers on the stroke of seven. Says she looked at her watch on entering the building, as she had meant to get there earlier and was surprised to find herself so late. Her story is that just as she was about to ring the bell she heard a man's voice inside the flat. It was answered by another voice which she took to be her grandfather's, but she admits that both voices were so indistinct as to make identification impossible. As her business with her grandfather was of a private nature she decided not to ring, but to wait until the visitor had gone; and not wishing to be found hanging about near the door, she went up on to the landing above, where she stayed for about a quarter of an hour. At the end of that time, hearing Johnson's voice, she came downstairs and discovered what had happened."

"Could she see the landing below from where she stood?" asked Gilroy.

"No. From her account she must have stood just outside the door of this flat. On the other hand, she could hear pretty distinctly. She says she heard Webb and Johnson come up the stairs, and waited deliberately, thinking that Johnson had met another of her grandfather's visitors and was ushering him in. It was not till he and Webb had gone into the flat that she made up her mind to come down and interview Johnson. One thing she is emphatic about. If any one had left her grandfather's flat while she was waiting on the landing she is certain she would have heard them. As she points out, that was the very sound she was listening for. And she heard no one; in fact, she is convinced that no one could have passed through the front door between seven and ten past. She is supported in this by Johnson, who declares that the wood of the front door is warped, and that it would be impossible to open and close it noiselessly. Webb, by the way, is convinced that the murderer slipped out of the building before Miss Braid's arrival, while he was waiting in his flat downstairs for Johnson to return. He was standing in the window of his study most of the time, watching for Johnson; but the window is a bow, and he says that he was looking up the street, with his back to the front door of the flats. From where he stood he would not have seen any one leave the building."

"On the other hand, it stands to reason that, if Sir Adam was alive at seven o'clock, and the flat was empty when Johnson went into it at seven-ten, whoever attacked him must have cleared out sometime during that ten minutes, after Miss Braid arrived," pointed out Gilroy. "Was anything taken, by the way?"

"A dispatch-box in the bedroom has been forced, and Johnson says the old man's gold watch and chain and certain other things are missing. He does not know what jewellery there may have been in the dispatch-box, but he thinks Sir Adam kept money there. He has seen him take money out of the box. With the exception of four pound notes and some silver which we found in Sir Adam's pockets, there is no money in the flat now. I think we may take it that robbery was the motive."

"You haven't overlooked the windows, by any chance?"

There was a mischievous gleam in Gilroy's eye.

"Oddly enough we did think of them," answered Fenn dryly. "They were all shut and latched, with the exception of the bedroom window, which was open at the top. It's got a patent catch, however, and that was fastened on the inside. No, the man, or woman, came and went by the front door."

Gilroy raised his eyebrows.

"There's no reason why the wound shouldn't have been inflicted by a woman," he admitted—"especially in a moment of rage. And the lady Webb heard seems to have lost her temper badly. In that case, the robbery is merely a blind."

"On the other hand," Fenn reminded him, "ladies don't usually call on even the most cantankerous old gentlemen with knives in their pockets—that is, unless the murder was premeditated. In which case, where's the motive? You don't deliberately plan the death of an old man just because he's habitually rude to you."

"Who benefits by Sir Adam's death?" asked Gilroy.

Fenn's usually cheery face clouded, and Gilroy realized that he was worrying badly over this case.

"That's where my trouble begins," he said slowly. "I shall know better where we stand when I have seen Sir Adam's solicitor; but, unless he has changed his will, Miss Braid stands to inherit every penny. And Miss Braid admits, quite frankly, that her object in wishing to see her grandfather privately was to persuade him to advance her some of the money that was to come to her at his death."

"She knew about the will, then?" put in Gilroy quickly.

With a sigh Fenn rose to his feet and stood gazing down into the fire. He looked suddenly older.

"She knew about the will," he admitted reluctantly. "She makes no bones about it."

Gilroy stared at him.

"Then what's biting you?" he exclaimed. "I admit that, so far, the evidence is purely circumstantial, but you've established some pretty useful facts. Ruling out Miss Braid's story, which, you must admit, is a bit thin, Sir Adam was murdered sometime between five minutes to seven, when Webb went back to his own flat, and ten minutes past. The murderer may, of course, have made his escape during the five minutes that ensued between Webb's departure and Miss Braid's arrival, but in that case she was lying when she said she heard voices coming from the flat when she arrived there at seven. And what possible motive can she have for lying if she is innocent? It's a rotten silly lie, I admit, but that doesn't make it the more convincing. Given that the woman's a fool and that she's up against it—"

"She's not a fool," interrupted Fenn. "Anything but! And yet, if she is guilty, she's showing about as much sense as the village idiot. She's made one damaging admission after another, of her own accord, too, and she's invented a story that's so thin that a child could see through it. It would have been the easiest thing in the world for her to say that she heard some one leave the flat while she was waiting on the landing above, but she sticks to it that no one did leave. She doesn't even pretend that she felt any affection for her grandfather, though she is shocked and horrified at his death. It's incredible that an intelligent woman could be so insanely foolish!"

"If she *is* being foolish," said Gilroy shrewdly. "The very baldness of her whole story inclines one to believe that it may, after all, be true. You must admit that you've reacted to it that way yourself. If she realizes this, she's playing a very clever game."

"You may be right," admitted Fenn wearily. "But, in normal circumstances, that aspect of the affair would affect me very little. I leave that sort of thing to the counsel for the defence, and he would no doubt make good play with it. My mind doesn't work that way. Facts are facts, and I stick to them. No, it isn't that that's set my mind wambling."

He paused for a moment, then faced Gilroy squarely.

"I give you leave to think what you like, and I admit that I am going against the principles of a lifetime, but this is my firm conviction. That child is so absolutely incapable of committing this particular crime that I am willing to stake my whole reputation on her innocence. I have put it strongly because I want to convince you that, insane as the contention must sound, coming from one in my position, I am prepared to abide by it. You can take my word for it, Jill Braid was not responsible for her grandfather's death."

Gilroy had seldom been so thoroughly taken aback in his life. He had known Fenn intimately since the days of his own boyhood, when the chief inspector had been with the uniformed force. He had listened entranced while Sergeant Fenn, as he was then, and his father, an overworked journalist with a taste for criminology, had sat over their pipes discussing the mentality of certain of the black sheep of the neighbourhood, and later, after his father's death, when he had set up for himself, and Fenn had been transferred to the Criminal Investigation Department, their friendship had persisted. He knew something of Fenn's hardworking persistence. The detective was not a man of great imagination, but he was possessed of a clear, logical brain and a power of co-ordinating his facts which Gilroy, a born researcher himself, could appreciate. He had never before known him to be biased by any personal equation. Fenn noted his amazement with a wry smile.

"I'm not mad," he said ruefully, "though I'm beginning to wonder at myself. I doubt if a man was ever in a more damnable position. I've known Jill Braid since she was a schoolgirl in pigtails, and I can remember the row there was when she shingled her hair and called me in to take her side against her father. I've taken an interest in her ever since he died and left her on her own. You wouldn't remember him, but your father knew him. He was police surgeon to our division in the old days, and we all knew his girl. She was the kind of jolly kid that made herself at home with every one. And she's the most transparently honest person it is possible to imagine. Hence all these damaging admissions. I don't suppose it's occurred to her yet that she could possibly be under suspicion; but even if she did realize it, she'd stick to the naked truth all the same, even though she's intelligent enough to know the inference that might be placed on it. You can take my word for it that she's acting true to type and there's no guile in her."

He relapsed into silence, and Gilroy could find no words with which to meet the situation.

"What are you going to do?" he asked at last.

"Properly speaking," said Fenn slowly, "I ought to retire from the case and hand it over to some one less biased than myself. But do you realize what that would mean? The facts, as you yourself pointed out, are too obvious to be disregarded. I might just as well ask for a warrant for her arrest as clear out now."

"You'll stick to it, then?"

Fenn nodded.

"Thank the Lord, I can honestly say that the evidence we have got so far does not, in my opinion, justify an arrest. Meanwhile, I shall hang on, and, if it's humanly possible, find the real murderer. But you see where it lands me. If I don't find him, and any further information comes to light, I shall have to arrest her."

Gilroy poured out the coffee, and the two men drank it in silence. It was not till Fenn rose to leave that Gilroy gave voice to his thoughts.

"I say," he said, his hand on the other man's shoulder, "you're sure you're not unduly prejudiced in her favour? The facts are against her, you know."

Fenn met his eyes squarely.

"I know exactly what you think of me," he said grimly, "and I don't blame you. But, you see, I know the girl. As for the case against her, I don't mind telling you that I've got a piece of evidence in my pocket now, which I've no intention of showing you, that would almost justify my making an arrest. Instead of which, I'm going to give her a chance of explaining herself. Now you know the full extent of my folly."

His face relaxed into a smile that was half rueful, half apologetic. Then, before Gilroy could answer, he was gone.

CHAPTER IV

"HAVE YOU EVER seen this before?"

Jill Braid started, taken unawares by the suddenness of the query.

It was the morning after Sir Adam Braid's death, and she and Fenn had met by appointment in the old man's study. The body had been removed to the mortuary, Johnson had packed his belongings and betaken himself to lodgings elsewhere, and the flat was in the hands of the police.

The study, airless and undusted, had a very bleak aspect in the cold November light that filtered in through the closed window. Fenn had drawn back the heavy curtains, otherwise the room was as Sir Adam had left it when he went to his death the night before. The ashes of the burnt-out fire still littered the grate; his pen lay on the bureau where he had placed it on rising from his seat; and the earphones still hung over the back of his chair, their long flex trailing across the carpet. No doubt his last action before leaving the room had been to place them there.

Jill took the sheet of paper that Fenn handed her and carried it across to the better light of the window. As she moved, a little shiver ran down her spine. She felt acutely conscious of her grandfather's presence in this grey, chilly room.

As she read the letter that broke off so abruptly at the bottom of the page, her eyes widened in consternation. When she raised them, to find Fenn watching her closely, they were horror-stricken.

"Have you ever seen it before?" he repeated.

Her glance did not waver.

"Never," she answered. "I—I had no idea he was going to do this! When I saw him last he was nicer to me than he had ever been. I don't understand it."

"He wrote it last night," said Fenn quietly. "Something must have disturbed him, and he left it unfinished. Johnson says that there was a half-written letter lying on the bureau, where I found this, when he went out last night. He remembers it because your grandfather hesitated when he asked if there was anything for the post, and, apparently, decided to send it later. You didn't know that he had any intention of cutting you out of his will?"

She shook her head.

"It's the last thing I should have expected. The last time I saw him he told me he was leaving me everything. I was surprised, because, though I am his nearest relation, he always hated my mother, and I had been quite prepared for him to leave me nothing. I can't think why he wrote this. I've done nothing to offend him."

"I think I can answer that question," said Fenn. "This letter from you was lying beside the other." The girl's face flushed.

"You mean it made him angry? I suppose it was a silly letter to write just after he'd told me he was leaving me the money, but I was desperate, Mr. Fenn. If I could have the money now, it would mean so much to me, and I asked for so little—just enough to keep me and pay my studio fees in Paris till I could start earning again. I thought he'd understand. He'd been through it all himself when he was young, and I took such trouble with the letter to show that I really wasn't being grasping and mercenary. It never occurred to me that he'd take it like that."

"From what I have gathered he seems to have had a fixed idea that his relations were out to get money from him; and no doubt, when he read your letter, he concluded that you were as mercenary as the rest, and simply sat down in a rage, then and there, to write to his lawyer. He'd probably have thought

better of it later. It's just the sort of thing irritable old gentlemen do. You're sure you did not know about this letter?"

She stared at him, puzzled.

"Why do you keep on asking me that? If he only wrote
it yesterday, how could I know about it? The last time I saw
him was when he called on me at my rooms, the day before
yesterday. I never came into this room at all last night; and if I
had, I shouldn't have noticed anything of that sort after what
had happened."

She paused. Then a flood of colour swept over her face.

"Mr. Fenn!" she exclaimed hotly, "surely you don't think—"

"I'm sorry to interrupt," broke in a discreet voice from the
doorway; "but the door was open, and as I'd stayed away from
the office on purpose to catch you, I ventured to come in."

Fenn swung round, to find Webb's mild little face peering
into the room.

"Come in, Mr. Webb," he said, trying to keep the irritation
out of his voice.

Mr. Webb came in with alacrity. He executed a punctili-
ous little bow in the direction of Miss Braid before addressing
himself to Fenn.

"My sister has some information for you," he said, "which
I thought I had better pass on at once. I only heard of it this
morning, and stayed away from the office, meaning to call
on you at Scotland Yard. When I saw you pass the window
I was really very much relieved. My time's not exactly my
own, you see."

"Yes?" put in Fenn encouragingly, as he paused for breath.

"Well, it's just this. According to my sister, a man has been
hanging about the Chambers for several days—rather a ques-
tionable type of person, in fact—and she feels certain now that
he was watching this house."

She would, was Fenn's inward comment, as he waited patiently for Webb's dramatic pause to come to an end.

"She says she noticed him first on Saturday evening, and wondered what he was waiting for. Then she saw him again on Monday, the day before yesterday—that is, about lunch-time. A rough-looking man, shabby and with no overcoat; not at all the sort of person one cares to have hanging about one's premises."

Webb cleared his throat and settled down to enjoy his own narrative.

"Well, you know what women are," he went on. "With all deference to Miss Braid, they *can* be a little fanciful, especially at a time like this—so that I was naturally inclined to take my sister's story with a grain of salt, as they say. But when she told me that she had been so impressed by this man that she had spoken of him to Ling, who keeps the paper shop at the corner, and that he had not only noticed him too, but agreed with her that he was probably up to no good, I began to take the matter more seriously. Ling is a very level-headed man with an intelligence distinctly above his station, and he and my sister had quite a talk about this man on the very morning of the day Sir Adam died, when she went to pay our weekly bill. It may be a clue or there may be nothing in it at all, but I thought it advisable to let you know as soon as possible. I give you the information for what it is worth," concluded Webb magnanimously.

"Much obliged to you," said Fenn. He did not wish to discourage the little man at this juncture. Boring and futile though he was, he might prove a useful source of information. As for his sister, her imagination had probably got the bit between its teeth and run away with her; but it might be worth while to interview this man Ling, and see if he had anything to report.

"I'll drop in on Miss Webb later, if I may, and get her to give me a more detailed description of the man," he went on, leading Webb firmly in the direction of the door. "Many thanks for the information."

"Not at all. Only too glad to be of service," and Webb trotted off, feeling very well pleased with himself.

Fenn turned to Miss Braid with an amused smile hovering on his lips. If he had expected any response from her, he was disappointed. All through Webb's visit she had been standing at the window, apparently absorbed in the contemplation of the mansions opposite. Now she turned on him, her eyes sparkling and a spot of vivid colour flaming on each cheek-bone.

"Mr. Fenn," she exclaimed, "is it true that you don't really believe that I was waiting upstairs yesterday evening? You don't think that I came *into* this flat when I first arrived, do you?"

Her whole bearing was a challenge, and Fenn had to meet it. The crisis had come sooner than he liked, but he answered her with absolute honesty.

"If you tell me that the first time you entered this flat last night was after Johnson had found your grandfather's body, I, personally, am ready to take your word for it. But it doesn't rest with me, you know. I've got to convince other people more important than myself, and if I'm to do that I must have facts. If only you had been seen or had spoken to some one on the landing upstairs, my job would be easier."

While he was speaking her eyes had been on his face. Evidently what she had read there satisfied her.

"You do believe me," she said, with obvious relief. "That's one comfort, anyway. But I'm beginning to understand what you're driving at. If my grandfather had been alone and had let me in when I came at seven I might have quarrelled with him. But I couldn't ever have murdered him! Surely you don't believe that?"

"I don't believe it, but, I put it to you, others might," answered Fenn, meeting her gaze steadily.

The colour faded slowly from her cheeks, but it was characteristic of her that, in spite of her consternation, she still pursued her own argument relentlessly.

"But why should I do such a thing, just when he was behaving decently to me for the first time in my life? And the tragic thing is that I'd just begun to realize that I could have been fond of him, if only he'd let me. I suppose it's the money you're thinking of. But money isn't as important as that."

"It is to some people," Fenn reminded her gently. "And, remember, you were within an ace of losing every penny of it."

She stared at him. Evidently she had not realized till then the difference it would have made in her life if her grandfather had had time to sign the letter.

"The letter, you mean, to his lawyers?" she said slowly. "I see now what you've been driving at. I suppose I was blind and stupid not to have seen it before. I might have gone in and seen the letter and killed him to prevent him from finishing it? Of course, I suppose it does look like that. It might seem like it to me, if it was anybody else; but when it's *me*, it seems so ridiculous!"

She shot a glance at him, half humorous, half apologetic, which was wholly enchanting. Even now she did not seem quite to realize the seriousness of her position.

"There's nothing ridiculous about it, I assure you," said Fenn gravely. "It's a very nasty state of affairs, from your point of view. You're sure there's nothing of any importance you haven't told me?" She made a little hopeless gesture.

"Nothing. I came here at seven, as I said, and waited; but there wasn't a soul on the stairs, and I don't suppose any one saw me all the time I was here. There's nothing to prove that I didn't come in here. I can see that."

"You're sure that you didn't hear a woman's voice when you were standing outside the door of this flat? If we could get on *her* track it would simplify matters."

"Certain. The voices I heard were men's. By the way, I can prove that the woman Mr. Webb heard was not me, if that's any help. I came straight here from Louis, the hairdresser's, and the man who cut my hair will know what time I left. I must have been there till about ten minutes to seven."

Fenn made a note of the hairdresser's address, and finding that there was really nothing more she could tell him, led the way out of the flat. As he stood aside to let her pass out, he felt a light touch on his arm.

"It seems impossible, but if—if there's any arresting to be done, could it be by you, please, Mr. Fenn?" said a small voice at his elbow.

And Fenn, catching sight of her face, realized that she was frightened at last.

He parted from her outside Romney Chambers and made his way to the local branch of the Northern Counties Bank. He interviewed the manager, but got, as he had expected, very little information of any value. One thing, however, he did ascertain. Sir Adam Braid had cashed a cheque for eighty guineas, and had taken the money away in pound notes, seven days before he was murdered.

"He had banked with us for years," said the manager. "And there was plenty of money lying to his account, but during the last two years he had developed a rather curious and, I considered, dangerous habit. Except for his rent and certain big payments he hardly ever drew a cheque on his account. It was his habit to cash any cheques that came to him in payment for his work and use the money for his current expenses. And there was a good deal coming in. I fancy he must have had plenty of old work stowed away to fall back on. Some of the cheques, especially those from American dealers, were for large sums, and after his exhibition last winter, I remember, he walked out of this bank with over six hundred pounds in cash in his pocket. I ventured to expostulate with him once on the danger of keeping such large sums of money in his flat, but I never did it again! He was a very peppery old gentleman."

"The chances are, then, that there was a considerable sum of money in the flat?"

The manager shrugged his shoulders.

"It's difficult to say, of course. I've no idea what he did with his money. But he has changed some largish cheques at varying intervals during the last six months, and, as I told you, he changed one for over eighty pounds only a week ago. If, as I have suspected, he had got into the habit of hoarding his money, there may have been a considerable sum in the flat."

Fenn produced an envelope from his pocket and took out four one pound notes.

"These were found in Sir Adam's pocket after his death," he said. "Seeing that they run in consecutive numbers it struck me that they might be part of a batch paid out by you for a larger sum. You've no record of the numbers, I suppose?"

The manager took the notes.

"We may be able to help you there," he said, "if you'll wait a minute."

He left the room, and was back almost immediately, carrying a slip of paper in his hand.

"They are part of the payment of eighty guineas which we made to him on the thirtieth of October," he said. "He had a prejudice against notes for big denominations, and the sum was paid in one pound notes. They were a series of new notes, and you may take it that any number between the two on this memoranda is part of the series. That will give you something to go on, anyway."

Fenn thanked him and departed with the paper in his pocket. He turned down Shorncliffe Street once more, and dropped into the paper shop Webb had mentioned earlier in the day.

He found Ling, the proprietor, seated behind the counter reading one of his own papers. He was a heavily-built man of about fifty, with a shrewd face and intelligent grey eyes. Fenn recognized in him the makings of a clear and conscientious witness. He remembered the man Miss Webb had noticed perfectly, and described him with some skill.

"You see, livin' on the corner as I do, I get to know most of the people round here by sight. Any one strange to the neighbourhood I seem to notice, without thinkin' like. This chap didn't belong round here, and when I see him hangin' about round this corner, I begun to wonder what he was up to. Seedy-lookin' chap, he was. Handkerchief round his neck and no overcoat on, in spite of the cold. Thin, with a stoop, and a long, thin face. I should know him again all right. You see, he stood for a good quarter of an hour under the lamp outside, and I got a good view of him. Looked to me as if he'd got his eye on one of the houses in Shorncliffe Street."

"How often did you see him?" asked Fenn.

Ling gave the matter his careful consideration before he answered.

"Well, now," he said at last, "I can check that pretty close. I'll tell you for why. I see him Friday last. He was out there between one and two, Friday afternoon. Now I know it was Friday, because I was makin' out my bills, which I always do on a Friday, seein' as there's a lot of the regular customers like to pay up on Saturday. Then I see him Monday last—the day before yesterday, that is—and I pointed him out to Ernie Bell, porter he is at the mansions, and *he* was payin' of his bill, which he always does of a Monday. And I see him again; but I can't say which day that would have been. One day last week, towards the end of the week, I should put it, and it was in the evening. I can't say no nearer than that. But I'd know him again. So would Ernie Bell, I should think."

Fenn made a note of Bell's address, and, very reluctantly, paid his somewhat belated visit to Miss Webb. He found her overwhelmingly full of information, and it was nearly an hour before he managed to wrench himself away. But her description of the loiterer, whom she already designated as "the murderer," tallied with Ling's. When Fenn asked her if she would know the man again she refused to commit herself.

"Knowing some one is one thing, but identifying him is another, isn't it, inspector?" she said brightly.

Fenn murmured something that might be taken for an affirmative, but the subtlety was beyond him.

As he was leaving the Chambers he ran into Gilroy. He refused his offer of lunch, but stood chatting for a minute or two.

"How are things going?" asked the doctor.

Fenn shrugged his shoulders.

"Pretty damnably, from my point of view," he said morosely. "The truth is, I'm beginning to hate my job."

"By which I gather you haven't managed to establish the innocence of your chief suspect. I'm sorry, old man. It's a beastly business, from your point of view. There's one thing, however. Until you've actually laid hands on the weapon that was used you can't be sure in whose possession you may find it."

"The weapon, as you call it, turned up last night," answered Fenn sourly. "One of my men found it under the mat outside Sir Adam's front door."

Then, in answer to Gilroy's unspoken question—

"Nothing doing. Both the blade and the handle had been wiped clean on the bath-towel in Sir Adam's room, and the knife is just a sheath-knife, the kind you can buy anywhere for five or six shillings. The sheath's missing, but there's very little chance of our stumbling on that now—burns too easily."

"Doesn't sound very promising. Nothing else has turned up, I suppose?"

"Nothing, except that Miss Webb has found the man who did it. She'll tell you all about it if you ask her."

"God forbid," murmured Gilroy, making a dive for the stairs that led to his own flat.

CHAPTER V

THAT AFTERNOON Gilroy had knocked off work at the Lister Institute rather earlier than usual, and was washing his hands preparatory to leaving, when he was rung up by Fenn. The chief inspector, who seemed to have recovered his temper since the morning, asked him what time he was likely to get back to his flat.

"I'm on my way there now," answered Gilroy. "Do you want to see me?"

"Heaven forbid!" was Fenn's ungrateful rejoinder. "Though I suppose you have your uses—as a Job's comforter! No, I want to stop Miss Braid before she leaves her grandfather's flat. I know she's got an appointment there with his solicitor at three-thirty this afternoon, and it struck me that if you're on your way home you might just catch her."

"What am I to do with the bereaved damsel if I do manage to get hold of her?"

"Simply ask her to wait at the flat till I come. I'll get down there as soon as I possibly can. I wouldn't have bothered you, but the only telephone in the building seems to be Webb's, and for obvious reasons I don't want him buzzing round."

"Ungrateful brute, aren't you? when you know he'd run his little legs off to oblige you! Right, I'll see what I can do."

Various small matters cropped up to delay Fenn, and it was past five when he reached Sir Adam Braid's flat. He was about to put the key in the lock when he noticed a card wedged into the flap of the letterbox. It was from Gilroy, and ran:

"Victim waiting for you upstairs."

Fenn chuckled softly.

"So friend Robert's been having a look-see for himself!" he murmured. "Webb's disease must be catching."

But he was not ill-pleased with the way things had fallen out. He had been reproaching himself for leaving the girl so long alone in the flat, with its gruesome associations. Also, he was not sorry that Gilroy should have an opportunity to judge for himself whether he had been unduly prejudiced in her favour.

He found her comfortably established in Gilroy's kitchen.

"I asked Miss Braid if she minded kitchen tea, and she said she didn't," Gilroy informed him, rather unnecessarily.

"If he only knew, it's just what I'm accustomed to," said the girl. She spoke gaily enough, but her voice sounded strained and tired. Fenn, glancing covertly at her, realized that she had lost much of her vivid charm since the morning. There were dark circles under her eyes and her shoulders sagged perceptibly under the weight of the well-worn dark coat which she had evidently put on as the nearest approach to mourning she possessed. He was also surprised to observe that there was an empty eggshell on her plate and an open box of sardines in front of her.

Gilroy caught his eye.

"I'm a better detective than you are," he announced cheerfully. "It took me just four minutes to find out that Miss Braid had had no lunch. Even if you don't eat yourself, you might give other people a chance, you know."

"I may occasionally miss my lunch, but I always make a point of having tea," answered Fenn, commandeering a cup from the dresser and calmly taking possession of the teapot. "There's no hurry. My business will wait."

"If you want me to go down to the flat, I'm quite ready," volunteered Jill Braid quickly.

"She isn't, whatever she may say," said Gilroy, who was performing feats of jugglery with a sardine between the box and her plate. "She never wishes to see the inside of that flat again. She's just told me so. And, what's more, no one but an unmitigated brute would make an appointment with a starving woman in such a place. It's the sort of thing one used to hear of in Russia, under the old regime. It's not done in England, you know."

Jill Braid laughed in spite of herself.

"Truly I can't eat any more sardines," she assured him. "Please put that back."

"Well, it's obviously got to go either on your plate or the table-cloth. I'd rather it was the plate, if it's all the same to you. Joking apart, don't take her down to that beastly flat, Fenn. I'll clear out, and you can have your interview in peace over your tea."

"No need for you to do that, Robert," Fenn assured him. "I've nothing private to discuss. It's merely this."

He took a typewritten list from his pocket and spread it out in front of the girl.

"I've managed to get a list of some of the missing articles from Johnson, and I wondered if you could check it for me. Of course, Johnson knows very little about the contents of the dispatch-box, but there are certain articles of jewellery which he declares are gone. Have you any idea what your grandfather did keep in that box?"

Jill shook her head.

"I know practically nothing about his things. You see, until lately, I hardly knew him. He never took the slightest notice of us as long as my mother was alive, and it's only since she and my father died that I've seen anything of him. Until last night I had never even set foot inside his bedroom."

She ran her eye over the list.

"I'm afraid I can't help you much," she said. "I remember the gold watch and chain. He always wore it, and it had his name inside the case. He showed it to me once. And the signet ring—if it's the one I mean—that should be easy to identify. My great-grandfather had several of them made for his sons, and grandfather had his copied, and gave my father one when he came of age. They're all exactly alike, with the crest and motto on them, and the name and date of the person they belonged to on the inside. Grandfather did not wear his, and I think he must have kept it in a little trinket box in his bedroom, as he fetched it once to compare it with my father's."

"Have you got your father's ring?" asked Fenn. She slipped it off her finger and handed it to him. "I always wear it. It's exactly like grandfather's, except for the name engraved inside."

Fenn added a careful description of the ring to the list.

"That will give us something to go on, anyway," he said, "provided the thief's fool enough to sell it. You don't recognize anything else?"

She shook her head.

"I'm afraid not; you see I knew so little about his affairs."

"It's unfortunate, from our point of view," admitted Fenn. "We know that a certain amount of jewellery is missing, if Johnson's account is correct, and we've reason to believe that quite a large sum of money may have been taken. There's also a waterproof which Johnson declares is missing from the hall. It had the maker's name inside the collar, and he's described it pretty accurately, down to a button missing off the belt, which your grandfather complained of a few days ago. However, you've helped us considerably over the ring and the watch. If anything else occurs to you, let me know, will you? Now, having picked your brains, I'll leave you in peace."

Jill rose and collected her bag and gloves.

"I must go," she said. "Thank you so much for the delicious tea, Dr. Gilroy. It saved my life. I should probably have been in a state of coma by now if you hadn't taken pity on me."

"Or gnawing your shoe-laces in that abominable flat downstairs! Why not wait and have a comfortable cigarette before you go?"

She refused regretfully.

"I've got work to do. You forget I'm still a wage-earner!"

"You know that your grandfather's lawyers will advance you anything you need," Fenn informed her. "That half-finished letter of his can't affect the will in any way."

She hesitated, her eyes on the glove she was buttoning. Then, with the colour deepening in her cheeks, she plunged.

"I've come to the conclusion that I can't take that money," she said. "I don't care whether the letter counts or not in the eyes of the law, but it's quite obvious that grandfather didn't mean to leave me anything. Surely that's enough. I can't take it on the face of that, can I?"

Fenn did not answer at once. He might have known, he told himself, that she would take a line that was typical of her, but he was at a loss as to how best to advise her. In view of her position she was doing a wise thing in refusing the legacy, but he, of all people, knew how badly she needed it. Gilroy said nothing, but he was watching her closely.

"I should think it over," said Fenn at last. "Don't do anything in a hurry. As regards your grandfather's letter, I shouldn't make too much of it. He wrote it in a moment of anger, and even then was obviously in no hurry to send it. If you had seen him and had the matter out with him when you first arrived at the flat he would certainly have destroyed it. Given a temperament like his there is every reason to believe that he would have thought better of it."

She lifted her eyes to his. They were transparently honest.

"Do you know, that sounds rather like sophistry," she said. "It's so exactly what one would like to believe, that it makes one suspicious. And there's another thing."

She hesitated again, then went on bravely.

"Mr. Compton *didn't* offer to advance the money. In fact, I think he kept off the subject on purpose. Just as he was going he said something about going into money matters after the inquest. His meaning was pretty clear, though he didn't put it into words. He's suspicious, too, you see."

She tried to smile, but her eyes were haunted. Then, with an obvious effort, she squared her shoulders and faced the two men gallantly.

"I'm not bothered about the money. I can manage, just as I've always managed. It was only that, when grandfather told me about the will, I saw a chance of chucking this beastly fashion-drawing business and getting some real training. I'll stick to my old job while you get on with yours, Mr. Fenn. But you will get on with it, won't you? It's getting rather important to me that you should!"

This time she did achieve a smile, rather a tremulous one, over her shoulder, as she was leaving the room.

Gilroy hurried after her to let her out, and Fenn was left to his own not very pleasant reflections.

"Well?" he queried, as Gilroy reappeared.

Gilroy stood frowning, his hands deep in his pockets.

"On my word, I don't know," he muttered. "She's a very fascinating person."

"She's more than that," said Fenn shortly.

Gilroy nodded.

"I'm quite ready to believe it. One thing's obvious, even on such short acquaintance. She's got brains. Don't overlook that fact, Fenn."

"I don't see why that should count against her," was Fenn's rather tart rejoinder. "You've got brains yourself, I presume, but I shouldn't put you down as a suspicious character."

Gilroy laughed.

"Thanks. But, joking apart, do you realize what an enormous pull a woman with looks, charm, and brains has with any man, even a well-seasoned policeman? If Miss Braid wasn't transparently sincere just now she's a consummate actress. Personally, I should infinitely prefer to think she was honest. But, then, I like her! That's why I'm walking warily."

"Walk as warily as you choose, but you won't catch her out," asserted Fenn. "And, remember, the cleverest criminal makes a slip, sooner or later. The true statement is the only one that is absolutely consistent. She's implicated herself right and left, but she's never once contradicted herself, and I'm ready to swear that she won't."

"I hope not," said Gilroy gravely, and left it at that.

If Fenn had been aware of the news that was awaiting him at the Yard, he would have been even more emphatic in his championship of Jill Braid. He had barely hung his hat on its accustomed peg in his office before he was constrained to snatch it off again and set out in response to a telephone call from the Chelsea police station.

The waterproof which had been taken from the hall in Sir Adam's flat had been traced and an arrest had been made.

The local inspector met him at the door of the station.

"We've pulled in the man," he said—"an out-of-work, name of Stephens. It was a smart bit of work on the part of the pawnbroker's assistant. The description of the waterproof was circulated early this morning, and when this chap tried to pawn it this afternoon, the assistant recognized it and passed the word to his master. The man gave a false name and address, but the pawnbroker sent his boy after him and traced him to a doss-house in Lawrence Street. We had no difficulty in getting him."

"Has he made a statement?" asked Fenn.

"Yes. He's quite willing to talk. Says he knows nothing of the murder, of course. Didn't know there'd been one. He hasn't seen a newspaper, according to his own account, or he wouldn't have tried to pawn the waterproof."

Fenn gave instructions that a message should be sent to Miss Webb and the newsagent, Ling, asking them to come to the station early next morning, then made his way to the cell in which the man Stephens was confined.

He found him easy enough to deal with. A gaunt, poorly-dressed man, with the broad shoulders and muscle-bound hands of one who has been a good worker in his day. Fenn saw at a glance that this was no habitual criminal. He showed none of the aplomb of the practised malefactor, and seemed only too anxious to give a frank account of himself.

"I ain't never been in trouble before, mister," he assured Fenn earnestly, his white face twitching and his gnarled hands clenched to stop their trembling. "And I shouldn't be now, if it wasn't for this blasted war. I was in good work when I joined up, but me job got filled while I was away, and, try as I would, I couldn't get nothing when I come back. It's been a couple o' days 'ere, and a couple there, and the last two months I couldn't get nothin'. Walked me feet off, I 'ave."

Fenn let him talk. He was watching him closely. The man was frightened, that was evident; but there was something, too, in his manner of the shamed consternation of a decent working-man who finds himself on the wrong side of the law for the first time.

"I pinched the coat all right," the hoarse, troubled voice went on. "But if any one'd told me a year ago I'd do such a thing, I'd 'a given them something to remember me by. Desperate, I was. I didn't know where to turn, then I 'eard some talk in a bar of the money the old gent kep' in that flat. I 'ung round and kep' an eye on the place for the better part of a week, but I couldn't bring meself to go up. Then last night, when I see the chap as works for 'im go out, I took me chance and slipped in. But I never got nothing but the coat."

"How did you get in?" asked Fenn. "Not into the building—I know the door downstairs is always open—but into the flat?"

"I found the door open when I got up there," asserted the man. "I'd brought a chisel, but I didn't 'ave no need to use it."

"What?" exclaimed Fenn, in astonishment.

Stephens nodded.

"Standin' ajar, it was, and, what's more, someone'd slipped the catch what 'olds the lock back. I know, because I left it like that when I went in. Thought it'd be easier to get out, like, if I 'ad to leave in a 'urry. Whoever left it like that did it a-purpose."

This was indeed news, in view of Johnson's emphatic statement that he had shut the flat door behind him when he left.

"How soon was it after the servant left that you went in?" asked Fenn.

"Not more than a minute or two. As soon as I see 'im turn the corner."

"Did you meet any one on the stairs or in the flat?"

"Not at first, I didn't. There was some one in with the old gentleman—a lady. I 'eard 'er talkin' when I went in. That's 'ow I knew the settin'-room door was open. I 'adn't counted on that, and, somehow, when the time came, I couldn't bring myself to go past it. That's 'ow I come to wait in the hall."

"Could you hear what was being said in the study?"

"Not clear, I couldn't. But the lady was in a proper temper. I remember 'er sayin' somethin' about 'avin' born' with 'im for years and not standin' it any longer; but I was too took up with what I was to do next to notice much of what was bein' said. I'd counted on the old gentleman bein' shut in the study, and I'd meant to get through to 'is bedroom, quiet-like. It was there they said 'e kep' 'is money. In a bedroom at the back."

"Who put you wise to all this?" demanded Fenn sharply.

"No one special. It was common talk in the bar, and if I 'adn't been so 'ard put to it for a bite to eat, I shouldn't 'ave taken no notice of it. I'm not keepin' nothin' back, mister. It was common talk, that's all."

He was obviously speaking the truth, and Fenn motioned to him to go on with his story.

"When I see the door was open and 'eard 'em talkin', I give it up and settled to 'ook it. Then, just as I was slippin' out, quiet, I see the waterproof 'angin' on the stand, and I pinched it. Honest, I never touched nothin' else, mister."

"Did you shut the door after you?"

Stephens shook his head.

"I didn't dare, on account of the noise. I'd just pulled it to behind me when I 'eard a step on the stair, and not wantin' to be seen, like, I goes up the passage a bit and gets behind a bit o' wall."

Fenn nodded. He had noticed the angle in the wall of the passage himself and knew that a man could stand there out of sight of the front door. He had to admit that the story rang true enough, so far. But there was more to come.

Stephens bent forward, his face almost touching Fenn's in his earnestness.

"There was some one went into the flat while I was standin' there, mister," he said. "I don't know who it was and I never see 'im, me not darin' to put me 'ead round the corner of the wall. I don't know whether it was man, woman, or child, but I'll take my solemn oath some one come up those stairs and went through that door, and, what's more, 'e shut it behind 'im. 'E was mighty quiet about it, but I 'eard the latch click."

"Did you see him come out?"

"Not me, mister! I wasn't waitin' for no one. As soon as I 'eard that door shut, I slipped out and got away as quick as I could. But there wasn't no murder done while I was there, and I didn't 'ave no 'and in it, and that's gospel truth I'm tellin' of yer."

"What time did you leave the flat?"

For a moment Stephens looked baffled, then his face cleared.

"It was soon after half-past six by the church clock when I went in, and I wasn't there not more than five minutes all told. And I do know as it was a quarter to seven when I started to walk to Waterloo. I looked at the clock, so did the chap as was with me."

Fenn was conscious of a sick feeling of disappointment. From the beginning he had been fighting against the conviction that the man spoke the truth, and now, if he could bring a witness to the fact that he was clear of Romney Chambers by six-forty-five, at which time, according to Webb, Sir Adam was still alive, suspicion was bound once more to revert to Jill.

"Can you produce this man who was with you?" he asked.

To his surprise Stephens shook his head helplessly.

"That's what the inspector asked me," he said. "And I've been trying to remember the chap's name ever since. You see, it was this way. I run into 'im just outside the door of those flats. 'E was a chap as I'd served on board ship with in nineteen sixteen and I 'adn't seen 'im since. It was 'im as reckernized me, or I shouldn't 'ave known 'im. When 'e see me 'e sung out and called me by name. 'Scotty,' 'e used to be known as, 'im bein' from the North. Come from Leith, I remember. But what 'is real name was, I don't know. And what I do know is, 'e ain't in London. I see 'im off myself by the seven-forty-somethin' for Southampton. Walked to Waterloo, we did."

"Let's get this straight," said Fenn. "You met this man, Scotty, directly after leaving Romney Chambers and walked with him to Waterloo Station. Is that right?"

"That's right, mister, only we didn't start at once, like. I suppose we must 'ave stood there talkin' for ten minutes or so. 'E asked me what I'd been doin' since I got me discharge, and 'e said, was I up against it, goin' by the look of me clothes and that, I suppose. I told 'im 'ow things was, and 'e passed me a quid for old time's sake and said as 'e'd look me up next time 'e was in London. I told 'im the branch of the Legion as would always find me, me knowin' Mr. Whitaker, the secretary. Then I walked with 'im to the station, and we 'ad a drink in the bar there, and I went with 'im to 'is train, and that's the last I see of 'im."

The statement was read over to him and he signed it.

"You've no idea whether the person you heard go into the flat was a man or a woman?" asked Fenn, as he prepared to leave.

The ghost of a grin came over the man's haggard face.

"You'd be hard put to it to tell one from the other nowadays," he said. "And the skirts don't make a noise now like they used to. And whoever it was was steppin' light, remember. All I do know is that some one went through that door uncommon nippy and shut it behind 'im."

And Fenn was left to make the best he could of that.

CHAPTER VI

IF FENN HAD NOT been worried by the uncomfortable conviction that Stephens was speaking the truth he would have been a happy man next morning, secure in the knowledge that his fears for Jill Braid's safety were definitely laid to rest and his credit at Headquarters enhanced by the capture of Sir Adam Braid's murderer.

He had his man paraded in the yard of the police station in the presence of Miss Webb, Ling, Ling's friend Bell, Isaac Samuel the pawnbroker's assistant, and two other witnesses the newsagent had managed to gather in early that morning. As regards numbers these made an imposing enough list.

With the exception of Miss Webb, who twittered and hesitated, and finally declared that, though Stephens looked exactly like the man she had seen hanging about the flats, she could not go so far as to say he *was* the man, the witnesses picked him out unhesitatingly from among a dozen others gathered at random.

Bell, who was in Ling's shop when the newsagent noticed Stephens for the second time, remembered the incident perfectly, and had taken a good look at the man when Ling pointed him out to him. As hall porter of one of the blocks of mansions in Shorncliffe Street it was his custom to keep a sharp eye out for any suspicious-looking characters. He identified Stephens easily.

Ling's two witnesses, Frederick Gibson, a chauffeur, who had seen Stephens on the evening of November the sixth, while waiting at the corner of Shorncliffe Street for the arrival of his young lady, and the young lady herself, Mabel Parry, a shop assistant, were even more valuable as witnesses, for Gibson had not only noticed Stephens and pointed him out to Miss Parry, but they had both actually seen him enter the flats. They were definite as to the time, Miss Parry having been a few minutes late for her appointment and Gibson having chaffed her about it. They gave the time as six-thirty-four, which tallied with Stephens' own account of his movements. Gibson happened to drop into Ling's shop and speak of what he had seen, and Ling, with the common sense and intelligence Fenn had noticed in him at their first interview, had commandeered the services of both of them.

Samuel, the pawnbroker's assistant, had no difficulty in identifying Stephens as the man who had pawned the waterproof. He had been too interested in the coat, owing to its resemblance to the one circularized by the police, not to take good stock of the man who brought it in.

On the whole, Fenn had as good a case as he could wish to take into court. Purely circumstantial evidence, of course, but it would take a clever counsel to knock a hole in it. On his own confession, Stephens had gone into the flat and stolen the waterproof, and Fenn could produce six unassailable witnesses to prove it. A cast-iron case, provided the hypothetical "Scotty" did not come forward; and, much as he would have liked to do so, Fenn could not quite bring himself to dismiss "Scotty" as negligible. In the course of his career he had learned to gauge pretty accurately the extent to which a man was perjuring himself, and Stephens belonged to a type which does not lie convincingly. Fenn had examined the statement the man had made when he was first charged, and it tallied exactly with the one he had himself taken later. And the station inspector, an experienced officer, was of the opinion that the man had not known of the murder until he was actually charged with it.

Fenn had a few words with the divisional surgeon, who happened to be on the premises, before leaving. He had his evidence cut and dried for the inquest. Braid had died as the result of a stab in the back of the neck, two and a half inches deep, which had severed the carotid artery. Sir Adam might have lived for a minute or so after the blow, but, given an old man with a heart that was none too strong, the chances were that death had been almost instantaneous. The surgeon would not commit himself as to the extent the assailant's clothes would be likely to be stained with blood, but he went so far as to say that, if his movements had been swift enough, he might escape with smears on his hand and sleeve. He had seen the bath-towel which had been found in Sir Adam's bedroom, and was of the opinion that the stains on it were those of human blood. There seemed little doubt that the murderer had wiped, not only his hands, but the knife on it, before leaving the flat.

"He left no other traces, I suppose?" asked the surgeon.

"None. He must have wiped his hands thoroughly before making his haul, unless, of course, he'd already taken the things when Sir Adam came on him."

"He was a pretty cool customer if he searched the bedroom after the murder. The servant might have come back at any moment."

"It depends when he actually did commit the murder. Johnson was so regular in his habits that he could be counted on not to get back before seven, at the earliest. I'm inclined to place the actual murder sometime between six-fifty-five and seven-fifteen, or possibly between seven and seven-fifteen. Miss Braid, unless she is mistaken, heard people talking as late as seven. Does that fit in with the results of your examination?"

Fenn knew only too well that at any moment now he might be forced to discredit Jill's evidence.

"Perfectly. Roughly speaking, I should say the old man had been dead about an hour when I saw him. Might have been more. It's difficult to be precise. The inquest's on Saturday, I hear."

"Yes. We shall ask for an adjournment, I expect."

The surgeon glared at him.

"Of course. Trust you fellows for that. That's another half-day lost for me."

"I thought you doctors liked that sort of thing," returned Fenn innocently. "You do cut rather a fine figure, you know. Barring the judge, you're the only person in court who can snub the prosecuting counsel with impunity."

He slipped out just in time to avoid the surgeon's sulphurous rejoinder.

He had not been back at the Yard ten minutes before a card was brought to him.

"Now we're for it," he groaned, for the name it bore was that of Daniel Whitaker, secretary to the branch of the British Legion to which Stephens belonged. Fenn remembered he had said that this man was a friend of his.

Mr. Whitaker proved to be a hollow-chested little man, with thin sandy hair and a white intelligent face. Fenn guessed rightly that he had been badly gassed in the war. He plunged straight into the business in hand.

"I hear one of my men is in trouble," he said.

"Pretty bad trouble, I'm afraid, and I'm sorry for it. It always goes against the grain to pull in a man with a good war record. He's all right, I suppose, from your point of view?"

"Very much all right. He was a Billingsgate fish porter by trade, one of those chaps who'd never seen the sea until they joined up. He served in the Navy from 1914 till 1919, was mined twice and torpedoed once. You've only got to look at his papers to see whether his country owes him anything. And there's only one thing he asks—work, and I can't get him any!"

The little man spoke bitterly, and he had Fenn's hearty sympathy. He knew something of the disappointments that fall to the lot of a conscientious Legion secretary.

"It's hard lines on the man," he agreed. "And if it was a case of theft, we should be very willing to speak for him. But this is a capital charge. If he can't prove that he left the building when he says he did, he'll stand a poor chance, I'm afraid."

"It all hangs on the production of this man he calls 'Scotty,' then?"

"If this man corroborates what Stephens has told us, he's cleared—of the murder charge, that is. The theft stands, of course; but he'll come under the First Offenders Act there, and his war record will stand him in good stead."

Mr. Whitaker rose, without wasting further time, and picked up his hat.

"Then it's up to us to find 'Scotty,'" he said briskly. "Will you back us if we ask for a wireless S.O.S.?"

Fenn held out his hand.

"Of course," he said, as the other took it. "We can't refuse, though we're putting a spoke in our own wheel! My job's to catch the murderer, and I don't mind telling you that I thought I'd got him! I should have felt better, however, if he'd been a habitual criminal. *They* go into the job with their eyes open, and they know what's coming to them, sooner or later."

He stood looking down at the little man with a humorous twinkle in his eyes.

"You're going to be a damned nuisance to us, you know," he added. "But I wish you luck, all the same."

His good wishes were genuine enough, but his spirits sank as he watched the door close behind Whitaker. There was something abominably efficient about the little man, besides which his own conviction that as regards Stephens they were barking up the wrong tree was growing in intensity.

Two days later he attended the inquest, and saw to it that it was "adjourned at the request of the police." He ran into Gilroy as he was leaving and accepted his offer of lunch. The truth was, he felt the need to unburden his soul to some one, and Gilroy, in spite of his exasperating North-country habit of caution, was a satisfactory person to talk things over with.

As they walked back to Romney Chambers Fenn told him how things stood.

"Now that we've narrowed the time of the murder down to between six-forty-five and seven-ten we're pretty well forced into choosing between Jill Braid and this man Stephens. And if Stephens' witness comes forward—"

"Why six-forty-five? Miss Braid heard voices as late as seven."

"It was you who insisted that we must take her evidence with reservations," Fenn reminded him.

Gilroy had the grace to look confused.

"I don't accept her evidence even now," he declared. "But we're bound to take into account the chance of its being true. Given the possibility that she did hear Sir Adam's voice at seven and that Stephens' pal does turn up and clear him, things look a bit blank."

"Considering that that leaves little Webb as our only suspect, they look perfectly damnable," was Fenn's whole-hearted rejoinder. "We've got the movements of every one else in the building. Adams, the caretaker, and his wife were walking in Battersea Park with a friend; Smith, the man above you, did not get back to his flat till seven-thirty, and you were at the Institute. That leaves Webb. After all, he was on the spot!"

"If you've got a more fantastic theory, produce it," said Gilroy, as he fitted his latchkey into the lock. "Poor little Webb was frightened out of his wits of Sir Adam. However, there's this about it, Webb would never dream of committing a murder without talking it over, in all its aspects, with his sister. You'd better go down and tackle Miss Webb after lunch."

While they were eating Fenn showed him a copy of Stephens' statement to the police. He read it through carefully.

"So he found the flat door open?" he said, when he had finished. "What do you make of that?"

"It rests between him and Johnson," said Fenn. "Johnson swears that he left the door securely locked. I'd give something to get to the bottom of Johnson!"

Gilroy laughed.

"On the contrary, you'd give a good deal not to," he gibed. "Johnson's altogether too easy a problem at present. He's got a cast-iron alibi, and even supposing that he did leave the door open on purpose, who on earth did he leave it open for?"

Fenn put down his knife and fork and leaned forward.

"Give your mind to this," he said. "Some one put Stephens wise to the fact that Sir Adam kept money in the house. Common talk in a bar, Stephens called it. And that some one knew that the money was kept in the old man's bedroom. Also, mark you, Stephens expected to find Sir Adam shut up in his study. And Johnson, we know, had just left him there. It's not such a wild theory."

"Johnson may have been in league with Stephens, of course," agreed Gilroy thoughtfully. "But given that he was, and that he left the flat door open for Stephens, and it turns out that Stephens did actually leave the flat before six-forty-five, where are you then?"

"Playing *Hamlet* without the Prince of Denmark," was Fenn's crestfallen rejoinder, "unless we cast Jill Braid for the part. That's where I'm up against it. If only you had been on the premises at the time it would give me something to build my hopes on! At least, you'd make a more convincing murderer than Webb!"

"Thanks! I was engaged on my lawful occasions and can prove it!"

He reverted unexpectedly to the subject when he was seeing Fenn out of the flat.

"Here's a little ray of hope for you," he suggested, under his breath. "If you're as hard up as all that, what about our top-floor tenant as a possible suspect?"

He jerked his head in the direction of a man who was mounting the stairs from the hall.

Fenn's answer was to step forward and place himself squarely in front of the new-comer.

"Hallo, Smith," he said pleasantly enough, but there was an undercurrent of authority in his voice that was new to Gilroy. He realized, with a certain glee, that he was being vouchsafed the spectacle of his old friend in his professional capacity.

The upstairs tenant halted in surprise. Then an engagingly frank smile illuminated his countenance.

"Why, it's Mr. Fenn!" he exclaimed. "I suppose it's the poor old gentleman downstairs that's brought you here."

"That's one of my little problems, certainly," admitted Fenn. "But I'm always willing to take advantage of an opportunity. It's a long time since we had a chat,"

The smiling eyes that never left Fenn's for an instant seemed to harden, but the invitation, when it came, was cordial enough.

"If you'd care to step upstairs, Mr. Fenn!" said the man, moving to one side and waiting for the detective to pass him.

Gilroy, watching him, thought he had never seen a man with his faculties more keenly on the alert.

Fenn passed him and went up the stairs. Smith followed in silence. Gilroy watched them as they disappeared round the bend of the staircase.

"Well, I'm damned!" was his comment, as he went back into his flat.

Once inside Smith's sitting-room, Fenn took up his position on the hearthrug, his back to the fire and his keen eyes roving round the room. It was a singularly characterless apartment. Beyond the fact that it contained the usual equipment of chairs and tables, and was clean and almost oppressively tidy, it gave no clue to the habits or occupations of its tenants. Except for an expensive gramophone in one corner and a woman's work things lying on the table, it might have been an unoccupied sitting-room in a second-rate hotel.

Smith seated himself on the edge of the table and waited.

Fenn knew only too well the lines on which the ensuing conversation would run. All through he would be forced to

take the initiative, Smith's task being to watch for any dangerous thrusts and parry them. And Fenn knew from experience
that Smith was a past-master in the art of evasion. He opened
his attack without any preliminary skirmish.

"I suppose you can give me an account of your movements
between the hours of, say, six and seven-thirty on the night of
November the sixth," he said briskly.

Smith's eyes twinkled with retrospective mirth.

"I had a visit from one of your men," he said. "A bright
young feller, but new to the force, I should say. He made a very
careful report, wrote it down in his little book and all that, but
it just happened that we'd never met before. I expect you'd
have found it more interesting if we had."

The shot went home. Fenn had been careless and he knew
it. He had accepted the Edward Smith, commercial traveller, of
the constable's report without question.

"You've dropped the 'Stanley,' I see," he remarked pleasantly.

"Edward S. Smith, Mr. Fenn," corrected Smith. "Stanley always was my second name, you know, and one naturally gives
one's right name to the police," he added virtuously.

Fenn nodded. Smith's godmother and godfather had, apparently, been unnecessarily generous in the variety of names
they had bestowed on him.

It was a phenomena peculiar to gentlemen of Smith's
persuasion.

He cast his mind back to the constable's report.

"As far as I can remember, you were not in the flat at the
time of the murder," he said.

"That's right," agreed Smith amiably. "I got in about seven-thirty. I'd been down to Luton on business. No, I wasn't
buying hats," he added, neatly forestalling the ironic comment
that rose involuntarily to Fenn's lips. "I don't travel in them. A
patent gas-saving device is my line at present. I'd like to sell you
one, Mr. Fenn, if you can spare me a few minutes later. It's a
peach! There hasn't been anything like it on the market before."

"I'm quite ready to believe it," commented Fenn dryly. "Where were you between six-forty-five and seven-thirty?"

"In Luton and getting back from Luton. My train arrived at St. Pancras at six-fifty. I went into the station bar and had a snack and then came on home. My wife'll vouch for the time I got back."

Fenn dropped his easy manner abruptly.

"That may be good enough for the local police, but it won't do for me," he said shortly. "I know you and I know Mrs. Smith! She's a good wife, but a bad citizen. You'll have to prove a better alibi than that, Smith."

For the first time Smith's composure seemed shaken. He hesitated.

"I didn't meet a soul," he said uncertainly. "The waitress in the station restaurant might recognize me. There was a crowd of people in the restaurant, though, and unless she's Pelman's pet pupil she's hardly likely to."

"Anybody see you get into the train at Luton?"

Smith shook his head, his lips twitching involuntarily. There was an answering gleam in Fenn's eyes. The detective had no doubt but that the confidence man's entry into the train had been as unobtrusive as possible.

"I don't know any one at Luton except the chap I was doing business with," was Smith's noncommittal reply.

"And your wife was here waiting for you?" pursued Fenn inexorably.

The mask fell from Smith's face. He became an ordinary, very perturbed, human being.

"My wife's not in this, Mr. Fenn," he said heatedly. "Why, she'd never even spoken to the old man."

Fenn pursued his advantage. He knew Mrs. Smith, a frail, delicate little woman, whose strength lay in her guileless eye and deft fingers. Unless she were actuated by an almost insane fury she was physically incapable of inflicting the wound from which Sir Adam had died, but having got Smith on the hop he meant to keep him there. It was on the cards that he might know something. The difficulty would be to persuade him to speak.

"We know that there was a woman in Sir Adam Braid's flat on the night he was killed," he said, his eyes on Smith's face. "She was there a few minutes before he was murdered and no one saw her leave this building. What's more, she was having high words with Braid. We're after that woman, Smith."

"You won't find her here, Mr. Fenn." Smith had grown perceptibly paler, but he spoke with conviction. "I'm not concealing anything from you. My wife was in the flat, I'm not denying it and I can't speak for her, because I was on my way home, as I said. But I'll swear she had nothing to do with that job downstairs. You know her, Mr. Fenn! It doesn't need me to tell you that she couldn't hurt a fly, even if she wanted to. As for housebreaking, it's not our line, and never has been. What should she do a thing like that for?"

"I might answer that travelling in gas contraptions isn't your line and never has been," answered Fenn dryly. "I don't say that either of you are actually under suspicion, but you'd better get a move on with that alibi, and for the present you'll both stay where I can lay my hand on you. If you or your wife can produce any kind of proof that she did not leave this floor of the building on the night in question, it may save a lot of unpleasantness. And if either of you saw or heard anything that may be of assistance to the police, you'd better look me up at the Yard."

Leaving Smith to digest this rather drastic dose he made his way out of the flat. He had barely reached the door, however, before the man was after him.

"I may as well spill it," he said. "You're bound to get on to it, anyway, once you get back to the Yard. If you want to know, I was pulled in on the morning of November the seventh for sharping. A mug of an American had lost a pot of money the day before on that train I was speaking of, playing with some chap he knew nothing about, and, of course, he went to the police about it. Well, I was charged all right, but when it came to a parade, the American couldn't identify and they had to let me go. I had nothing to do with it, anyway. I'd come up from Luton by an earlier train, and I was in this flat by five o'clock that evening. I was here with my wife, as she told your people, and I can vouch for it that she never left this flat while I was in it. That's the truth, Mr. Fenn."

Fenn glared at him.

"Chock-full of alibis, aren't you?" he growled. "Just seem to take your choice, according to the circumstances. You told me five minutes ago that you were not in this flat because you were on that very train from Luton!"

"Well, wouldn't you have done the same yourself?" was Smith's unabashed reply. "When you first sprung the murder on me I naturally got the wind up, and that blooming train seemed the best way out. I didn't know then that you were on to the wife. But I *did* come up by the earlier train, as I told the police at the time, and seeing that I was here and in a position to swear that we neither of us left this place that night, what could I do but tell the truth? It wouldn't have been fair to her if I hadn't. It *is* the truth this time, Mr. Fenn."

"Take my advice and make up your mind which of the two crimes you haven't committed and stick to it, and we'll pull you in for the other," was Fenn's dour comment as he departed.

On arriving at the Yard he went at once to the Record Office. There, sure enough, was the report of Smith's arrest on November the seventh for card-sharping on the London train on November the sixth. The American, on whose complaint he had been charged and who had lost over a hundred dollars, had confessed to being so inebriated on the day before as to have no clear recollection of the appearance of the ingratiating gentleman who had cleaned him out so neatly. He had been unable to pick out Smith when he was paraded before him, and on Mrs. Smith's added evidence that he was in their flat at the time the offence took place, the charge against her husband had fallen through.

By confessing that his wife's evidence was false and pleading guilty to the minor offence of card-sharping, the confidence man could have cleared himself completely of any complicity in the murder of Sir Adam Braid. Rather than leave his wife to face the music alone he had deliberately placed himself under suspicion.

Fenn, who shared the conviction of the detective who had run Smith in that the man was guilty of the card-sharping offence and had only escaped identification by a miracle, took off his hat, metaphorically speaking, to Smith.

CHAPTER VII

THREE MORNINGS LATER, Fenn was sitting in his room at New Scotland Yard, his hands deep in his pockets, his pipe in his mouth, and his gloomy eyes fixed on the ceiling with an absorption that suggested he was deriving some obscure comfort from the contemplation of cracks and cobwebs. He was wishing, with all his heart, that whoever murdered Sir Adam Braid could have done so on a day when his granddaughter was not on the premises, in which case he would have been free to give his whole mind to a case which promised to be as involved as any he had come across in the course of his career. As it was, he pursued his investigations doggedly, with the conscientiousness that was part of his nature, but never ceasing to dread the possible results of his efforts.

The news that Miss Webb was asking to see him did not serve to lighten his depression.

He rose to his feet as she bustled in. She seemed even plumper and more ineffectual looking than usual.

"I know how busy you are, inspector," was her greeting, "and I'm only going to keep you a minute. It *is* important, or I should never have had the courage to beard you in your den! It's rather terrible, you know, to feel oneself positively surrounded by policemen! I suppose you're so used to it that you don't notice it!"

"Well, I'm one myself, you see. Perhaps that has something to do with it," suggested Fenn, with a noble effort to be amiable, as he placed a chair for her.

"I ought not to sit down," went on Miss Webb, seating herself firmly. "What I've got to tell you won't take a moment, after which I must fly."

She bent forward and spoke in an impressive undertone.

"It's about some people in Romney Chambers. Of course, I know how particular the landlord is about references and all that, and Adams really is an excellent and most conscientious caretaker. He really *does* keep an eye on the tenants, which is more than you can say for some of the porters in much more pretentious buildings, and what with his collecting the rents, and his wife working for most of us, he's pretty well *au fait* with what goes on in the building. If he noticed anything irregular, out that tenant would go. I often say that I don't know what the landlord would do without him. He's an ex-soldier, you know, with such a *good* record. My brother has seen his papers."

She paused for breath, and Fenn, who, though prepared to let her have her head to a certain extent, had other things to do that morning, took the opportunity to lead her gently back on to the track.

"Is it about Adams you want to see me?" he asked.

"Oh dear no! On the contrary, I was just saying what a trustworthy man he is. In fact, it's partly what Mrs. Adams told me, added to what I couldn't help noticing for myself, that made me feel I ought to come to you. Of course, not knowing the flats, you wouldn't realize what a very pleasant little coterie we have always been till now. Until this terrible thing happened to poor Sir Adam there has never been the smallest unpleasantness. The place had a nice atmosphere, if you understand me. I can't think of any other way of expressing it."

Fenn, stifling a sigh, hoped devoutly that she would not try.

"And now something further has happened?" he suggested.

"Not happened exactly. It's more that a strange element has crept into the flats. I know there are others who feel as I do."

She paused again, leaving Fenn completely puzzled.

"Until a short time before Sir Adam died we were, as I said, a very congenial little community: neighbourly and friendly, people of the same kind, if you know what I mean. Then the flat above Dr. Gilroy's changed hands. The old lady who had it went to live with her married daughter in the country, and, I assure you, nobody was more sorry than myself. That may have made me a little prejudiced against the new-comers, but I don't think I was unfair, and I know my brother agrees with me. You've seen these people, the Smiths, haven't you, inspector?"

"I had an interview with Mr. Smith not long ago," said Fenn non-committally. Bless the woman, did nothing escape her? "It was just part of the usual routine."

"Then you'll understand what I mean when I say he's not the kind of person we've been accustomed to. Ever since they moved in there's been something—well, I won't go further than 'fishy'—about the Smiths."

The corners of Fenn's mouth twitched in spite of his efforts.

"Is that what you came to tell me?" he asked.

"Oh no. However I might feel privately about them, I should never have said anything. This is something much more peculiar. I am practically certain, inspector, and so is Mrs. Adams, that the Smiths are hiding some one in their flat!"

She sat back in her chair triumphantly, her little round eyes bright with excitement. Certainly she had succeeded in jerking Fenn out of the apathy into which he had fallen.

"What makes you think this, Miss Webb?" he asked.

"I'll tell you. Mrs. Adams, as perhaps you know, works for most of us. Dr. Gilroy has his own charwoman and I have some one in to do the rough work, but Mrs. Adams comes every day to do the cooking, and until now she has always put in a couple of hours first in the Smiths' flat. Well, the day after Sir Adam Braid died, Mrs. Smith told her that she couldn't afford to have extra help just at present and would have to economize for a time and do her own housework. Mrs. Adams wasn't surprised, really, because, as she said to me, she had always looked upon the Smiths as happy-go-lucky people, the sort who are rich one day and poor the next. It was only when she noticed that they were taking in just twice the quantity of bread and milk that she began to think their way of economizing was rather odd."

Fenn looked dubious. He had hoped for something better than this.

"If that's all you have to go on—" he began.

But Miss Webb cut him short.

"But it isn't! Mrs. Adams sweeps down the stairs every morning. That's how she came to notice the provisions standing outside the door. Two days ago she was doing the landing outside the Smiths' flat when the door opened and a woman came out and took in the milk. And the woman was not Mrs. Smith!"

"But there's no reason why they shouldn't have a guest. I mean, it doesn't even follow that she was sleeping in the flat, does it?"

Miss Webb's voice was almost tart as she answered.

"What else should she be doing at half-past six in the morning? Besides, if they have a guest, why not say so? I happened to meet Mrs. Smith in the hall yesterday evening, and she stopped and said something about the weather. She was carrying a parcel of rubbish down to the dust-bin, and I made some quite harmless remark about her finding the housework rather trying with a guest in the house. She simply looked at me as if I'd insulted her, and said she didn't know what I meant. So then I asked her point-blank whether she hadn't a friend staying with her, and she flatly denied it. Now, that was not true, inspector. The Smiths have got some one in their flat, and, what's more, that some one *never* goes out! She is never seen on the stairs; and living, as I do, on the ground floor, I should certainly have caught sight of her if she'd ever left the flats. I've kept a sharp look-out, I assure you!"

Fenn was quite ready to believe her. And knowing what he did about the Smiths, her story was not without interest. It was quite on the cards that they were shielding some friend who was temporarily "in trouble." The questions in Fenn's mind were: To what branch of Smith's precarious profession did that friend belong, and did she make her appearance at the flat before or after the murder?

He was only speaking the truth when, after thanking her warmly for her trouble, he told Miss Webb that he would look into the matter at once. It was no doubt her anxiety to get back at once to Romney Chambers, so as to be there when he made his first move, that made her so easy to get rid of. In the course of bidding him good-bye, however, she managed to sandwich in various extraneous bits of information.

Gilroy, it appeared, was seeing a good deal of Miss Braid. She had met them twice on the stairs, and, for her part, she considered them an excellently matched couple: especially as she understood that Miss Braid was inheriting the whole of her grandfather's money. Matrimony seemed to be in the air, as it were. Johnson, also encountered casually, had told her that he was setting up a small tobacconist's business. Was Fenn aware that he had moved out of the flat and was living in the next street? Fenn, who, ever since he closed the flat, had been keeping Johnson under observation, thanked her gravely for the information, closed the door firmly behind her, and having given her time to get clear of the premises, went out to lunch, marvelling at some people's capacity for collecting information.

He was to have immediate proof that at least one item of her news was correct. When he got back to the Yard he was told that Dr. Gilroy and Miss Braid were waiting to see him.

He greeted them with becoming gravity, and there was nothing in his manner to suggest that he had had to wait outside the door of his room for a full minute to compose his countenance before entering.

"I persuaded Miss Braid to take a morning off at the Zoo," explained Gilroy, avoiding his old friend's eye. "The fact is, we both needed a holiday. I very nearly rang you up to see if you could lunch with us."

Fenn made a somewhat sardonic note of the "very nearly," but contented himself with saying that he had gone out early and that they probably would not have caught him.

"It's really my fault that we're bothering you now," said Jill Braid apologetically. "But Dr. Gilroy told me something at lunch that I think you ought to know. He doesn't consider it important, but, as I told him, every little thing matters, from my point of view."

She flashed an appealing glance at him.

"I'm grateful for any grist that comes to my mill," answered Fenn. "What is it?"

"Pure gossip, for all I know," said Gilroy disgustedly. "Honestly, I don't think there's anything to it. Only you seemed so pally with our friend Smith the other day that you may like to add this to your bag. The funny old party who works for me, Mrs. Cotswold by name, came to me this morning full of a story that seems to be going round the flats that the Smiths have got some one tucked away in their flat, and that, for some reason, they're keeping it dark. I shouldn't have thought twice about it if it wasn't for the fact that more than once lately I've heard the voices of two women talking and laughing late at night overhead. The floors are pretty thin, you know, and I should imagine they were probably calling to each other from the bedrooms. Unless Mrs. Smith has suddenly developed a habit of talking to herself there is an extra person in the flat. I don't suppose it's of the smallest importance, but I give it you for what it's worth."

"It's all my fault," said Jill apologetically. "I simply had to drag him here. He said it made him feel exactly like Miss Webb!"

She was totally unprepared for the Homeric peal of laughter that Fenn was unable to control. It was some time before he could speak, and when he did, he declined to give an account of himself.

"Sorry," he said, mopping his eyes. "But the thought of Miss Webb was too much for me. I'm all right now, so you can take that professional look out of your eye, Robert. I'm not hysterical. What's your programme for the afternoon?"

"Miss Braid's got to get back to work, so she declares," Gilroy informed him.

Jill nodded.

"I've got to make attractive drawings of three perfectly hideous dresses and get them off to my paper this evening," she said. "The only bright spot in my sad life is that they don't ask me to compose the appalling captions that will go underneath them. Some other poor wretch will tear her hair over those."

"Then I'll keep Robert, if you don't mind, and pick his brains some more. There may be something in this Smith affair. Anyway, you were quite right to bring him."

"Sure you'll get home all right?" asked Gilroy, with such unnecessary solicitude that Fenn turned away to hide a smile.

"Her faith in you is rather pathetic," he went on, after she had gone. "She believes you'll clear her."

"If you were a fair example of the average juryman, I'd undertake to do it," was Fenn's dry rejoinder.

Gilroy's face flushed a dull red. For a moment it seemed as though he were going to take offence at the implication, then his sense of humour triumphed and he laughed in spite of himself.

"I suppose I've been asking for it," he admitted. "But I have honestly tried to be impartial, Fenn, difficult though it's been. I've never been much of a lady's man, and I'm a bit uncomfortable with them as a rule—I suppose because I'm no good at small talk and that sort of thing. But you can't help getting on with Miss Braid, somehow. I put it down to the fact that she's a worker herself."

Fenn bent down to poke the fire.

"I've no doubt you're right," he agreed, in rather a stifled voice. "Am I to understand from this that you've abandoned your strictly scientific attitude?"

"Very funny, aren't you?" said Gilroy serenely. He had regained his composure, and showed no reluctance to discuss his attitude towards Miss Braid. "Roughly speaking, my point of view is this. I may be as big a fool about her as you are, but I have tried to keep an open mind. If she's not the most transparently honest person I ever set eyes on I'll eat my hat. And she couldn't possibly be guilty of this particular crime. Given the circumstances, I suppose we're all capable of killing in a fit of rage, but a deliberately-planned murder for money is a different thing. I agree with you that she is incapable of that. I'm willing to accept her word that Braid was alive at seven o'clock."

"That gives the murderer twelve minutes, roughly, in which to kill his man and get away," remarked Fenn. "It doesn't help us much."

Gilroy agreed, gloomily enough. Then an idea struck him.

"Who searched the flat when the murder was discovered? Webb or Johnson?" he asked.

"Johnson. Miss Braid was there by then, and Webb stayed with her in the passage, ready to intercept anybody who tried to get out. Johnson swears there was no one in the flat."

"And then Webb and Miss Braid went downstairs and left the flat empty and the road clear for any one who wished to get away."

Fenn nodded.

"Except for Johnson. It's funny how things come round to him. I've had him and Stephens on the mat and I can get nothing out of them. Stephens is, apparently, only too anxious to talk, and Johnson's in such a state of nerves still that I don't believe he'd be capable of concealing his connection with Stephens if there was one. I cannot bring myself to believe that there was."

"Then we come back to the old problem. If Johnson did leave the door open, who was he expecting?"

"Not Stephens. For one thing, the chisel he said he was carrying to force the lock was found in his pocket when he was arrested. I'm not saying that that's conclusive. He might have had it handy for any drawers or boxes in the flat, but it does serve to corroborate at least part of his story. And, you must remember, he's a man with very little power of invention."

"So Johnson's still nervy, is he? He ought to have got over the shock by now."

"If you ask him a sudden question he swerves like a shying horse. But, try as I will, I can't corner him. One thing, though, I did get out of him. He admits now that Braid kept large sums of money in the flat and that he knew of it. Says he used to feel nervous about it, so nervous that he never spoke to any one of it outside. He swears he never mentioned it at 'The Nag's Head.' Stephens, by the way, declares that he has never been inside that particular pub, and he certainly is not known there. I've had that looked into. I tackled Johnson as to why he'd kept back such an obviously important piece of information when I asked him if anything of value had been taken from the flat and he said he had not thought it of any importance at the time."

"Johnson's not such a fool as all that, by any means," said Gilroy. "Does he know where the money was kept?"

"Some of it, the money Braid used for current expenses was in the dispatch-box; but Johnson declares now that the old man had a larger hoard that he kept elsewhere. Where he kept it, he doesn't know. We went over the place pretty thoroughly, and Compton, Braid's solicitor, has looked through everything since. We've neither of us found anything."

Gilroy rose to his feet impulsively.

"Let's go down there now and give the place a look over," he suggested. "If the old man had a hiding-place it's pretty obvious it wouldn't jump to the eye."

Fenn agreed. He wanted to see Smith, in any case, and could take the flat on the way.

Gilroy proved a systematic worker. He fetched tools from his flat, had the carpet up in the bedroom, and even pried up a couple of loose boards under the hearthrug. But the accumulation of dust underneath showed that they had not been moved recently. Fenn confined his attention to the drawers and cupboards, and drew a complete blank.

As a last resort he dragged a table over to the wardrobe, climbed on to it, and peered over the cornice at the top. His explorations were rewarded by a cloud of dust.

"It doesn't look as if the old gentleman had been in favour of spring cleaning," he remarked. Then, with quickened interest, "Hallo, that's queer!"

On the top of the wardrobe, near the centre, was an oval-shaped space, completely clear of dust.

"Something stood here and has been moved quite recently," he said. "A hat-box, by the look of it. I'm certain there was nothing on the top of this cupboard when we went through the flat after the murder."

He climbed down and dusted his hands.

"Johnson will have to give an account of this," he said. "And I hope, for his sake, it will be satisfactory."

"A hat-box is as good as anything for hoarding money in," commented Gilroy, who was engaged in putting back the carpet. "Get off the edge, that's a good chap, while I give it a pull."

He was on his hands and knees by the wardrobe, tugging at the edge of the thick carpet. He sat back on his heels and looked up at Fenn.

"How tall was Sir Adam, would you say?" he asked unexpectedly.

"Getting on for six feet, I should think. I remember noticing his height when they were putting him on the stretcher. He was a tall man, though he'd obviously shrunk as he grew older. Why do you ask?"

Gilroy was staring at the carpet.

"I'd have given him all of that myself," he agreed. "If he had climbed on a chair he could have reached the top of the wardrobe easily. Come and look at this."

Fenn bent down. On the thick pile of the carpet, in front of the wardrobe, were a number of small round impressions. Amongst them he could see the fainter square indentations made by the table he had just used himself.

"Chair legs," he said. "And made by that chair, if I'm not mistaken."

He pointed to a heavy carved oak chair that stood by the wardrobe.

"He used it pretty often, too," added Gilroy, "by the look of the carpet. I think we've found out where he kept his money, all right."

"We haven't found out who took it, though," said Fenn. "Johnson's shorter than I am. He couldn't have used the chair, and there's only the one set of table legs."

"That's not conclusive," objected Gilroy. "He's lighter than you are, for one thing, and I doubt if even those marks you've made are permanent. Sir Adam was a very heavy man and he must have used the chair pretty often, otherwise the traces would hardly be so clear. Remember, it would be easy enough for Johnson to add a hat-box to his other luggage when he moved out of here. It wouldn't arouse any comment."

"It ought to be easy enough to find out if he did. By the way, he's setting up as a tobacconist, so I'm told."

Gilroy grinned.

"'So I'm told' means that it's not official. Therefore, source of information probably Miss Webb," he deduced.

"Of course. That woman ought to be in the force. She's wasted here."

The front door bell pealed loudly.

"Talk of the devil!" ejaculated Gilroy.

However, when Fenn opened the door, it was not Miss Webb who stood outside, but Ling, the proprietor of the newspaper shop.

"There's a phone call for you, inspector," he said. "It's from Scotland Yard, I think. They told me I should find you here."

Fenn thanked him.

"I gave your number in case they wanted to get me," he explained, ignoring an audible chuckle from Gilroy, who was aware that the Webbs were on the telephone. "You might come along, Robert, then I can have a few words with you when I'm through with them. I probably shan't have time to come back here."

They followed Ling back to his shop. The telephone stood at the end of the counter, the receiver lying by its side.

Fenn picked it up.

"Yes," he said. "Oh, he has, has he? A steward on a liner? What name? Macnab. No wonder they called him 'Scotty'! When? Thanks."

He rang off and turned to Gilroy.

"That was Whitaker," he said. "Stephens' witness has materialized. The S.O.S. reached him. He's a steward on a liner, and Whitaker has had a wireless message from the captain. They are due at Southampton on the morning of the twenty-fourth, and the man will be in London that evening."

The eyes of the two men met for a moment, then they both looked away. They had but one thought: Jill Braid.

CHAPTER VIII

DISCONCERTING AS the telephone message from the Yard had been, it contained no demand for Fenn's presence, and he decided to go back with Gilroy to Romney Chambers and look into the matter of Mr. Smith's mysterious visitor.

"By the way," he said, as he was parting with Gilroy at the door of his flat, "this charwoman of yours, is she a Chelsea woman?"

"Mrs. Cotswold? Born and bred in 'the village,' I believe. Why?"

"If she's inclined to gossip, and I never knew a 'char' yet who wasn't, you might encourage her. It's amazing the amount these old women manage to pick up, and they won't open their mouths to the police. You can get more out of her in five minutes than we should in a month. See if she knows anything more about the Smiths, or Johnson, for instance. For all we know, she may have a husband who is a regular customer at 'The Nag's Head.' Local gossip isn't to be despised."

Gilroy did not look over-pleased.

"She'll gossip all right! I've only just managed to stem the flow sufficiently to get my breakfast in peace, and now I've got to undo the good work of months! She's a nice old body, but, lord, how she talks!"

"Let her!" was Fenn's unsympathetic injunction as he disappeared up the stairs.

He found both the Smiths at home, and though Smith accorded him a friendly, if sardonic, welcome, Mrs. Smith seemed to him nervous and ill at ease.

"It struck me that I might as well have Mrs. Smith's corroboration of your account of your movements on the night of November the sixth," he said briskly. "She was at home when you got back, I understand?"

Mrs. Smith's rather sallow face flushed a bright scarlet.

"You won't get anything of the sort out of me!" she exclaimed surprisingly. "Ned didn't set foot inside this flat till half-past seven that night, and I'm ready to swear to it!"

Smith crossed the room and put his arm round her shoulders.

"Steady, old girl!" he said soothingly. "The truth is, she's a bit worked up, Mr. Fenn, and doesn't rightly know what she's saying. That business downstairs has upset her."

"It hasn't upset me so much that I don't know what time you got in last Tuesday night. Considering I'd kept your supper hot and waited for you and then was told you'd had it at the station! Where he'd been or what he'd been doing, I don't know, but he wasn't in this flat, Mr. Fenn!"

Her husband shot a glance, half anxious, half deprecating, at Fenn.

"I've told Mr. Fenn where I was, and he can judge for himself whether I'm speaking the truth or not. If he can prove that I didn't come up by the earlier train, or that I was the man that stung that poor can of an American, let him. There's no need for you to butt in."

"Let's get this straight," interjected Fenn. "Mrs. Smith, here, was ready enough to speak for you when you were charged the other day. She said then that you were with her in this flat at the time you were supposed to be taking that money off the American."

"I did, and I lied!" snapped Mrs. Smith. "I knew he hadn't anything to do with any American, but a lot of good it would have done to tell the police that! If he'd taken the money off him I should have seen it, shouldn't I? Goodness knows, we've wanted it badly enough lately, and I can testify there hasn't been a dollar bill inside this place. Knowing what I did, there wasn't anything for it but to say he was here with me. And I said it!"

"And now you propose to go back on it! You're a nice couple, I must say," was Fenn's exasperated comment. "I've had two conflicting accounts from your husband already, and now I find you contradicting your own statement to the police! I'm a patient man, Mrs. Smith, but you can't play fast and loose with us like that. It's time I got the facts from both of you."

"You've had them from me," stated Smith sullenly. "I came up from Luton by the three-fifty and went straight to this flat. That's what I told the sergeant when he charged me, and it's what I'm telling you now."

"But it's not what you told me three days ago," remarked Fenn. "Now, Mrs. Smith, let's have your version."

"Ned got back to this flat at seven-thirty, not a minute earlier. Where he'd been, I don't know."

Fenn struck swiftly.

"Sure he wasn't in the flat downstairs?" he suggested.

Her face whitened as she realized the trap into which she had fallen. Smith gave a long, low whistle.

"See what you've done now, old lady," he murmured. "Better to have let things lie."

Fenn noticed that, though he was obviously nervous as to the lengths to which his wife's tongue might lead her, he was not seriously disconcerted. Mrs. Smith, on the contrary, was fast losing her head.

"He wasn't anywhere inside this building," she cried, her voice shrill with alarm. "I can prove it—"

"None of that!"

Smith's exclamation cut like a knife across the sentence, and with a frightened look at him Mrs. Smith relapsed into silence.

There was a short pause, broken by Smith.

"So that's how it stands, Mr. Fenn," he said, in his silkiest voice. "You'll have to choose between us. But if you knew women as I do—"

The words died on his lips.

With a quickness few would have given him credit for, Fenn had crossed the room and thrown open a door leading, presumably, into the little dining-room of the flat.

"I thought so," he said quietly, standing aside so as to leave the doorway clear. "I think I'll have to ask you to join our little party."

Smith, with a shrug of his shoulders, strolled over to the table and helped himself to a cigarette.

"Sorry, Gertie," he said. "It wasn't any fault of mine."

The new-comer, a big, handsome woman whose clothes, in their expensive but quiet good taste, were in marked contrast to her surroundings, laughed good-naturedly.

"It was my own darned bad luck," she said. "If I hadn't fallen over my own feet coming out of the bedroom it wouldn't have happened. What can I do for you, Mr. Fenn?"

"Save me and yourself a lot of trouble by coming along quietly, for one thing," said Fenn. "In the meanwhile, if you've anything to say about this business here, I shall be glad to hear it. Subject to the usual warning, of course."

Gertie Anderson, "wanted" in Liverpool for shop-lifting, was an old acquaintance of Fenn's. Oddly enough, when reviewing the list of any possible fugitives Smith might be suspected of sheltering, he had omitted to take her into account, possibly because it was several years since she had operated in London.

There was no malice in her eyes as she looked across at the detective. Gertie was a philosophical creature when her temper was not roused.

"I'll come," she said shortly. "I'm tired of lying low, anyway. I've had a pretty thick time of it, I may tell you. But I don't know anything about the job downstairs. I only came up from Liverpool three nights ago."

Fenn grunted.

"Then it's a pity, for your sake, that you weren't spotted at the station," he remarked.

"But I wasn't. And for why? Because I was motored up by a friend. And if you ask me who the friend was, I'm not telling. So you can whistle for an alibi."

"I fancy it's you who'll do the whistling when the time comes," said Fenn dryly. "However, that's your affair. Anybody see you off at Liverpool?"

She shook her head.

"Not a soul! I just faded out, in a manner of speaking. Matter of fact, I couldn't stand it any longer. As soon as I knew the splits were after me I went to May Heally. I don't mind telling you that, because she's out of the country now for good. It was all right there till her Phil came out of stir. That's what she'd been waiting for, and, as soon as she could, she went off with him. Fed up with England, both of them, and I don't blame them. And there was I on my little lonesome, sneaking out at night to get a tin of sardines and polishing the oil-cloth in May's flat in the daytime for want of something to do. It was a proper picnic, I can tell you! Then, three nights ago, I got the chance of a lift up to town, and came to Ned and Carrie here. That's the story of my sad life up to date. Sorry I can't do more for you."

"That's right," agreed Smith. "The missis found her waiting outside the door on Saturday night. She doesn't know anything."

Fenn sighed. Accustomed as he was to this kind of interrogation, he had seldom had to face so many wilfully contradictory statements. That the Smiths were trying to shield each other and making a nice muddle of it in the process was evident. The one story he saw no reason to doubt was that of Gertie Anderson, and of the three people before him, she was the one most likely to have been involved in the murder of Sir Adam Braid. For Gertie, in spite of her robust good-humour, had a reputation for violence, and in her far-away youth had been convicted of house-breaking, in company with a man who had since done more than one stretch for burglary. In any case, she was the least of his problems. A warrant was out for her arrest, and for the next few weeks she would be where he could place his hand on her. The Smiths were a more difficult proposition. He could hardly arrest them on suspicion at this stage of the inquiry.

He turned to Mrs. Smith.

"Assuming, then, that you were alone in the flat on the evening of November the sixth—" he began.

"She wasn't," cut in Smith at once. "I was with her, and you can take it from me that neither of us know anything about this ruddy murder!"

His temper had got the better of him at last, and at any other time Fenn would have taken swift advantage of the fact. But he was not attending to Smith. The words had hardly left his lips when the detective intercepted a glance full of meaning between the two women, and was seized with a sudden conviction that they shared some secret which Mrs. Smith had not chosen to communicate to her husband.

Acting on impulse, he rose, picked up his chair, and planted it opposite to that of Mrs. Smith. As he sat down, he saw her eyes widen with fear and then dart helplessly from the other woman to her husband, and he knew that he had not been mistaken.

"We've had enough of this fooling," he said, with a note in his voice that made her shrink. "Something happened here on the night of the sixth. What was it?"

All expression faded from Mrs. Smith's face.

"Nothing," she muttered.

"Think again," pursued Fenn. "Any statement you make now is voluntary and I can't force you to speak, but you may as well make a clean breast of it now as wait till you find yourself under oath in the witness-box. You're not doing yourself or Smith any good by keeping things back."

"Aw, let him have it, Carrie," broke in the other woman unexpectedly. "What's the good of holding out now?"

"There's nothing to tell," said Mrs. Smith stubbornly. "I was here by myself, as I said, and I never went out of the flat."

"Then you heard or saw something," countered Fenn sharply. "What was it?"

"If you ask me," remarked the irrepressible Gertie, "she heard the old man downstairs bumped off. I've been telling her all along to go to the station and say so; but she got the wind up about Ned, though she knows he wasn't within a mile of the place at the time. Spit it out, Carrie; you're only getting us all in wrong with the police. Ned and I can look out for ourselves."

"What did you hear, Mrs. Smith?" asked Fenn patiently.

Under this combined attack Mrs. Smith's nerve began to desert her. Her voice rose hysterically as she replied—

"She means a noise I heard in the flat downstairs. I didn't think anything of it then, and I don't now. If it hadn't been for the way she's been bothering me about it I shouldn't even have remembered it."

"She never said anything to me about it," exclaimed Smith.

He was evidently genuinely taken aback at the turn the conversation was taking.

"I take it that, by 'the flat downstairs,' you mean Sir Adam Braid's flat?" said Fenn.

She nodded.

"I suppose his window was open, just as mine was," she volunteered reluctantly. "If I hadn't been leaning out I shouldn't have heard it."

"What did you hear?"

"Only a bump that might have been a chair falling. And then a sort of cry."

"What do you mean by 'a sort of cry'?"

"It sounded like 'My God!' but I couldn't be sure. It was a man's voice—that I do know. I thought Johnson had probably dropped something. I know he told Ned once it was as much as his life was worth to break anything in that flat."

"Where were you when you heard this?"

"In my bedroom. I was getting ready the dinner in the kitchen when I remembered some gloves I'd hung outside the bedroom window. I've got a line there I use for drying things. I didn't want to leave them out all night, and I thought I'd better take them in while I remembered it. I opened the window wide, and leaned well out to reach them. It was then that I heard the noise below."

"What time was it?"

"Just on a quarter to seven," stated Mrs. Smith definitely.

Fenn stared at her, his disbelief plainly written on his countenance. Up till now, it had seemed more than probable that it was Sir Adam she had heard. But Sir Adam, according to three independent witnesses, was alive and entertaining a visitor in his study up till seven o'clock.

"What makes you so sure of the time?" he asked.

"Because when I remembered the gloves I looked at the clock in the kitchen, to see whether I'd time to bring them in then. It was just on a quarter to seven, and I decided I had, and went straight into the bedroom."

"Is your clock reliable?"

"Quite. It's set every morning by the church clock and it's never more than a minute out. You can see the church clock from this window."

"You're sure you didn't make a mistake? I don't mind telling you that we've established the fact that Sir Adam was alive after a quarter to seven."

Mrs. Smith cast a triumphant glance at Gertie Anderson.

"It's what I've said all along. What I heard had nothing to do with the murder. The time's all right, I know, because I was expecting Ned home at seven-thirty and I wanted him to find his supper ready when he got back. And then he went and had it at the station."

Evidently she could not get over this matter of the supper. In her mind it seemed to rank above the murder in importance. Her indignation served to convince Fenn that whatever Smith's movements may have been that evening, he did not get back to the flat till seven-thirty.

"Why didn't you come forward with this information at the time?" he demanded.

"I tell you, I didn't think anything of it."

Fenn's temper failed him at last.

"Nonsense!" he exclaimed. "You don't tell me that you're not aware that information of that sort is important. I've seen your statement to the officer who called on you after the murder. In it you declared quite definitely that you had neither heard nor seen anything suspicious."

It was Gertie Anderson who answered.

"Put two and two together, Mr. Fenn," she said, "and if you're lucky it makes four. The constable saw Ned first, before he saw Carrie, and Ned didn't say anything about any cries, or chairs falling, for the simple reason that he hadn't heard them and Carrie hadn't thought of telling him about them. A couple of hours later Carrie was up at the station, swearing till all was blue that Ned had been in the flat here with her all the evening. She wasn't likely to take the risk of having him questioned about a thing he hadn't heard, was she? She's been all kinds of a fool this evening, but she's not such a soft fool as that!"

"Then I may take it that Smith did not get in till half-past seven on the night in question?" said Fenn blandly.

"Take it any way you like," agreed Miss Anderson cheerfully.

Smith swung round, muttering something under his breath which sounded suspiciously like "Damn all women!" and walked over to the window, where he remained during the rest of the proceedings. Evidently he had washed his hands of the affair.

Fenn inspected the bedroom, and found that it was above Gilroy's room, which, in turn, was immediately above that of

Sir Adam Braid. He also tackled Mrs. Smith once more as to the exact time at which she had heard the sounds from below. But she was not to be moved, and, to the best of his knowledge, she could have no possible object in lying.

Then, accompanied by Miss Anderson, who showed herself a chatty and philosophical companion, he left the flat.

On the way to the police station she favoured him with her opinion of Mrs. Smith's statement.

"If Carrie didn't hear that poor old chap's last words, I'd like to know what she did hear," she said. "And that's a straight story she told you, Mr. Fenn. If she says the time was a quarter to seven you may be pretty sure she's right. She's got a good enough head when she keeps it. What she told you is, word for word, what she told me the night I came to the flat. The trouble with Carrie is that she'd swear herself black in the face to save Ned. Fairly soppy about each other, those two are. But she wasn't lying just now, you can take my word for it."

And Fenn, though he had little enough opinion of her word, was, for once, inclined to accept it. He went back to the Yard feeling tired and disheartened.

If it were Sir Adam Mrs. Smith had heard, her information opened out an entirely new vista and one which he did not much care to contemplate. Her suggestion that the voice was that of Johnson was, of course, inadmissible, seeing that Johnson was at "The Nag's Head" at that time. Given that the cry had come from Sir Adam and that he had actually met his death at that moment, the dispute both Stephens and Webb had heard going on in the study could only have been between two unknown people, a man and a woman, presumably in league with Braid's assailant. For Webb had arrived outside the flat and had stood listening to two people quarrelling at the precise moment that Mrs. Smith had heard the cry from the bedroom.

In his endeavour to reconcile Mrs. Smith's account with that of Webb, Fenn began, for the first time, to realize how misguided he and Gilroy had been in their too hasty assumption that the voice in the study had been that of Sir Adam Braid. Webb, misled by the violence of the speaker, had at once jumped to the conclusion that he was listening to Sir Adam; Jill Braid had stated frankly that she could not identify the voice as that of her grandfather. Fenn now found himself confronted with the possibility that, instead of one intruder, there had been three in the flat that night, and that the man and woman in the study, on hearing the front door bell, had raised their voices purposely, with the object of drowning the sound of a struggle going on in the bedroom.

This, as a theory, seemed plausible enough, but what Fenn found difficult to believe was that, fifteen minutes later, Sir Adam's assailants should still be engaged in loud conversation in the study whilst the body of their victim was actually lying in the room across the passage. And yet, if Jill Braid's account were true, this is what would seem to have happened.

Fenn reviewed his list of suspects. If Stephens' witness was prepared to substantiate his statement—and it seemed, judging by the message Fenn had that afternoon received from Whitaker, that he was about to do so—he must have been clear of the flat before the murder took place. This left the two Smiths, Gertie Anderson, and Jill Braid, none of whom, so far, had been able to produce any convincing proof that they were not in the flat at the time.

Disregarding Mrs. Smith's statement, the voices heard by Stephens at six-thirty-five and Webb between six-forty-five and six-fifty-five might have been those of Mrs. Smith and Sir Adam, or Jill Braid and Sir Adam, or Gertie Anderson and Sir Adam.

Taking Mrs. Smith's evidence as true, the voices heard by Webb and Stephens might have been those of Smith and Gertie Anderson, or Jill Braid and a man at present unknown.

Or, provided that there was a third person in the bedroom and that the cry Mrs. Smith had heard had emanated from him and not from Sir Adam, the disputants in the study might have been: Gertie Anderson and Sir Adam, or Jill Braid and Sir Adam.

Accepting Jill Braid's, Stephens', and Webb's accounts, and ruling out Mrs. Smith's, there would seem to have been a man and a woman (Smith and his wife, or Smith and Gertie Anderson?) present in the flat, the woman between six-thirty-five and six-fifty-five, and the man at seven.

There was also Stephens' evidence to take into account that some one, man or woman, had entered the flat soon after six-thirty, when he was standing in the passage.

And this person had entered without a key. If Stephens was speaking the truth, this admitted of three explanations: Either Johnson had left the door unlatched deliberately; or the man whose voice Stephens had heard in the study had failed to shut it when he entered; or Sir Adam had opened it himself after the departure of Johnson.

That night Fenn dreamed that he had surprised Webb and his sister in the act of stabbing Mrs. Smith, their excuse being that she was not the kind of person they were accustomed to.

It was a nice, straightforward case compared to the one he was engaged on in his waking hours.

CHAPTER IX

THREE DAYS LATER Fenn, on coming down to breakfast, found a letter addressed in Gilroy's small, neat handwriting lying beside his plate.

"Dear Fenn," it ran, "taking the estimable Miss Webb as my model, I have, I think, squeezed the last ounce of information out of old Cotswold. She has, as you so sapiently suggested, a husband who frequents 'The Nag's Head.' Here are her contributions, for what they are worth. Johnson puts his money on horses, with very little judgment, going by results. He does most of his betting through Ling (the chap at the corner of the street, who, it appears, runs the usual newsagent's little side-show, in addition to his legitimate business), and, a short time ago, is known to have owed money right and left. Two days ago he paid up what he owed to a pal of Mr. Cotswold's, and at the same time he settled up with two other men to whom he owed money. The general impression is that he has had a windfall of some sort. This seems a bit significant, in view of the disappearance of the hat-box, and might very well account for his nerviness now. Mrs. C. has no information worth reporting concerning the Smiths, and has never heard of Stephens. Says her husband knows most of Johnson's pals, and, egged on by me, she questioned him, but drew a complete blank there. She is sure that Stephens was not a regular frequenter of 'The Nag's Head.' Mr. Cotswold *is*, according to his long-suffering wife! Let me know if there is anything else I can do.—Yours, Robert."

Fenn rose from the table feeling considerably cheered. He had reached a pitch at which he was grateful for any evidence that pointed away from Jill, though, at the most, it seemed doubtful whether Johnson could have been guilty of anything more heinous than theft. He had undoubtedly had ample opportunity to rifle the flat immediately after the murder, and, if he knew of the hat-box, could have helped himself to its contents while Jill was telephoning from Webb's flat. Why he should have taken the hat-box, instead of merely abstracting the money it contained, was a mystery. That Ling should run a betting agency on the side was not surprising. It would have been more so if he hadn't! Nearly every little shop of the sort in the poorer districts of London acts as a blind for traffic of that sort, and the mere fact that Ling thought it worth while to install a telephone had given Fenn a pretty good inkling as to his real business on the occasion of his first visit to the shop. But if his morning had begun well, it was destined to end badly.

He had not been at New Scotland Yard more than ten minutes before he was rung up by the manager of the Chelsea branch of the Northern Counties Bank.

"Four of the notes we issued to Sir Adam Braid on October the thirtieth have returned to roost," he said. "Shall I send our clerk round to you, or will you drop in and hear what he has to say?"

"I'll come round now," was Fenn's answer, little recking of the shock he was to receive when he got there.

"You'd better see our man yourself," said the manager, as he greeted him. "He'll give you the facts. But I'm afraid they won't help you much, seeing where the notes came from."

He sent for the clerk, who gave his name as George Soames, and produced four one pound notes which he handed to Fenn.

"These were handed in just before closing time last night by a Mrs. Sutherland, who has banked with us for several years," he said. "She owns a couple of houses in Chelsea, which she lets out in rooms at a weekly rental. She collects these rents every Wednesday, and usually pays the results into her account on Thursday. These notes were part of her payment."

"You've no idea which of her lodgers they came from, I suppose?" asked Fenn.

"As a matter of fact, I have," answered Soames. "I recognized the numbers at once, but I didn't know whether you wanted her suspicions roused, so I didn't question her directly. I merely made a joking comment on the fact that we had paid out these very notes not so long ago and had not expected to see them back so soon. Fortunately she rose to the bait and told me of her own accord where she had got them. Apparently some of her tenants slip their rent into an envelope, and drop it, with their rent book, into her letter-box. I actually saw her take these out of the envelope in which she had received them, so her information was probably correct. I'm afraid it won't lead anywhere, though. She got them from the one person in whose hands one would naturally expect to find them."

Fenn caught his breath.

"Who is that?" he asked.

"Miss Braid, Sir Adam Braid's granddaughter." There was a silence while Fenn slowly tucked the notes away in his pocket-book.

"We'll keep these, if you don't mind," he said at last, "though I admit it would have been more satisfactory, from our point of view, if they had come from almost any other source."

He went straight from the bank to Mrs. Sutherland's. The landlady was at home, and he questioned her closely, taking the line that if the notes had really been paid in by Jill, who had a legitimate right to them, there would be no point in pursuing that avenue of investigation any further. Mrs. Sutherland assured him emphatically that they had. She also volunteered the information that Jill Braid was a lodger after her own heart, quiet and hardworking, and that she would have been prepared to stretch a point and meet her half-way even if she had, after all, failed to come up to the scratch with the rent.

"What's that?" demanded Fenn.

The landlady hesitated.

"I don't want to say anything against her," she said at last. "As I told you, she's a good tenant. But money's been pretty tight with her lately. She was quite frank about it. All my tenants are supposed to pay by the week; it's the only way in which I can make sure of getting my rents. They're a 'here to-day and gone to-morrow' lot, most of them. Well, Miss Braid owed me four weeks' rent when she paid up the other day, and knowing how things were with her, I was very glad to get it. A pound a week she pays for those rooms, and that's less than I charge the others."

"I suppose she told you the money was part of her grandfather's legacy?"

"No. She simply said that she had come into a bit of luck. I thought she meant she'd sold some of her drawings."

Fenn went on from there to Jill's lodgings, but there he drew a blank. She was out, and the music student who shared the top floor with her could not say when she might be expected back. All she knew was that she had gone off with a parcel of drawings to Fleet Street early that morning.

As he walked briskly away down the street, Fenn's mind dwelt bleakly enough on this, the latest of his problems. Unless Jill had some convincing explanation ready, he saw nothing for it now but to take out a warrant for her arrest.

Before going back to the Yard he turned off King's Road and went round by the newsagent's shop. Ling was sitting behind the counter as usual. He looked up with a gleam of interest in his eyes as Fenn entered.

"Anything I can do for you, inspector?" he asked.

"You can tell me how much Sir Adam Braid's man, Johnson, has dropped to you during the last few months," said Fenn briskly; "and whether he has paid any of it back yet."

Ling stared at him. His face was inscrutable.

"I'm afraid I don't get you," he answered. "Sir Adam had a running account here for papers, and I was going to ask you where I should go for my money. But Johnson, he paid for any he bought on the spot."

"I'm not talking of bills," said Fenn, going straight to the point. "Look here, Ling, it's no affair of mine if you do keep a betting joint. That's a matter for the local police. But if I can't get my information one way, I'll have to get it another. You don't want this place raided, though I daresay it's not the first time you've had a visit from the police."

"They can come, for all I care. They won't find nothing here."

"Which means you've got a room somewhere else you're using," asserted Fenn cheerily. "Well, I've no doubt a good many people know where it is, and there's generally one squealer at least when it comes to a betting raid. Better not risk it."

Ling waited till he had finished tying up a bundle of old newspaper remainders before he spoke.

"What do you want to know?" he asked, and Fenn knew that he had gained his point.

"Just what was against Johnson on your books and whether he has paid up," he said.

"He owed me close on fifteen pounds," admitted Ling reluctantly. "Mind you, I'm not saying he'd been betting. It was a private debt. He was fed up with service, and had some idea of buying up a tobacco business and retiring. He said he could double the money if I'd lend it to him. That's what he told me, anyway. Well, I knew he was getting steady money, and I let him have it. And he paid me back all right, too."

"When?"

"Last Thursday week. Two days after the murder, that'd be."

"Did he say where the money came from?"

"Come to think of it, he didn't. But I know as he'd got some money in War Loan that he hadn't wanted to touch till he bought the business. Likely he sold that. I'd been pressin' him a bit, I admit." Then, as Fenn turned to go—

"You're not trying to fix the murder on him, are you, inspector? He wasn't nowhere near the flats at the time, and besides, he wouldn't hurt a fly, Johnson wouldn't."

There was a suspicion of contempt in his voice. Evidently he had a poor enough opinion of the man.

Fenn shook his head.

"We've got nothing on Johnson," he said, with an assumption of frankness. "But certain notes which we believe to have been in the possession of Sir Adam Braid when he died have been traced, and we're trying to locate the person who paid them in. How did he pay you? In pound notes?"

"Two fivers, and the rest in pound notes," answered Ling promptly. "I banked the fivers and stuck the rest in the till. They may be here, or I may have paid them out. There's no telling."

He opened a drawer in the counter and took out a tin box.

"This is where I keep any notes as come in. His may be among them, but I've changed a cheque or two for customers in the last few days and, as like as not, I used them."

Fenn looked through the little bundle of notes he handed him.

"None of my numbers here," he said, as he gave them back. "I needn't tell you we don't want this to get about."

"It won't be my fault if it does," Ling assured him. "There's enough gossip goin' on as it is over that affair at Romney Chambers. They're sayin' as the old gentleman's granddaughter's mixed up in it now."

Fenn did not miss the inquisitive gleam in the man's eyes.

"Trust them for getting hold of the wrong end of the stick," he said carelessly. "Miss Braid didn't get to the flat till some time after her grandfather was killed."

"She was in the building, though, by all accounts," was Ling's shrewd rejoinder.

"Who told you that?" asked Fenn sharply.

"Johnson was speaking of it when he was in here the other day."

"Then if he told you that much, he'll have told you that he saw her enter the flat himself."

Ling shrugged his shoulders.

"I don't take no stock of what people say," he said. "I've got me own affairs to attend to. And what if she was in the building? She wasn't the only one, as I told Johnson."

Fenn took him up sharply.

"What are you trying to say?" he demanded. "If you've got any information to give, let's have it."

But Ling declined to commit himself further.

"If I'd any information I'd have been to you with it by this time," he said. "I know my duty. I'm not sayin' nothin' and I'm not accusing anybody. But there's some queer customers got flats in Romney Chambers, and I've an idea you know it, inspector."

Fenn met his eyes with a glance as shrewd as his own.

"The question is, how do you come to know it, Mr. Ling?" he parried.

"Well, I'm not a betting man, as a rule," explained Ling virtuously. "But I do a bit of racin' now and again like any one else. And twice I've travelled up from Kempton in the same carriage with a gentleman I see sometimes going in and out of the flats. The last time we came up together and the coppers were waitin' for him at this end." Fenn laughed.

"In that case, you'll be interested to hear that he's travelling for a gas-fitting company at present," he said. "He tried to sell me a contraption of some sort the other day."

"I'll take your word for it he's travelling," was Ling's cynical rejoinder. "And I've no doubt he tried to take some money off you. It's what happened the only two times I met him."

Fenn worked late that night at the Yard, and it was close on eight o'clock when he gathered up his papers preparatory to departure. He was about to rise from his table when he was arrested by the buzz of the telephone at his elbow. He took off the receiver. "That you, Fenn?"

The voice was that of Gilroy.

"Fenn speaking. What is it?"

"Look here, Fenn, a pretty rotten thing's happened. I'm speaking from the Piccolo Restaurant. I asked Miss Braid to dine with me here tonight and arranged to call for her at her rooms. I'd nearly reached them when I passed a chap who was standing on the other side of the road and recognized him. He was one of your men, that fellow Garrison, who used to be in your room at Scotland Yard. I had a suspicion of what he was up to, and I took a squint out of Miss Braid's window after I got in. He was still there, and he was obviously watching the house. I didn't say anything to Miss Braid, but I kept my eyes open, and he's here now, in this restaurant, sitting at a table near the door. What are you going to do about it?"

"Have Garrison on the mat for making such a conspicuous ass of himself. He ought to know better than that by now."

Fenn's tone was not conciliatory. He was tired and jaded, and had spent the afternoon fighting a black depression.

"Good lord, you don't mean to say it's your doing?" Gilroy's voice was hot with resentment. "I made sure some fool department or other had been butting in behind your back. I say, old chap, you'll have to call him off! The next thing will be that she'll notice something, and what do you suppose she'll think then? She's feeling rotten enough already over this business."

"Oblige me by going back to your dinner, Robert, and leaving me to handle this case in my own way," said Fenn wearily.

Gilroy exploded.

"You can't take that line, Fenn! Either you believe she's innocent or you don't! Considering the things——"

Fenn cut him short.

"Don't be a fool, Robert! Or, if you must make an ass of yourself, come and do it here instead of over the telephone! As for Garrison, I'll call him off to-morrow if I think fit. If you take my advice you'll say nothing of this to Miss Braid."

He rang off before Gilroy could answer. He saw no reason to tell him that he had already written to Jill Braid, asking her to call on him at his office, without fail, next morning.

CHAPTER X

FENN CAST a wary glance at Jill Braid as she came into his office next morning, but it was evident from her manner that Gilroy, in spite of his indignation, had kept his discovery of the ubiquitous Garrison to himself. Her greeting was as natural and friendly as usual, and if she felt any misgivings as to the reason of Fenn's hasty summons she did not show them.

Intent on getting an unpleasant business over as soon as possible, he opened his drawer and took out the four notes he had received from the bank. As he spread them out before her he watched her face closely, only to find that she was regarding his manoeuvres with a faint, amused smile on her lips.

"What a pleasant sight!" she said. "Have you got any more like that, Mr. Fenn?"

In spite of himself, Fenn's official attitude relaxed.

"As a matter of fact," he retorted, "that was the very question I was going to ask you. But, first of all, I wish you'd tell me where you got these."

"But they aren't mine," she answered, with a little frown of perplexity. "I haven't lost any money that I know of."

"I don't suppose you'd recognize them, but these were paid by you to your landlady last Wednesday. I've got a special reason for wishing to know where they came from."

Her face cleared.

"I can tell you that exactly," she answered frankly. To his relief she did not show the slightest sign of embarrassment. "My grandfather gave them to me."

"When?"

She hesitated.

"So much has happened since that it's difficult to remember. He came to my rooms. It was the first time he'd ever been there."

Then, as the recollection came to her—

"Of course! It was the day before he died. Why he came, I don't know exactly, but I fancy he'd seen a drawing of mine in a paper I work for, and liked it. At any rate, he spoke of it and said something about my talents being wasted. I told him frankly that I couldn't afford to do anything else. He was extraordinarily nice and sympathetic," she finished sadly. "I wished I'd realized before that he could be like that. And when he left, he just took out his pocket-book and gave me the money."

"How much did he give you?" asked Fenn.

"Twenty pounds. It was an immense sum for me. I hadn't had so much money in my pocket for a long time. You see, one of my best papers had changed hands, and the result had been a new fashion editor. That's always fatal to a free-lance like myself."

"You were pretty hard up then, I gather?"

"I was broke," she answered frankly. "I owed for my rent and various other things besides. My grandfather's visit seemed like a sort of miracle at the time."

Fenn glanced at the calendar that stood on his table.

"Your grandfather's visit took place on Monday, November the fifth," he said. "If you owed money for your rent the natural thing would have been for you to pay it on the following Wednesday, which, I understand, is the day your landlady collects her rents. Can you give me any reason why you didn't do this?"

Jill glanced swiftly at him as though there were something in his voice she did not understand. For the first time in the course of the interview she looked troubled.

"I forgot," she said simply. "Tuesday was so awful, and next day I could think of nothing but grandfather and what had happened to him. Mrs. Sutherland, the landlady, is a decent old thing, and she knew that I was upset, and didn't bother me. Then, having missed one rent day, I suppose I naturally waited for the next."

"Did you pay any other bills out of the money Sir Adam gave you?"

"Yes. There was a milk bill and some money I owed to a little restaurant that sometimes lets me have meals on tick."

"Can you tell me how much you've got left of the twenty pounds? I'm sorry to bother you, but I've got to try to get this clear."

"I can tell you exactly," she answered. "I was making up my accounts last night. I've got seven pounds, thirteen shillings left. Mr. Fenn, is there anything queer about those notes?"

"Nothing. But they are part of a batch that was issued to your grandfather by his bank, and we naturally had to account for them."

She nodded abstractedly. Then, as the result of her reflections—

"You mean that the person who killed my grandfather might have taken them?" she said slowly. "I don't wonder you wanted to see me."

"It seemed advisable to hear your explanation," agreed Fenn guardedly.

She gave a little sigh.

"I don't seem to have much luck, do I?" she murmured, and she looked so pitifully young and helpless that Fenn's heart smote him. He tried to infuse a reassuring note of confidence into his voice as he answered her.

"It's just as well you had a convincing explanation to offer. That was all that was needed."

But his words lacked conviction, and he knew it as he met her eyes. They were wide with apprehension, but they did not waver.

"All that you needed, you mean," she said gravely. "I believe you do know I'm speaking the truth. But I can see how it must look to other people. I'm in a pretty bad hole, aren't I, Mr. Fenn?"

"You're innocent, and that's half the battle," he hedged, with a smile so full of kindness and good-comradeship that a little of the dread was lifted from her heart. "There's one thing, though, I want you to remember. Anything you can tell me, not only about that night, but about your dealings with your grandfather in the past week or so, may be of use to me. If I'd known about that money, for instance, I need never have dragged you down here to-day. Why didn't you tell me before about it?"

"I never thought about it. There were so many things to put it out of my head. But I see what you mean. If there's anything that occurs to me, I'll come to you at once."

"That's a bargain, then," he said. "And now about those notes. If you'll let me have them, I'll see that you get the equivalent in cash. Are they at your rooms? Then I'll call for them. Let me see, to-morrow's Sunday. Shall I find you at home in the morning? Good. Then I'll come about eleven," he said cheerfully, as he shook hands and accompanied her to the door.

But it was as well for her that she did not see his face as he moved heavily back to his seat at the table.

Gilroy was waiting for her in a little underground restaurant in Victoria Street. He kept a sharp eye on the door as he greeted her. Had he but known it, Garrison, the C.I.D. man, had been called off by Fenn that morning, and his substitute, who was at that moment settling himself comfortably in the first-floor window of a teashop on the other side of the street, had never, as yet, crossed his horizon. It was unlikely, therefore, that his feelings would be lacerated again.

"Well, how did you get on?" he demanded, as he helped her off with her coat.

"Mr. Fenn was a dear. He always is," she answered. "Let's forget it for a little, please. It's all so beastly."

She did not allude to the subject again till they had finished lunch and were sitting over their coffee.

"I'm beginning to lose my nerve, I think," she said suddenly. "I know now what it must be like to feel that every policeman you pass in the street is against, instead of for you. Until now, I've always looked upon them as being there for my own special convenience and protection."

"Considering that one of your oldest and best friends is a policeman—" began Gilroy banteringly.

But she cut him short.

"Don't laugh, please," she said, and there was a tenseness in her voice that he did not like. "I've kept telling myself, all along, how absurd the whole thing is, but now I'm frightened. It's like being trapped. Whichever way I look, there's no way out. Mr. Fenn's worried too. He did his best to hide it, but I knew."

Gilroy tried to reassure her, much as Fenn had done, but his methods, too, lacked conviction. He was consumed with a quite unreasoning rage against the detective for having frightened her.

"I'm fed up with police methods," he exclaimed angrily. "Old Fenn's a good sort and I know he's doing his best, but it's about time he arrived at something definite."

Jill's colour rose.

"I don't see what more he could do," she said warmly. "I don't suppose any one's ever had a better friend than he's been to me over this business. I'm not so blind as he thinks, and I've been wondering lately whether, if any one else had been in charge of the case, I should be at liberty now."

Gilroy, who knew how near she was to the truth, had no wish to pursue the subject. He capitulated.

"I'm sorry," he said. "Only I'm beginning to think there's a good deal to be said for the system they have abroad. There they can arrest people on suspicion, and it's up to them to clear themselves. In Italy there'd be a dozen people in prison over a case like this."

"Which would be all right if the murderer happened to be among them. And there's one thing you forget."

"And that is?"

"That I should be one of the dozen people in prison," she retorted.

They were both homeward-bound and he walked with her to her rooms. Half-way down King's Road he halted abruptly.

"Now, where's *he* off to?"

She followed his eyes and saw Johnson on the other side of the road, walking briskly in the direction of Sloane Square. He was carrying a couple of suitcases and was clad in garments of suspicious newness. Equally suggestive was the festal appearance of the tall, handsome girl who accompanied him.

"If Johnson wasn't married this afternoon, I'll eat my hat!" exclaimed Gilroy. "I wonder where they are going."

"Margate, probably, judging by the lady's clothes. I can't imagine Johnson married, somehow."

"I wonder if Fenn knows he's leaving London? Probably not, poor innocent," gibed Gilroy, whose soreness against the detective had not completely evaporated. "And he'll tell us afterwards that he had been meaning to keep him under observation. By that time Johnson will be in Boulogne!"

He was being childishly petulant, and he knew it, but the sight of Sir Adam's servant carrying his luggage openly to the station, under the noses of a dozen constables, made him feel fractious.

"But there's nothing against Johnson, is there?"

"Nothing definite, but I don't fancy Fenn wants to lose sight of him just at present. It might be as well to ring him up. Only, the last time I interfered, he told me to leave him to conduct this case in his own way, and I'm uncommonly inclined to take him at his word. I'll tell you what I should like to do, though!"

Something in his voice made Jill turn and stare at him. To her surprise, his usually serious face was alight with impish glee.

"I'd give something to have a look at Johnson's rooms! And now that the coast's clear it seems a shame not to take the opportunity. It would be fun to steal a march on old Fenn. If you're game, we'll do it!"

An answering spark lit up Jill's eyes.

"I don't see how we're to get in, though," she said doubtfully.

"That's not worrying me," answered Gilroy. "I'm wondering how we're to get hold of his address without rousing Fenn's suspicions."

"I've got it," said Jill unexpectedly. "He gave it to Mr. Compton, the lawyer, when he left the flat, and I made a note of it, in case I heard of any one wanting a valet."

She opened her bag and took out a tiny notebook. Gilroy looked over her shoulder.

"We're in luck," he said cheerfully. "It's just round the corner. Come on!"

Ten minutes later, somewhat to Jill's surprise, they were standing in Johnson's little sitting-room.

She had not expected it to be so easy, but, fortunately for them, Johnson's landlady had proved to be of the fat, easy-going kind. Also, she was already slightly bemused by her Saturday libations.

"'E's gone to Brighton," she announced, in answer to Gilroy's inquiry. "And 'e won't be back for a week, so 'e said. Didn't you know as 'e was gettin' married to-day? Fine goin's on, there's been, up at 'is wife's aunt's place. Married from there, they was, and I must say she give 'em a lovely clock. Solid marble, with two of them angels in gold on it."

"We thought the wedding was on Monday," stated Gilroy mendaciously. "This is Miss Braid. He used to work for her grandfather, and she had a special reason for wanting to see him. It's a bit of bad luck for him that we should have missed him. You haven't his address, I suppose?"

"'E left it on a card on the mantelpiece in 'is room. If you'll step in, I'll give it to you."

They followed her into a front room on the ground floor. The address was, as she had said, on the mantelpiece. So was the clock that had aroused the landlady's admiration. Gilroy rose still further in her estimation by his shameless eulogy on its beauty.

"It would save time if we could write a letter here and post it on our way back," he said. "I suppose you couldn't oblige us with an envelope? I've got a pen and a half-sheet of paper in my pocket."

His quick eye had already spotted a rack containing a couple of dusty envelopes.

"There's one 'ere, if you can make do with it," said the landlady. "And 'e did 'ave a blotter, but I don't know where 'e kept it."

Gilroy was skilfully manoeuvring Jill into a chair at the round table that stood in the middle of the room.

"Don't trouble," he said. "We can manage, if you don't mind Miss Braid's writing it here."

The woman moved to the door.

"You're welcome," she assured him. Then, over her shoulder, "p'raps you won't mind lettin' yourselves out."

"Not a bit," was Gilroy's hearty rejoinder.

They heard her heavy footsteps lumbering down the stairs into the basement.

Gilroy went quickly to the door and closed it. He did not latch it, however.

"If she comes back we're bound to hear her," he said. "You might just address that envelope and stick it up, then we shall have something to show for our visit if we see her again."

He cast a swift glance round the room.

"There's nothing here. Step lightly if you move, by the way. She's probably just underneath."

He opened the built-in cupboard that stood by the fireplace.

"Nothing here. I wonder if that's his bedroom."

"What are you looking for?" asked Jill, who was watching his movements with mingled amusement and apprehension.

"A hat-box. Probably one of those old-fashioned leather contraptions. I shan't know for certain till I see it. Good egg, this *is* his bedroom. Will you stay here and listen for all you're worth, while I have a look round. Let me know if you hear any one."

He disappeared through the communicating door into the room beyond.

Jill stood by the table, feeling more uncomfortable each moment, and wishing, with all her heart, that he would come back. There was a parcel lying on the table with a letter tucked under the string with which it was tied. A belated wedding present, she decided. In her nervousness she slipped the envelope out, and stood turning it over and over in her hands while she listened anxiously for the sound of the landlady's feet on the stairs. But there was no movement from below.

When Gilroy came back into the room and peered at her through his thick glasses he gave a low chuckle at the sight of her face.

"Cheer up," he said. "The worst's over! But I'm afraid we've wasted our time. It's not there."

She looked down, and for the first time realized that she had been holding the letter in her hand. At the sight of it she gave an exclamation of dismay.

"It's open," she said. "It must have come unstuck while I was fiddling with it!"

Gilroy took it from her.

"At the risk of shocking you, I'm going to look inside," he said. "It isn't done, I grant you, but I'm certain that there's something fishy about Master Johnson, and I'm going to take advantage of an obviously heaven-sent opportunity. We can stick it up again afterwards. Whoever licked it in the first place scamped his job badly."

He drew it carefully out of the envelope. As he did so, two pound notes fluttered out on to the table.

Then he ran his eye over the letter, and a slow smile spread over his face.

"Little Webb again," he murmured. "How they do crop up!"

He handed the letter to Jill. It ran:

"To Johnson, with best wishes from Bella and Everard Webb."

"Depressingly unincriminating," commented Gilroy, "but so funny that it was worth sacrificing the principles of a lifetime for. They *would* be the only people who knew the exact date of Johnson's wedding!"

He picked up the notes and folded them, preparatory to putting them back in the envelope.

"Have you got two one pound notes on you?" asked Jill suddenly.

"I have. *Do* you want to make Johnson a wedding present?"

"No. But if you've got two more to put in their place, I'm going to keep these for Mr. Fenn. He's trying to trace the money that was taken from the flat on the night of the murder."

Gilroy took a couple of notes from his pocket-book and placed them, with the letter, in the envelope. Then he stuck down the flap and slipped the whole thing back under the string of the parcel.

A couple of minutes later they were in the street.

"Surely you haven't got to the point of suspecting little Webb?" exclaimed Gilroy.

Jill laughed rather shamefacedly.

"It does seem absurd, doesn't it? And yet, I don't know why we all take it for granted that he couldn't possibly have had anything to do with it. He was on the spot, and we've only got his sister's word for it that he was with her at the time."

"But you don't suspect him, all the same!"

"One simply can't, somehow," she admitted. "But these notes have come from Romney Chambers and, though it's only the forlornest of chances, there's no harm in showing them to Mr. Fenn when I see him to-morrow."

"What's he up to to-morrow?" asked Gilroy. "You don't mean to say that the indefatigable beggar works on Sunday?"

She gave him the gist of her interview with Fenn that afternoon.

"Bad luck," was his only comment, but she could see that he too was perturbed.

"I'm a fool to let it get on my nerves," she said, when she had finished. "But I feel sometimes that if this goes on much longer I shall begin to think I did do it!"

For a moment he did not answer her, then—

"I wish you could get away for a bit, out of all this," he exclaimed. "It isn't Fenn's fault, I know, but if he wants to break your nerve he's going the best way about it. Look here, couldn't you take a week-end out of town?"

Even as he made the suggestion he realized that there would be Fenn to reckon with. It was hardly likely, at this juncture, that he could afford to let her go.

"I could manage it, I suppose." Jill's voice was not enthusiastic. "But it would be pretty beastly at this time of year."

"There's Brighton, of course," began Gilroy vaguely. Then, with sudden enthusiasm, "What about it? Running down to Brighton, I mean, and taking a squint at Johnson and his bride? I don't suppose they'll do anything very startling, but we could keep our eyes open and see if they've got any friends there and whether Johnson's very free with his money. You never know what may crop up, and, anyhow, it will be an excuse to get out of London. I can get away for four days at least, next week, and there's a chap I used to dig with in London who'll put me up. You could go to a hotel, and we could carry on the good work together. Say you'll come!"

He was as enthusiastic as a boy of fifteen, and, in spite of herself, Jill found his mood infectious. She had not been exaggerating when she said that the situation was getting on her nerves, and she found the temptation to get away very strong.

In the end she gave in, helped to her decision by the fact that one of her editors had that morning paid up, and that she was sufficiently in funds to be able to afford a short holiday.

That Fenn might have any objection to the plan fortunately did not occur to her.

CHAPTER XI

PUNCTUALLY at eleven o'clock next morning Fenn knocked at Jill's door. To his relief she was already fully dressed.

"I didn't realize what an outrageous nuisance I must be making of myself," he said apologetically, "until I saw the bottles of milk reposing outside the doors as I came up. Yours is the only one that has been taken in, so far, and I'm afraid that's my fault for forgetting that Sunday is a day of rest."

Jill laughed as she drew a comfortable chair up to the fire.

"We have got rather a habit of what my charwoman calls 'layin' up' on Sundays," she admitted. "But, then, we do work pretty hard during the week. As a matter of fact, I've been up for hours. I was too busy to stay in bed."

Fenn nodded sympathetically.

"I know," he said. "Even if one's only going away for a day or two, there are all sorts of odds and ends that crop up at the last minute to keep one busy."

Jill stared at him. It was true that she had been engaged in packing her suitcase when he knocked, but her bedroom door was now closed and the sitting-room bore no sign of impending departure.

"How did you know?" she asked. "I only made up my mind to go last night!"

"Once the vast machinery of New Scotland Yard is set in motion," intoned Fenn ponderously, "little passes that does not come to the ears of the Big Four! I'm quoting from my favourite author. As a matter of fact, Gilroy rang me up last night and told me you were off to Brighton. I can see nothing against your going, provided you leave me your address, in case of any unexpected development." Jill gave him the name of a cheap boarding-house at which she had sometimes stayed with her father, and watched him as he made a note of it in his book.

"I'll stay if you think I'd better," she said. "I don't want it to seem as if I was—well, running away. It hadn't occurred to me that it might look like that."

"It doesn't," Fenn assured her. "It'll do you good to shake all this off your shoulders for a day or two, and I may very possibly have some news for you when you get back. Anyway, try to forget it all for a bit. And keep an eye on Gilroy. He's one of the most puzzling aspects of this blessed case."

Jill, who was bending over the fire, stiffened.

When she spoke her voice sounded strained and breathless.

"Mr. Gilroy? Surely he's got nothing to do with it?"

"With your grandfather's death? Nothing. It's Gilroy himself that's got me guessing. Do you realize that he's ten years younger than he was a week ago? Perhaps you don't, seeing that you haven't known him as long as I have, but you can take my word for it that that young man was rapidly degenerating into a sober, middle-aged scientist. In another year or so he'd have forgotten how to play. Then a tragedy occurs which is making us all old before our time and Gilroy becomes positively skittish! You may be able to account for it. I can't".

Jill caught the twinkle in his eye, and turned away to hide the red that stained her cheeks. Fenn helped himself to a cigarette from the box she had handed him and sat smoking placidly. He was meditating over his next move. His rather heavy pleasantries had not been without a motive, for he had an unpleasant duty to perform, and the less official the atmosphere, the easier it would be to break to her at least one of the reasons for his visit.

"You spoke of your charwoman," he said casually. "Does she come to you on Sundays?"

"No. Most of them get Sunday off."

"You do your own housework then, I suppose?"

"On Sundays, yes. As a matter of fact, I've been economizing lately and she's only been coming twice a week, so I'm pretty well used to it. It doesn't take long in rooms like these. I'd finished before ten this morning. Did you want to see her?"

He stood up and threw the stump of his cigarette into the fire.

"Lord, no! I only wondered whether the place was ship-shape. If it is. I'd like to take a look round."

"Of course you can look at it," she answered in surprise. "There are only these two rooms, and a kind of cupboard, with a gas ring, on the landing. Why do you want to see it?"

Fenn realized that it was no good beating about the bush any longer.

"It's simply a matter of routine," he explained carefully. "You were on the premises when your grandfather died, and, properly speaking, we ought to have had a look round here before, but I didn't want any one but myself to do it. It's always an annoying business for the people concerned. Besides which, I wanted to be able to say that, to my own knowledge, there was nothing here that could have any possible bearing on the case. If you're going away, we may as well get the thing over and done with."

Jill caught her breath. So this was what it had come to—an official search of her rooms!

"Of course," she answered, trying to speak naturally, in a loyal attempt to support his efforts to spare her feelings. "Will you begin with my bedroom?"

"If you don't mind. You just sit here and smoke a cigarette."

On his way to the door he halted in front of her.

"Don't let it worry you," he said. "As I told you, it's just a matter of routine, a pure formality."

He disappeared into the bedroom, and Jill, with a little shiver, drew her chair closer to the fire. She wondered now why he had been so willing to let her go to Brighton, and then, with a shock that sent her heart beating wildly in her throat, she realized the truth! Probably every step she took from now onwards would be known to the police.

She was huddled over the fire, dejection in every line of her figure, when Fenn came back into the sitting-room. But she responded gamely to his cheerful assumption that a police search was an every-day occurrence in most well-ordered lives.

"I'll go into the other room while you have a look round," she said, forcing herself to smile. "It'll be easier if we play Box and Cox."

When he opened the door to tell her he had finished she had regained a little of her self-confidence and was able to review the situation more calmly.

"Nothing doing," he announced cheerily. "That's over and done with, and I can leave you to get on with your packing. Now I'll have those notes, if you don't mind."

He counted out seven Treasury notes on to the table and exchanged them for those Sir Adam had given her. The transaction reminded her of Webb's wedding present to Johnson, and she was just going to speak of it when Fenn forestalled her.

"By the way," he remarked, regarding her with a disconcerting twinkle in his eye, "what were you and Gilroy doing in Johnson's rooms yesterday? If you'd asked me I could have told you that he was away on his honeymoon."

Then, catching sight of her horrified face—

"You needn't look so guilty," he assured her dryly. "You've got a perfect right to call on your grandfather's valet if you like."

"You've made me feel an awful fool all the same," she admitted frankly. "I very nearly rang you up last night to tell you that Johnson had gone away."

"Why didn't you? I should have taken it in the spirit in which it was meant, though I don't mind telling you that I've had Johnson under observation for some time now. My man saw you go in, and reported it to me as a matter of course."

He was afraid for a moment that she might jump to the fact that his man had been shadowing, not Johnson, but herself. Fortunately, her thoughts were elsewhere.

"Did he tell you we were burgling?" she asked demurely.

"If he had I should have been obliged to put a few rather unpleasant questions to our friend Robert. What mischief has he been leading you into?"

For answer she fetched the notes which she had placed in readiness in an envelope and gave him an account of what had happened.

He listened to her with marked disapproval.

"Look here," he said, as he placed the envelope in his pocket-book, "this has got to stop. I've no doubt Robert means well, but he's taking a greater risk than he realizes, besides making my job even more difficult than it is already, by blunders of this sort. Make him understand this, will you? As regards this trip to Brighton, I don't know what Robert has up his sleeve, but I am relying on you, if you do run into Johnson, not to do or say anything that may put him on his guard."

His voice was stern, but when he had finished he tempered his little homily with a kindly smile.

"I'm not saying, mind you, that I shan't be grateful for anything Johnson may let drop in the course of conversation. Anything you can report may be of use to us. But do impress the fact on Robert that if he tries to act independently of the police he may do irretrievable mischief."

So convinced was he of the futility of Gilroy's ill-advised action that he did not even go to the trouble of opening the envelope Jill had given him till late that night.

He had begun to undress, and was turning out the contents of his pockets on to the dressing-table when the sight of his pocket-book reminded him of the Treasury notes. He took them out and compared them with the numbers on his list.

As he had expected, those that Sir Adam had given to Jill came within the limits of the numbers he was looking for. Then he opened the envelope she had handed him and took out Webb's two notes. At the sight of the numbers they bore he gave a sharp exclamation and bent down to examine them more closely. There was no doubt about it.

They were two of the eighty Treasury notes which had been issued to Sir Adam Braid on October the thirtieth.

By eight o'clock next morning he was knocking at the door of Webb's flat. He was shown into the little study, where the brother and sister were breakfasting.

"Delighted to see you, inspector," beamed the little man, his eyes alight with curiosity as to the object of Fenn's visit. "You'll join us in our meal, I hope."

Fenn, assuring him that he had breakfasted already, produced the two Treasury notes.

"Can you tell me anything about these?" he said. "I understand that they were given by you to Johnson, Sir Adam Braid's servant."

Webb eyed them with interest, and immediately deluged the unhappy Fenn with a flood of irrelevant information.

"I sent Johnson a small wedding present from Miss Webb and myself in the shape of a crystal wireless set," he explained. "It only cost a matter of fifteen shillings, so we decided to add a couple of pounds to the present, so that he could get himself a pair of decent headphones as well. He was a very pleasant and obliging sort of fellow, and had done us more than one small service while he was living here, and we both felt that some little tribute was due from us. These may be the notes I sent him, but, of course, I cannot say for certain. He has never had any other money from me."

"Can you tell me where you got these notes, Mr. Webb?" asked Fenn, wondering whether, after all, there might not be something behind the little man's verbosity. He remembered now how difficult it had always been to pin him down to any definite statement. Even now he seemed incapable of giving a plain answer to a plain question.

"Ah! there you have me," he said, cocking his head on one side and peering up at the detective. "I changed, let me see, two cheques last week—"

"I gave you those notes out of my housekeeping money," broke in Miss Webb, who had been listening, mouth and eyes wide with curiosity, absorbing every detail of the little scene. "Don't you remember? You were short of change and I had a little over from the week before."

Webb looked manifestly relieved.

"Of course. I bought the set in the afternoon, I remember, and in the evening we talked it over and decided to add a small sum to our present. I give my sister a cheque every week for our joint housekeeping expenses," he explained redundantly, "and these notes came out of that money."

"Where did you change your cheque, Miss Webb?" asked Fenn patiently.

"At the paper shop. I always change my housekeeping cheque there. I must say Mr. Ling is very obliging in that way."

A new light began to dawn on Fenn.

"You're sure there's no other source from which those notes could have come?" he suggested. "There was no other money in your possession?"

"I keep a reserve fund in my jewel case," she answered, "but I hardly ever touch it. These notes were part of the cheque I changed at Ling's shop. I am sure of it."

Fenn, having with difficulty stemmed the flow of questions that poured, without intermission, from both brother and sister, and assured them that the notes in question related merely to certain payments of Sir Adam's that he was trying to trace, escaped from their clutches and made his way to the newspaper shop, acutely conscious of the scrutiny of two pairs of eyes glued to the ground floor windows of Romney Chambers.

Ling, whose working day began with the early morning newspaper delivery, was standing in his doorway. He greeted the detective with a somewhat surly nod.

"Can I see you alone for a moment?" asked Fenn, indicating the boy who was sorting papers in a corner of the shop.

Ling gave him a keen glance, then picked up a couple of monthlies from the counter.

"Here, Bert," he said, "nip over to Mr. Carter's with these. Tell him they only sent 'em up last night."

The boy once out of the way, Fenn produced his two notes and explained his mission. Ling examined them.

"Come from me, did they?" he asked. "Well, if Miss Webb says so, I'm ready to take her word for it. I did change a cheque of hers, same as usual."

He looked at Fenn meaningly.

"Stands to reason I can't say nothin' for certain," he said slowly. "But it looks to me uncommon likely that these two beauties were part of that fifteen pound odd Johnson paid me. Mind you, I don't say they were, but it looks like it."

Fenn nodded.

"I thought as much," he said. "It's a pity you can't be a little more definite, though. You've no reason to think they're not part of that payment, I suppose?"

"None," was the man's decisive answer. "As I told you, I just shoved the notes Johnson gave me into that there box, along of whatever other money I might have had in it. I can't rightly say what there was in there already, what with people comin' in and payin' their bills and me changin' cheques for customers. All I can say is that those notes got paid out with the rest, and there's no reason why Miss Webb shouldn't have got them, same as any one else."

Fenn took a pencil from his pocket and jotted down a couple of numbers in his notebook.

"You might keep that handy," he said, tearing out the leaf and handing it to Ling. "If any of the numbers between those two turn up, ring me up at the Yard and make a careful note of where they came from."

Ling glanced at them and tucked the paper into his waist-coat pocket.

"I'll remember 'em," he said. "I've got a good head for figures. But if you're after Johnson, inspector, you can take it from me you're on the wrong tack. Like as not, that money was part of his wages."

"I've no doubt you're right," answered Fenn noncommit-tally. "I hear he's married, by the way."

Ling looked up quickly. Fenn had a feeling that he was going to volunteer information of some sort. If he had meant to, he evidently thought better of it.

"So I'm told," he said. "He's a chap as'll be all the better for having a woman to look after him."

Fenn was very thoughtful as he left the shop. His mind went back to his first interview with Johnson after the mur-der. He remembered the white, strained face, the restless eyes focusing themselves for a second on his in answer to a direct question and swerving the moment the effort of will was over. The man had been a bundle of jangled nerves; the extent of his collapse out of all proportion to the shock he had received. And yet his account of his actions had been clear and straight-forward, and had been confirmed by too large a number of independent witnesses, to be anything but true.

Fenn was inclined to the opinion that Johnson had had no hand in the murder, but had seized his opportunity, during the confusion that followed, to rifle either the dispatch-box or the missing hat-box. Hence his obvious nervousness. That the hat-box had not left Johnson's rooms, Fenn had reason to know, but he doubted if it had ever been there. The pity was that he had not discovered its traces directly after the murder. As it was, the man had had time and to spare in which to get rid of it.

So far as the notes were concerned, Fenn had ascertained from Sir Adam's solicitor that the old man had been in the habit of paying his servant's wages at the beginning of each

month, and that, unless Johnson were lying, the last payment
had been made on October the third, close on a month before
the notes Fenn had succeeded in tracing had been issued to
Sir Adam by his bank. Johnson had applied to the solicitor for
money due to him after Sir Adam's death and had been paid a
month's wages in lieu of notice, his explanation being that his
master frequently let a week or more elapse before he remembered to pay him, and that, owing to his irritability, he had
not liked to remind him that his wages had been due on November the first. There was, of course, the possibility that the
man had actually been paid by Sir Adam at the beginning of
November and had been guilty of a barefaced attempt to get
the money twice over, but the solicitor had seen no reason to
doubt his statement, and had paid him without questioning it.

Whichever way one looked at it, Johnson's honesty seemed
open to criticism, and Fenn decided that the sooner he tightened the strings round him the better.

CHAPTER XII

JILL BRAID AND Gilroy arrived at Brighton on the Sunday
night, and it was not until Wednesday afternoon that they first
caught sight of Johnson and his bride. The weather had turned
bitterly cold, short, fitful spells of pallid sunshine alternating
with rain and east wind, with the result that the piers were
deserted in favour of cinemas and teashops, and even the most
hardened of the trippers showed themselves as little as possible
out of doors. Gilroy's scheme for running accidentally into
Johnson seemed doomed to failure.

On the other hand, the bracing air and absence of anxiety were working wonders with Jill. Her old buoyancy had
returned, and with it the pluck that had enabled her to face
life so gallantly after her father's death, when it had been a
question of finding a market for the only work she could do,
half-trained though she was, or throwing herself on the charity

of her grandfather. She had chosen the former, and only she knew how hard the struggle had been. And then, just when it seemed as if she had won the respect and affection of the cantankerous old man who could do so much for her if he wished, the ground had been cut away under her feet, and she found herself on the brink of an abyss blacker and more terrible than anything she had ever been called upon to contemplate.

But now, as her nerves responded to the keen air and the stimulus of Gilroy's company, she regained her fighting spirit. Some one, she told herself, had killed her grandfather, and if Johnson, as Gilroy and even Fenn seemed to think, held the clue to the riddle, she was prepared to take a hand in the solving of it. She set herself to the task of running Johnson to earth with a fervour that tickled Gilroy's sense of humour, though, as she reminded him, he had been the first to suggest the possibility of achieving something in that direction.

Oblivious of the vile weather, she dragged him, unresisting, from one second-rate place of entertainment to another; and he, who had worked so hard and played so little in the course of his life, found himself growing lighter-hearted and more easily amused each day.

It was not, however, in any of these places that they eventually ran their quarry to earth. Taking advantage of one of the infrequent spells of good weather, they had decided to brave the bitter wind and go on the pier.

Gilroy, who was talking to Jill and had not observed the couple who were immediately ahead of him, was suddenly aware of her hand on his arm.

"Look!" she whispered.

He followed her gaze and saw Johnson in the act of paying for his ticket. And he was paying with a Treasury note!

Gilroy fumbled wildly in his pocket and produced a handful of coins. As he counted them he thanked his stars that in the last shop he had been to he had been given his change in silver.

He stepped into the place Johnson had just vacated.

"I suppose you couldn't give me a pound note for this?" he asked, placing his accumulation of half-crowns and shillings on the ledge.

The ticket clerk, who was in the act of putting away Johnson's note, laid it down while he counted the money.

"Right," he said, handing the note over to Gilroy, who pocketed it, paid for the tickets with the last odd shillings left to him, and passed through with Jill on to the pier.

They could see the Johnsons battling with the wind ahead of them, and knew that there was no fear of losing them now.

"Do you know the numbers of those notes Fenn is after?" he asked.

Jill shook her head.

"It doesn't matter, though," she said. "We can send him the number of this one. Note collecting seems to be our forte at present."

Gilroy took her arm and drew her to one side.

"My suggestion is that we take it gently and meet them on their way back. We don't want it to look as if we'd followed them. If we run into them near the gate they'll take it for granted that we've only just arrived."

In theory the scheme was excellent, but by the time the other couple had lingered at the end of the pier and strolled slowly back towards the entrance, Gilroy and Jill were blue with cold.

"If we get anything more exciting than influenza out of this I shall be surprised," murmured Gilroy. "Come on. Now's our moment!"

They started briskly forward in the path of the approaching couple. At his first clear view of them Gilroy decided that Johnson's honeymoon was not being a complete success. He was stalking ahead of his bride, his hands buried in his pockets and his chin tucked into the turned-up collar of his coat. She followed, her high heels slipping precariously on the damp boards, her skirts whipped about her knees by the wind. Together they presented as perfect an illustration of sullen discomfort as it was possible to imagine.

The sight of Jill Braid did not serve to lighten Johnson's gloom, though he greeted her civilly enough. If he was surprised to see Gilroy he did not show it. They exchanged the usual commonplaces about the weather, Gilroy wondering when he was going to introduce the girl who stood close behind him, her chin held high, her dark eyes glowing more dangerously each minute. It was not until she lost patience and emphasized her presence by a sharp dig in his ribs that her husband deigned to notice her.

After that the two groups fell naturally apart, Jill trying to hold Mrs. Johnson in conversation with a view to giving Gilroy a free hand with Johnson. Gilroy, conscious of the short time at his disposal, was debating how best to approach the topic he had in mind, when Johnson surprised him by introducing it himself.

"Have they found out anything about Sir Adam's death, sir?" he asked. "I saw in the papers that they'd made an arrest, but they don't seem to be giving much away."

"It's a mysterious business altogether," answered Gilroy. "You've got no ideas yourself, I suppose, on the subject?"

He saw the man's eyes flicker.

"Me? None. Sir Adam hadn't no enemies that I know of, and if it was a thief, it might have been any one."

"I was discussing it with Miss Braid just now," went on Gilroy. "She was telling me that her grandfather sometimes had quite a lot of money in the flat. You've no idea where he kept it, I suppose?"

"The only money I ever saw, he took out of the dispatch-box in his bedroom. The chap as did the job got into that all right. If there was any other place, I've never seen him go to it."

"What do you make of this story of Mr. Webb's about some woman he overheard quarrelling with Sir Adam?"

Johnson's answer was emphatic.

"I don't make nothing of it, sir. Mr. Webb's a very pleasant gentleman, but he's on the imaginative side, if you understand me. I wouldn't bank too much on anything he might say, if I was the police."

"All the same, there seems no doubt that there must have been some one talking to Sir Adam, and according to Miss Braid, who heard them laughing, it was some one he knew pretty well."

A dull flush crept over the man's white face.

"There wasn't anybody there when me and Mr. Webb went in," he stated, with a hint of defiance in his voice. "I'll answer for that. It's what I've told the police all along, and I stick to it. It's no good them coming bothering me about it."

Gilroy was conscious that Jill's conversation with Mrs. Johnson was hanging fire. She caught his eye, and intimated clearly that she wished to go.

He led the way to the entrance, stepping naturally into Jill's place at the other woman's side.

"I hope you've found some nice lodgings," he said, smiling at her. She was a fine, handsome woman, and so tall that her dark eyes were on a level with his.

"Not so dusty," she answered, "though they're a bit out of the way. If I'd known as Vinor Street was right up by the station I'd never have let Ned take the rooms. Not as it matters much; we shall be back in London soon enough, thanks be to goodness!"

Gilroy made a mental note of the road she had mentioned. It tallied with the address Johnson's landlady had given him. Evidently he was making no secret of his whereabouts.

They parted at the entrance, Johnson obviously relieved to see the last of them, his wife with a provocative flash of her fine dark eyes in Gilroy's direction.

"How did you get on?" he asked Jill, as soon as they were out of hearing. "The address we got is all right, which is something. That chap's as nervous as a cat at the mere mention of the murder. I'd give something—"

He broke off in amazement. Jill had stopped short and was clutching his arm, her eyes blazing with excitement.

"There's something wrong, frightfully wrong, about Johnson," she stammered. "And I don't know whether we ought to go to the police here or try to get hold of Mr. Fenn. That woman, Mrs. Johnson, was wearing my grandfather's ring!"

Gilroy could only stare at her.

"Are you sure?" he said at last.

"Of course I'm sure! It's unmistakable! It's exactly like the one I'm wearing now, which grandfather had copied for my father. I don't suppose there are any others quite like them in the world."

"Did she see yours?" asked Gilroy swiftly.

"No. I thought of that, but, thank goodness, I'd got my glove on. But Johnson may have guessed I'd seen it. In which case, even if we go straight to the police here, we shall be too late. What are we to do?"

"I don't know," answered Gilroy slowly. "But I fancy we'd better try to get on to Fenn. As you say, if Johnson has spotted the fact that you've seen it, he'll have taken steps by this time in any case, and we shan't gain anything by dragging in the local police. Did she see you looking at it, do you think?"

"I'm sure she's got nothing to do with it," said Jill decisively. "I don't like her much and I think Johnson's caught a Tartar, but she never tried to hide the ring; in fact, I think she's proud of it. She was quite frank about their plans, too. I'm sure she's got nothing to hide."

"Is there a telephone at your place?"

She shook her head.

"I'll see you back to your lodgings, then, and after that I'll go straight to the nearest public call office and try to get Fenn. He'll have to take back one or two things he's said lately about our little efforts."

"Did you ever come across a more unsatisfactory honey-moon couple?" asked Jill, as they hurried in the direction of her lodgings. "I've never seen two people look more fed up in my life!"

"Some people never know their luck," agreed Gilroy, with a glance in her direction. Then, receiving no encouragement, he went on hurriedly, "Johnson looks sick, physically and mor-ally. Did you get anything out of her, by the way?"

"Nothing, except that she seems to have a pretty poor opinion of her husband! She told me that they were starting a tobacconist's business, and that she intended to serve in the shop and see that the money they took went into the till. She volunteered the information that 'Ned' was soft about money and that he'd have to give up betting, or else there's going to be trouble. She's evidently going to make him toe the line! I may be wrong, but I got an impression that he'd wriggled rather at the last moment, and that, in the end, she'd pinned him down in spite of himself."

"She may know something and have used her knowledge to bring him to heel."

"It's possible," said Jill doubtfully. "But one thing I'm cer-tain of, she wasn't nervous to-day and she wasn't hiding an-ything. Johnson was anxious to get away all the time he was talking to you, but she was quite prepared to be friendly."

Gilroy lingered on the steps of the boarding-house, making plans for the evening, while she waited for the door to open. He arranged to call for her after dinner and take her to a cin-ema. By that time he would know what steps Fenn proposed to take as regards the ring.

"There's a gentleman called to see you, Miss Braid," said the maid, when she opened the door. "He's in the sitting-room."

"To see me?" exclaimed Jill in astonishment. "I don't know a soul in Brighton!"

"He asked for you by name, and when I told him you were out he said he'd wait," volunteered the maid.

Jill and Gilroy stared at each other. The same idea had struck both of them. Johnson!

"I think I'll just stand by, if you don't mind," said Gilroy significantly.

Jill nodded and led the way into the sitting-room.

Planted firmly on a small plush sofa in the centre of the room, his bowler hat on his knee, his eyes fixed contemplatively on a flourishing aspidistra, was Chief Detective-Inspector Fenn!

CHAPTER XIII

GILROY'S TRIUMPH was short-lived. When Fenn compared Johnson's note with the numbers on his list it did not tally.

Fenn handed it back to him with a smile.

"Sorry, Robert," he said. "It was a smart bit of work and you deserved better luck, but I'm afraid this one's innocent. Not that it makes much difference, the ring's good enough for us. We can hold him on that."

"Are you going to arrest him?" asked Jill.

Fenn did not answer immediately. He sat staring into the crown of his hard hat, lost apparently in meditation.

"Look here," he said at last, turning suddenly to Jill. "Supposing he did take the ring in a moment of temptation, do you wish to prosecute? It will rest either with you or Sir Adam's solicitors, and I don't know that we need drag them into it."

She hesitated. She had never disliked Johnson, and, to the best of her knowledge, he had served her grandfather well.

"Unless you think he was concerned in the murder—" she began uncertainly.

Fenn smiled at her.

"If I knew that, it would be all over but the shouting," he said. "To be honest with you, I'm keeping an open mind about it, and that's all I can say. There's been something on the man's mind all this time, and if he did do a bit of pilfering, we know

now what it is that's been worrying him. If he's fundamentally honest, as he very likely may be, the fact that he was tempted and fell would be enough to account for his manner. If it wasn't for one thing, I'd be inclined to acquit him of any hand in the murder."

He paused.

"I know what's in your mind," said Gilroy—"the open door."

Fenn nodded.

"He sticks to it that he shut the front door of Sir Adam's flat when he went out. Five minutes later Stephens, according to his own account, finds it open and, what is still more significant, declares that the person he heard enter the flat acted as though he expected to find it open. All this may be sheer romancing on Stephens' part, but one can't overlook the fact that, whereas he has nothing to gain by lying, Johnson may have excellent reasons for not speaking the truth. Now that he has given himself away over the ring, we may get the whole story from Johnson. We haven't got it yet."

"He certainly hasn't the makings of a criminal, poor chap," said Gilroy thoughtfully. "He might kill in a moment of blind panic, though."

"He didn't. Assuming that he killed and robbed his master before leaving the flat, it's inconceivable that his accomplices should have stayed on, talking loudly, for a good half-hour after his departure. And if they weren't his accomplices and did not reach the flat till after he had gone, how did they get in? We are assuming, remember, that Sir Adam was already dead by then."

"They got in through the door Johnson had left open, presumably," said Gilroy. "In fact, we've got Stephens' word for it that that's just what they, or he, did do."

"If you're going to ask me to believe that Johnson, having killed his master, deliberately left the flat door open so that any one might walk in and stumble on the evidence of his crime,

I flatly refuse to do anything of the sort. No, there's no reason that I can see to doubt that one of the voices both Webb and Stephens heard was that of Sir Adam. Even you cannot say for certain that the person you heard speaking was not your grandfather," he concluded, turning to Jill.

"I've no reason to think it wasn't," she admitted.

"What made me doubtful was that I had never known him in such a cheerful mood. The people I heard were talking and laughing. Pretty loudly, too!"

"Which shows how apt one is to jump to conclusions," pointed out Fenn. "You took it for granted that it was not Sir Adam because he was in a laughing mood. Webb, on the contrary, decided definitely that the voice was that of Sir Adam because he sounded angry. I, personally, am of the opinion, in spite of certain things that have come to my knowledge lately, that it was Sir Adam you both heard, and that Johnson was not in the flat at the time he was killed. But it doesn't follow that Johnson is not in the hands of some one a good deal cleverer than himself. Johnson hasn't got the nerve or the brain to carry through a thing of this sort, but he's the kind of chicken-hearted fool that makes the best tool."

"Do you want me to prosecute?" asked Jill.

"I don't," said Fenn bluntly. "At least not at this stage of the game. He can't slip through our fingers now, and I've an idea that the more rope we allow him the better. Johnson under lock and key for petty larceny, with a whacking good alibi for the time of the murder, is no good to me; but free, goodness knows where he may lead us."

"I'll leave you to do as you think best," said Jill.

"So far as the ring is concerned, I shouldn't prosecute if the circumstances were normal. I should be quite content to let it drop, provided he returns it and anything else he may have taken. After all, we don't even know for certain whether he did take the money."

"We know he's dishonest, whichever way you look at it; whether the notes he gave Ling were part of his wages—in which case he's managed to get them paid twice over—or they weren't, but were stolen by him after Sir Adam's death. He's for it, either way. But it isn't Johnson I want, but the man behind him, if there is one. And, frankly, I'm not even sure that there is. But if we keep him on a string we're likely to stumble on something."

"When you've finished your business with Johnson, why not stay on over to-night and go back with us in the morning?" suggested Gilroy. "The chap I'm staying with would put you up, and both Miss Braid and myself have got to be back at work on Friday morning."

Fenn shook his head.

"I must get back to-night, I'm afraid," he said, rising reluctantly to his feet. "It's a dog's life, a policeman's. And now to put the fear of God into Master Johnson!"

The door of the cheap lodging-house which Johnson had chosen for his honeymoon was opened by a slatternly girl with a cold in her head, and a permanent grudge against anybody misguided enough to ring the front-door bell.

"I dunno if 'e's in. I'm sure," she said, in answer to Fenn's inquiry. "But I can see, if yer like to wait."

But Fenn did not wait. Instead, he followed her as she flapped wearily up the narrow staircase, and was close behind her when she stopped outside a door on the third floor.

"'Ere! what yer doin'?" she snapped, realizing his presence for the first time. "Why didn't yer stay downstairs like I told yer?"

"I'm here to ask questions, not to answer them," said Fenn, and there was something in his voice that brought a quick gleam of suspicion into her sharp eyes. "You knock at that door, and if Mr. Johnson's in he'll see me."

"You ain't the police, are yer?" she queried, under her breath.

For answer Fenn stepped past her and knocked at the door.

At the sound of a man's voice from within he placed his hand on the girl's shoulder and gave her a gentle push in the direction of the stairs.

"You trot along and finish your washing-up," he said. "I'll let myself out."

He waited till she was safely round the corner of the staircase, then he opened the door and went in.

He found himself in a small, none too clean bedroom. Johnson was lying on the bed in his shirtsleeves reading, and a woman, presumably his wife, was sitting by the empty grate darning a stocking.

"What the hell—" began Johnson, and then thought better of it. "Come in, Mr. Fenn," he finished weakly, as he swung his feet to the floor.

Fenn shut the door and stood leaning against it, his hands in his pockets.

"I want a few straight words with you, Johnson," he said grimly.

The man's face turned from white to a dirty grey.

"You'd better clear out, Ruby," he muttered, with a jerk of his head in the woman's direction.

"Mrs. Johnson can stay where she is," snapped Fenn. "She's in this too."

The woman, who had been staring at him in amazement, sprang to her feet, her cheeks crimson.

"I ain't done nothing!" she exclaimed shrilly. "And I'd like to know by what right—"

"That'll do," cut in Fenn, and with a sidelong glance at her husband she relapsed into silence.

"Before we go any further," he went on, "I'll have that ring you were wearing this afternoon."

She slipped her left hand out of the stocking she had been darning, and he saw that it was ringless.

"I don't know what you're talking about," she said sullenly.

Johnson crossed the room and picked up his coat.

"That's right, Mr. Fenn," he said earnestly, as he inserted his arm in the sleeve. "We don't know nothing about no ring."

In a couple of strides Fenn was across the room and, before the man realized his object, had the coat in his hands.

"Here, you've got no right to do that!" squealed Johnson, making a futile snatch at him.

"If you'd rather it was done at the station, say so," was Fenn's answer, as he went deftly through the pockets. "But I warn you, you won't get so good a chance to explain matters there."

He had extracted a fat pocket-book from the breast pocket of the coat and was running through its contents. In a small compartment intended for stamps he found the ring. Holding it and a wad of Treasury notes in his hand, he threw the coat and pocket-book on the bed and turned to Johnson.

"Now, what about it?" he said.

Mrs. Johnson suddenly found her voice.

"That ring's mine!" she exclaimed. "It was given to me—"

"Hold your tongue, will you!" snapped Johnson furiously. "And leave this to me."

"If Mrs. Johnson's got anything to say, I'm ready to hear it," said Fenn, his eyes on the woman's face.

But it was too late. Something in her husband's voice had warned her. She relapsed sullenly into her chair and picked up her darning.

"If I don't know nothing, I can't say nothing, can I?" she muttered.

Fenn examined the ring. It was identical with the one he had seen Jill wearing.

He turned to Johnson.

"I'm going to give you a bit of advice," he said sharply. "Whether you choose to act on it or not is your own affair. You can either talk now and explain how you came to be in possession of Sir Adam Braid's ring, or you can wait till I've charged you. But I tell you frankly that it depends on what you say to me whether Miss Braid decides to prosecute or not.

She's willing to make allowances for you, which is more than they'll do in the charge-room. Which is it going to be?"

Johnson hesitated, then, catching his wife's eye, drew himself up with a gesture of bravado that was not very convincing.

"If you charge me with theft I can't help but go with you," he said. "But you've got to prove it, and you won't get a word out of me till I've seen a lawyer."

"That's right, Ned," exclaimed his wife triumphantly. "Don't let him put it over on you."

Fenn shrugged his shoulders.

"Have it your own way, then," he said quietly. "What Miss Braid may do is her own affair. But if I charge you, it won't be with theft."

The man's jaw dropped.

"What do you mean?" he exclaimed.

"What I say. The man who fixed the safety-catch of the lock of Sir Adam Braid's front door so that the door would not shut on the night of November the sixth was an accessory to the murder." Johnson's face betrayed him.

"I wasn't anywhere near the flat when Sir Adam was killed," he stammered.

"I'm not saying you were; I'm only pointing out to you that things don't look any too good for you as it is, and that the franker you are, the better it will be for you in the long run. I'll go further, just to prove that I'm playing fair with you. I'm pretty well satisfied that that door was left open by you, and though I can't prove it, I've got evidence enough against you to make it worth my while to take a chance and pull you in. Now, if you've got anything to say for yourself, let's have it."

Johnson put his hand up to hide his twitching lips.

"That door was shut and locked when I left the flat," he said stubbornly.

"I've only got your word for that. How do I know that this little lot isn't your share of the swag?"

He thrust out the hand containing the ring and the notes.

What little nerve Johnson had left deserted him completely.

"I'll tell you everything, Mr. Fenn," he gasped. "I took the ring. I saw it lying on the table in the bedroom when I went the round of the flat after Sir Adam's death. I never meant to; but I owed money and they were pressing me, and I thought I could sell it. And then Miss Braid asked me if it was gone, and I didn't dare mention it when I gave you the list of the things that were missing. That's how it was. I didn't take nothing else, I'll swear, except a couple of notes that were in the drawer in the study."

Fenn unfolded the notes he had taken from Johnson's pocket-book and glanced through them. Not one of them bore the numbers he was looking for. So far it would seem that the man's statement was correct. But Fenn had not forgotten the missing hat-box, and was not blind to the possibility that there had been more money in the flat than the eighty pounds Sir Adam had brought from the bank on October the thirtieth. He did not by any means feel convinced that Johnson had come by the money honestly.

"Where did you get these?" he asked.

"They're mine, sir," answered the man eagerly. "I sold out a bit of War Loan to pay up some money I owed, and this was what was over. It was some I'd saved, but I was hoping I shouldn't have to touch it."

Fenn balanced the notes thoughtfully in his hand.

"I'd be more inclined to take your word for that," he said, "if I knew what Ike Sanders was doing in this house on Monday evening."

Johnson flinched perceptibly. His hunted eyes roamed helplessly round the room as he tried to frame an answer to Fenn's question. At the sound of his wife's voice he started convulsively.

"Ike came to see me, if you must know," she said, looking up from her darning. "I've known him since I was a kid, and he came to see how I was getting on. There's no harm in that, I suppose?"

"None, if what you say is true. I've sent word for him to call at the Yard to-morrow morning, and I shall know better when I've heard what he's got to say," answered Fenn, with what was, for him, lamentable lack of discretion.

He handed the notes back to Johnson.

"I'll take your word for it that you came by these honestly," he said. "But I warn you, Johnson, that you'd better deal straight with me from now on. It rests with Miss Braid whether I charge you with the theft or not. If she doesn't prosecute, you'll have better luck than you deserve. Those notes you say you took from Sir Adam's drawer, what did you do with them?"

Johnson hesitated, then—

"I used them to make up the money I owed," he said sullenly.

"To whom?"

"A man called Ling."

"And you took nothing but those two notes and the ring?"

"Not a thing. I swear it."

"Do you know anything about a hat-box that's missing from Sir Adam's flat?"

The question was so sudden that it seemed as though the man were bound to betray himself. But he met Fenn's eyes with no sign of embarrassment.

"I don't know nothing about a hat-box. If it's the one that used to be on the wardrobe in the bedroom, it's a month or more since that disappeared. What Sir Adam did with it, I couldn't say."

Seeing that there was no more to be got out of him, Fenn went on his way. But he was far from satisfied. Johnson had been altogether too glib with his explanations, and it struck Fenn that he was fortunate in having married a woman a good deal more astute than himself.

He might have been inclined to alter his opinion if he could have heard her ultimatum to her husband, delivered immediately after his departure.

She had risen from her seat and moved to the window, where she stood watching till Fenn had turned the corner. Then she swung round on her husband.

"I spoke up for you this time, Ned," she said. "And I'd like to know where you'd have been without me. But I'm not going into this blindfold, and so I tell you. What call had you to say as you'd taken that there ring off the old gentleman? I thought there was something queer when you made such a fuss about me wearing it, and if you'd told me what was in your mind then, instead of behaving like a dirty bully, I'd likely have listened to you."

Her husband shifted his feet uneasily. He was no match for her, and he knew it.

"The less you know about this business, the better for both of us," he muttered. "You can take that from me, my girl."

She approached him until her face was close to his, and when she spoke it was in a low voice, full of meaning.

"You know where I found that ring," she said. "And you're going to tell me why you took on yourself to lie about it. For lying you were, and unless that split's a bigger fool than he looks, he knows it. I'm waiting, Ned,"

For a moment it seemed as if he were about to give in; then, in a frenzy of helpless rage, he turned on her.

"Mind your own damned business!" he shouted, and, with the short-lived violence of a weak man who knows that he is cornered, pushed her roughly on one side and left the room, banging the door behind him.

Mrs. Johnson went back to her seat by the grate and picked up her work.

"And you'll come back blind to the world, my lad," she said. "And then we'll see what you've got to say for yourself."

CHAPTER XIV

AT THE CORNER of Vinor Street stands a small druggist's. A well-polished shop window makes an admirable mirror, and the elderly, rather shabby-looking individual who was standing apparently absorbed in the contemplation of a stock of patent medicines did not turn his head at the sight of Fenn, neither did he miss the almost imperceptible signal that the detective made as he passed behind him.

Once round the corner of the street Fenn paused. A second later he was joined by the man whose attentions to Jill Braid's movements had roused Gilroy's ire only a few days before.

"You'll find yourself back in London this time to-morrow, Garrison," said Fenn, "unless I'm mistaken. If the woman makes a move of any kind, let her go. I don't think she'll lead us anywhere. But if Johnson telephones or sends a wire, report at once. You're sure it was Johnson Ike Sanders was after?"

Garrison nodded.

"Dead sure. That's why I reported at once. They showed themselves together at the window. And if you've been putting the wind up Johnson, sir," added the detective, who had stationed himself at an angle from which he could keep an eye on the door of the house Fenn had just left, "I can tell you what his first move will be."

In answer to his superior's questioning glance he lifted his elbow significantly.

"So that's what's the matter, is it?" murmured Fenn.

"Been at it ever since I've been on the job," answered the man. Then, with a gesture of warning, "He's coming now, and I'm willing to bet I know where he's going."

They strolled up the street and took refuge in a shop doorway, from which they could see Johnson hurry round the corner and across the road. Without a glance in their direction he dived through the swing doors of a public-house.

"He's safe for the next half-hour, sir," said Garrison. "And when he does come out, he'll be past knowing whether he's being trailed or not. His head's as weak as his nerves, from the look of it."

"He's a poor creature," agreed Fenn. "For which we're going to be properly grateful if our luck holds."

He glanced at the time-table he was carrying, and found that he could just make the London train, in spite of which he risked missing it by entering the nearest call office and ringing up the Yard. The instructions he gave were brief and to the point, and he caught his train by the skin of his teeth.

A constable met him as he entered the portals of New Scotland Yard. Fenn listened to his report.

"Bring him along," he said briskly, when the man had finished.

It was a distinctly nervous individual who was escorted, a few minutes later, up the stairs and along the forbidding corridors to Fenn's office. Though there was nothing very heinous on his conscience at the moment, he was afflicted with a constitutional dislike to anything connected with the police.

Fenn, who had not come in contact with him before, thought he had never seen a more unlovely object. Ike Sanders, the name on whose passport was, curiously enough, Jacob Finkelstein, had already been quite adequately described by the police officer who gathered him in.

"Sit down," said Fenn, pointing to a chair.

Sanders perched himself on the extreme edge, clutching the brim of his hat with both hands as though he expected it to be snatched from him.

"When did you get back from Brighton?" asked Fenn abruptly.

Sanders's black eyebrows shot up to meet his hair.

"Brighton, thir?" he queried, in blank surprise.

Fenn nodded.

"A favourite health resort on the East Coast. I fancy you must have heard of it, or you wouldn't have taken the trouble to go down there on Monday night."

Sanders looked pained.

"And if I did go to Brighton for a bit of a blow, what about it?" he asked.

"Only that I hope you got it," answered Fenn unsympathetically. "Those little streets near the station are apt to be a bit stuffy compared to the sea front."

The man shifted uncomfortably in his chair.

"There'th nothing againtht a feller combining buthineth with pleathure, I thuppothe?" he queried uneasily.

"The trouble with your kind of business is that it so rarely coincides with other people's pleasure. Not that I'm under the delusion that you went to Brighton on any job of your own. See here, Sanders, I'm not asking you who you went to see that night, because I know, and if I don't know what your business with him was, I can make a shrewd guess. What I'm asking you is, who sent you?"

"Nobody thent me. You've got it wrong, I athure you," Sanders assured him earnestly. "I had my own reathonth for wanting to thee thith feller. I'm being perfectly honetht and above-board with you."

Fenn stretched out his hand and placed his finger on the button of the electric bell attached to his table.

"Have it your own way," he said resignedly. "But you've been sent up once for doing other people's dirty work, and if you're mug enough to fall for it again, I can't help you. If you've nothing to say, you can go. But I'd have you remember that your friend Johnson was in Sir Adam Braid's service at the time of his death, and that my job is to lay my hands on the man that killed him."

The man's face had changed colour.

"Here, don't ring that bell, mithter," he gasped. "What'th thith about murder?"

"You heard me," answered Fenn. "You've run your head into a very nasty business, Sanders. I'm giving you a chance, and I advise you to take it. Who paid your fare to Brighton on Monday night, and what was the message he gave you?"

"I didn't have no methage, honour bright, I didn't! I don't know any more about thith buthineth than a babe unborn! I jutht handed in the letter like I wath told to. I don't know what wath in it."

"You're not going to tell me that you carried a letter all the way from London to Brighton without having a look inside?" said Fenn incredulously.

But Sanders was impervious to insult.

"How could I look inthide when the envelope wath thealed?" he demanded aggrievedly.

"Well, you know where the letter came from. You're wasting my time, Sanders."

"I'm telling you all I know. You wouldn't have me invent thingth, would you?" urged Sanders. "On Monday a feller I know came round to my plathe and athked me if I'd do him a favour and take a letter down to a pal of hith in Brighton. Well, there didn't theem no harm in that, and I'm one that'th alwayth ready to do a friend a good turn. That'th me!"

He paused as though to give proper weight to this virtuous sentiment, but Fenn knew that his wits were working double time on the question of how much of his information it would be safe to suppress.

"And then?" he demanded. "Get on with it."

"Then I naturally athked him, what about my fare? And he paid it, and I went," concluded Sanders.

"And now perhaps you'll tell me the name of this philanthropist," said Fenn blandly. "You'd have saved yourself time if you'd mentioned it in the first instance."

Sanders's face was the picture of innocence.

"That'th just what I don't know," he said. "I've known him, mind you, on and off, for a long time, but I've never heard hith name mentioned."

"You knew where to take the answer to the letter, I suppose?"

"There wathn't goin' to be no anthwer."

Fenn stretched out his hand once more towards the bell. As he did so, he leaned forward, his eyes on the man's face.

"It's a murder case, Sanders," he said softly.

Sanders's forehead grew damp. He gulped and cleared his throat. Then he spoke, huskily.

"I've remembered now; they call him Eddie Goldstein. That'th between ourthelveth, though. I wouldn't thqueak on a man," he finished virtuously.

"Eddie Goldstein? Are you sure that's all you know?"

Fenn's voice was gentle, but the little man shivered, and he was undoubtedly sincere as he answered.

"Honeth, that'th all I can tell you, thir. There'th one thing Eddie did thay, though, that I remember. He told me the letter wathn't hith, but had been given him to take, and that, properly, he ought to have gone down with it himthelf. But it wathn't convenient for him to be away that night, hith old father being ill, I think he thaid."

"I've no doubt he did," said Fenn dryly, making a mental note to have an inquiry made into the Monday night activities of Goldstein and his friends.

Sanders was hardly out of the building before the order had been passed to all stations to bring in Eddie Goldstein. But as the night wore on and the reports began to come in, it became evident that that gentleman had temporarily forsaken his usual haunts.

Fenn, running through them on his arrival at his office next morning, began to wonder whether, at last, he had not sighted his quarry. Johnson's depredations were undoubtedly taking on a deeper and more sinister significance than he had at first imagined; and whereas before they had seemed merely to confuse the trail, they now appeared to be leading to a very definite objective. He had already applied for a search warrant for Johnson's rooms, and had every intention now of putting it into execution at the first opportunity.

As it happened, both Gilroy and Jill Braid were in his office when, at six o'clock that evening, Garrison telephoned to say that the Johnsons had returned to London, but had gone to the cinema and that the coast was clear. His report was satisfactory, inasmuch as it confirmed Fenn's prediction that, on learning that Sanders had been summoned to the Yard, Johnson would try to get in touch with him. As it turned out, he had returned to his lodgings in Brighton the night before too helplessly drunk to travel and had gone straight to bed; in spite of which he and his wife had left Brighton by an early morning tram and been in London by lunch-time. Leaving Mrs. Johnson to make her way back to Chelsea with their bags, Johnson had gone straight to Sanders's lodgings in Camden Town. There, as Fenn had foreseen, he drew a blank. Sanders, after his experience at the Yard, knew better than to put his neck further into the noose, and it was doubtful whether Johnson would succeed in laying eyes upon him for some time to come.

Blissfully unaware of these recent developments, Johnson had spent the afternoon hurrying from one to another of Sanders's associates, none of whom was able to give him any information as to Sanders's whereabouts. According to Garrison, he was a badly worried man by the time he got back to his rooms in Chelsea. Also, he was anything but sober, and it looked as if his wife had dragged him to the cinema in an attempt to keep him out of the public-house.

"I suppose you can't let an outsider in on this?" suggested Gilroy tentatively, when he heard of Fenn's intention to search the man's rooms. He had not forgotten their brush over the telephone, and though neither of them had alluded to the in-

cident since, he was painfully conscious of having made rather
an offensive fool of himself.

Fenn was aware of his diffidence, and liked him all the better for it. After all, he had been in a devil of a temper himself
that night.

"Of course," he answered heartily. "I shall be glad to have
you. And if there are any filthily dirty carpets to be dragged up,
I'll see that you do it."

Gilroy grinned over his shoulder at Jill as they followed
Fenn down the side staircase.

"You haven't seen the sleuths at work," he said. "It's quite
according to tradition. The tall, good-looking young doctor,
with his head under the bed in a cloud of dust, and the little insignificant fellow, with the big head, tucked away in the
only comfortable armchair, writing down the clues in his little
book as the doctor—that is to say, I, produce them. Every now
and then I say, 'My God, Fenn, how do you do it?' and he an-
swers, 'Brains, my dear Gilroy, just brains!'"

Fenn stopped suddenly in his descent.

"Brain, my dear Gilroy, not brains," he corrected gently. "I
never, in my wildest moments, accused you of that!"

They dropped Jill at her rooms, and dismissing the taxi,
walked from there to Johnson's lodgings.

The man who had relieved Garrison was waiting for them.

"There's nobody in the house, sir, but the landlady's old
mother," he reported. "The daughter's gone to the pictures
with the Johnsons. I've had a word with the old lady. She
won't make any trouble. She's none too fond of Johnson as it
is, owing to his drinking habits."

He led the way up the steps and pushed open the front
door. If the old woman in the basement was aware of their
entrance, she made no sign.

"The key's under the mat, so she tells me," said the detective. He bent down, then straightened himself with it in his

hand. Unlocking the door he stood aside while they entered the room.

Gilroy made a swift inspection. It was much as it had been when he and Jill had paid their visit, though now it showed more positive signs of occupation. A coat of Mrs. Johnson's trailed over the back of a chair and a paper-backed novel lay face downwards on the table, but little had been done to alter the cheerless aspect of the room.

Fenn made straight for the door leading into the bedroom, and Gilroy followed him.

Here there was more confusion, owing, no doubt, to the fact that Johnson had not had time to unpack his things since his return. The suitcase that stood open on the bed was still full of clothes, and Fenn ran through the contents swiftly before turning his attention to the cupboard.

"You won't find the hat-box there," volunteered Gilroy—"that is, unless he had it in Brighton with him. I went through that cupboard the other day."

Then seeing that Fenn, disregarding his remark, had started systematically on the contents of the cupboard, he strolled into the sitting-room and embarked on a more thorough search than he had been able to make on the occasion of his former visit. But he had no better luck than before, and when Fenn joined him he had given it up and was absent-mindedly fingering the small wireless set which stood on a little table near the window.

"Any luck?" he asked. "There's no sign of it here."

Fenn, who had opened the table drawer and was going through its contents, looked up vaguely.

"What? Oh, the hat-box!" he answered. "He's not likely to have hung on to that as long as this. I was hoping I might pitch on something else, but it was a very forlorn hope and I'm afraid we're beaten."

As he spoke, his eyes fell on the grate. Earlier in the day a fire had been burning there and a little pile of dead coals still remained. He crossed the room and bent over it.

From the grey, feathery deposit on the top of the still warm ash it was evident that papers had been burnt there, but the job had been done so effectually that no portion of them was left. Fenn knelt down, put his head into the grate, and peered up the chimney.

Suddenly his hand shot out, and with infinite care he detached the charred fragment of a piece of paper that had evidently blown up the chimney and lodged behind the edge of the ventilator. One glance at it was enough.

"Done it!" he exclaimed, as he scrambled to his feet.

Gilroy peered over his shoulder, and read what was evidently a fragment of a letter. The unburnt portion was easily decipherable.

> out. The splits
> traced two of the
> they come to you stick
> we arranged.   Keep
> I gave you next
> till you can send
> She has enough

Unfortunately the signature was missing. The writing was firm and clear, but evidently that of an uneducated person, and the paper was of the ruled kind that is sold in cheap blocks.

"Now at least we know what took Sanders down to Brighton," said Fenn, with satisfaction. "If this is Goldstein's writing we've got him. You were just two days too late when you collected that note of Johnson's, Robert. He'd been warned."

Gilroy gave a low whistle.

"So that's what you were after!" he exclaimed. "I must say you're in luck's way! If a little more of this enlightening communication had been burned we should have been none the wiser. As it is, it speaks for itself."

"Yes, and the third line is significant. If 'they come to you, stick (to the plan or explanation) we arranged.' I thought Johnson was a bit too glib with his confession, when it came to the point. 'She,' in the last line, presumably refers to Johnson's wife. The note you intercepted probably was supplied by her."

Gilroy stared at him.

"This narrows things down a bit, doesn't it?" he said. "How many people knew you were on the track of those notes?"

Fenn smiled.

"All the police stations within the Metropolitan area, the banks, post offices, and any small tradesmen the police saw fit to warn. No, that's not going to lead us anywhere. Webb's two notes are more significant. Sanders took this letter down to Brighton on the Monday night. By lunch-time on Monday the fact that those notes were in my possession was known only to the Webbs, Ling, and myself. By Monday evening, no doubt, the knowledge had been pretty widely circulated. Unfortunately, we can take it for granted that the Webbs probably spread it wholesale."

"All the same, I find it difficult to believe that little Webb has criminal associations! His gossip would be pretty harmless."

"Would it?" was Fenn's dry comment. "Take it that Miss Webb prattles to the porter's wife while she is working at their flat. She tells her husband, and he spreads the glad news in the bar of the nearest pub. It's in the bars that the crook gathers his most valuable information. It's there that the servants and the charwomen gossip, and he's only got to listen to find out where the Smiths keep their silver, when a flat is most likely to be left empty for an hour or so, or what beautiful jewellery Mrs. Brown's got. I've heard them at it myself, and it's a wonder any of these small flats escape. I could have warned the Webbs, but I knew it would be worse than useless. They're constitutionally incapable of keeping a tit-bit like that to themselves."

"What about Ling, the newsagent?"

"Ling's a different proposition. I did warn him, and if he spread the news, he did it deliberately. From the look of him, I shouldn't say he was a talker. Apart from his betting proclivities, which are not in any way unusual, he's a respectable tradesman, and, so far, he's done all in his power to help the police."

A sudden thought struck Gilroy.

"This chap Goldstein is a member of a race gang, isn't he?"

"I doubt if he's a member of any actual organization," answered Fenn. "These little tipsters join forces with each other when the occasion arises, but they're always changing their associates. Both Sanders and Goldstein have been 'inside,' and on more or less the same count. On each occasion a bookie got badly beaten up one dark night, but whereas Sanders worked with two other men, Goldstein did the job single-handed. I see what you're driving at: Ling's racing connections. But you must remember that men of the Goldstein kidney are the sworn foes of the small bookmaker. It's unlikely that there would be any connection between Goldstein and Ling. However, it's worth looking into."

He put the bit of paper carefully away in his pocket-book. As he did so, his eye fell on the crystal set in the window.

"Hallo, that's Webb's little tribute, I suppose," he said. "Know anything about wireless?"

Gilroy laughed.

"I used to be rather keen on it. As a matter of fact, I've been chuckling over that set. If he gave more than ten shillings for that contraption he was cheated. And the pathetic thing is that Johnson's evidently spent the morning coupling a loud speaker on to it! If he expects any results, I'm afraid he'll be disappointed."

"He must have been in a hurry to lay out Webb's two pounds," remarked Fenn, as he picked up his hat, "considering he only came home from Brighton this morning and has spent a pretty busy day since!" Gilroy shook his head.

"He was lucky if he got that second-hand for forty shillings," he said. "It's a beauty. Besides, I saw it in his cupboard when I was here the other day. It was probably a wedding present."

"If it wasn't, he seems to have done pretty well out of his 'bit of War Loan,' as he calls it," was Fenn's sceptical comment as they left the house.

CHAPTER XV

CHIEF INSPECTOR Abel Fenn was the fortunate possessor of a tiny house on the towing-path at Putney. He had bought it when such houses were cheap, and could have doubled the price he paid for it easily during the last ten years, instead of which he had divided it into two small flats, letting one to a friend, a fellow-bachelor, and living very comfortably on the upper floor himself.

After leaving Johnson's rooms he had gone back to his office, put the finishing touches to his day's work, dined on his way home, and at last settled down gratefully to the enjoyment of a long peaceful evening by the fire. There was little or no traffic on the towing-path, and except for the gentle lapping of the tide, caused by the wash from the long strings of barges that filed like grey ghosts past his windows, there was hardly a sound to disturb him. He had the book on his knee that he had been saving for just such an evening, but his mind reverted obstinately to the Braid case, and he did not open it. Gradually the warmth and stillness laid its spell on him, and he drifted off into that pleasant state that is half sleep, half incoherent meditation.

He was roused by the buzz of the electric bell which connected the front door with his flat. He looked at his watch, and was annoyed to find that he had let the evening slip by and that it was past ten o'clock. With an exclamation of impatience he strode to the window, threw it up, and peered out into the darkness.

His heart sank as he recognized the uniform of the man standing below, and, without wasting time in further parley, he went downstairs and opened the door.

The constable who stood on the steps saluted and handed him a letter.

"From Inspector Flamborough, sir," he said.

Flamborough was one of the inspectors attached to the Putney police station and an old acquaintance of Fenn's, who consigned him mentally to the devil as he opened the letter.

His face changed at the sight of the contents.

"Tell the inspector I'll be with him in ten minutes," he said, as he turned and ran upstairs to his flat.

He was as good as his word.

"Sorry to disturb you," said Flamborough apologetically, "but I understand that you were inquiring after this man yesterday. Straker, here, used to be on duty at Epsom, and he identified him at once. I thought it better to let you know."

"Quite right," answered Fenn. "This will save me a journey from the Yard to-morrow. Any idea how the thing happened?"

"Looks as if he'd been slugged and then dumped into the river. The surgeon's seen him and his verdict is, 'death from drowning,' but there's a crack on the back of the man's head that didn't come there after death. Will you see him?"

Fenn nodded.

"When was he found?"

"Six-twenty this evening. Warren, one of the Thames lightermen, who was out in a skiff, saw something half under a barge and went to have a look at it. The man couldn't have been in the water more than half an hour. Warren, who knows the river well, is of opinion that he was taken out in a boat and slipped overboard. He must have been sucked under the barge and held there by the current, like that poor chap who fell off the bridge last year."

To Fenn, fresh from the hospitable warmth of his fireside, the mortuary seemed cold and dank as the river itself, and, hardened though he was through long experience, a shudder ran through him as Flamborough drew aside the sheet that covered the bit of human wreckage that was stretched on the stone slab.

He drew a long breath.

"It's Sanders, right enough," he said soberly. "Have his people been notified?"

"His wife's up at the station now," answered Flamborough. "He was brought in about seven, but Straker, who was on his beat, didn't see him to identify him till close on eight. As soon as I got his name I applied to the Yard and got his address from them there. It was they who suggested that I should notify you, that's why I didn't do it earlier. Meanwhile I'd sent a man down to his place, and he brought the wife back with him. She's in a proper stew, poor woman. I left her in charge of the police-woman, and I can tell you I was thankful she was still on duty. If some of those old jossers had a few of our dirty jobs to do, they wouldn't blow a lot of hot air about women police being an unnecessary extravagance. The poor soul's in the family way and it's a woman's job, not a man's, looking after anybody like that whose man's just been pulled out of the river."

Fenn nodded. He entirely agreed with him.

"I'd like to see the contents of the pockets," he said.

As they entered the police station they almost ran into a little group of people coming out. One of them, a big woman in a thick tweed coat, was leaning on the arm of a police-woman. Her heavy features were swollen with weeping, but she seemed to have exhausted her first paroxysm of grief.

"Mrs. Sanders?" queried Fenn, under his breath.

"Yes," answered Flamborough. "Do you wish to speak to her?"

Fenn turned to the policewoman.

"If she feels equal to it," he said, with his kindly smile. "If not, to-morrow will do as well."

Mrs. Sanders raised her dazed eyes to his.

"What is it now?" she asked heavily.

Fenn glanced into the waiting-room. It was empty.

"Only that, if you feel you can stand it, I'd like a few words with you. I won't keep you long, and it might be easier for you if we got it over now. You're as anxious to get to the bottom of this as I am, I expect, and anything you can say would be a help to me."

A sudden flush stained the woman's sallow skin as she stared at him.

"He was done in, Ike was. You know that?" she demanded.

"Yes," said Fenn gently. "And I'd give something to know who did it."

"If I knew, I'd tell you right enough. I wish to God I did know!" she finished passionately.

"You've no suspicion of anybody?"

She hesitated, her fingers tearing at the sopping handkerchief she held.

"I've got my own ideas about it," she muttered at last. "You're welcome to them, if they're any good to you."

Fenn took her by the arm and led her into the waiting-room.

Once there she broke down once more. Fenn fetched her a glass of water and waited patiently until she was able to speak. There was little enough he could say to comfort her.

"He was a good husband, Ike was," she said at last, drying her tears with the apology for a handkerchief. "And goodness knows what me and the kids'll do without him."

"Do you know if he had any enemies?" asked Fenn.

"Ike and the lot he went with was bound to have enemies," she admitted frankly. "But there wasn't one of the regular lot would have done this. He's been set on, Ike has, before now, like any one else. This is different."

"He never said anything to you to make you think he was in any danger?"

"If anything was said, it was by me! And he wouldn't listen! I told him, when that dirty beast, Goldstein, started his little game that I wouldn't have him inside my place, and I warned him he wasn't up to no good. And, in spite of all I said, he just walked into it."

"What did Goldstein want with him? He wasn't one of his regular pals, was he?"

"Him? There's been bad blood between them ever since I can remember. There aren't many as will work with Eddie Goldstein, and them as does gets the dirty done on them before they've finished. So that, when he started suckin' up to Ike somethin' over a week ago, with a lot of talk about lettin' bygones be bygones and bein' able to put money in his pocket, I was worried, and I told Ike what I thought. And, in the end, Ike backed out and wouldn't have nothin' to do with it, and I thought it was all right. But he got round him the second time, right enough, curse him!"

"What did he want with him?"

"I don't know. Ike wouldn't say. But he came up one night and called Ike out on to the landin', and I overheard something. From what I could make out, there was a job down Southampton way he wanted Ike for, and Ike wouldn't take the risk. He didn't like the look of it then, and what with me speakin' so strong against it, he did refuse it in the end."

"You've no idea what the job was?"

"None, but it was the kind Eddie wouldn't touch himself and wanted some one else to do for him. It must have been pretty bad for him to feel that way about it. Ike was to go to Southampton or thereabouts, that I do know. And, if you ask me, Ike knew too much after that. He wouldn't be the first that Eddie had got put out of the way."

"You really think Goldstein's responsible for this?" asked Fenn thoughtfully.

"I don't think, I know!" she exclaimed passionately. "And I'll wager he got some one else to do his dirty work for him, the same as he always does. When he came back that second time, sayin' he'd make it worth Ike's while to take a letter for him, I knew he wasn't up to no good. But Ike would have it that it was all straight and above-board, and there you are!"

"I don't see why Goldstein wanted to employ Sanders. Surely there were plenty of men among his own lot he could have given the job to?"

"And had it traced to him afterwards!" was Mrs. Sanders's shrewd comment. "That's Goldstein all over. Him and Ike had never worked together and every one knew it. Whatever Ike might do, no one would think of Goldstein being at the back of it. Oh, he'd got good enough reason for usin' Ike, and good enough reason for gettin' rid of him afterwards too. And there's this. Ike told me about his seein' you at the Yard. You may be sure there were others besides me knew about that. What he told you, I don't know. He didn't say, but, if he spilled anything, or the Goldstein lot thought he had, he'd be for it!"

Fenn nodded.

"That's likely enough," he agreed. "He didn't ask for police protection or he could have had it. I wish now he had. I want a word with Goldstein on my own account, and I can promise you that, if he's had a hand in this, he shall answer for it. Meanwhile, keep your suspicions to yourself, if you want to see justice done. By the way, did you ever hear your husband speak of a man called Ling?"

She shook her head.

"Never. I've never heard him or any of his pals mention no one of that name. If he'd ever worked with him I should know."

"You're sure he didn't mention him in connection with this business of Goldstein's?"

"Certain. He told me Goldstein was workin' alone on this and didn't want to bring any of his pals into it. That's what made me smell a rat." Fenn thanked her and handed her over to the police-woman. Then he made his way to the inspector's room and went through the heterogenous collection of limp and sodden objects that had been found in the dead man's pockets. They provided no clue as to how he had met his end, but, adhering to the wet lining of a cheap purse, Fenn discovered a pound note, and that note bore one of the numbers he was looking for.

With a sigh he added it to his collection. Sanders, the only person who could have told him where it came from, was dead, and, so far, his attempts to trace any connection between Goldstein and either Ling or Johnson had proved abortive. Mrs. Sanders was no doubt speaking the truth when she declared that her husband had been merely a tool in Goldstein's hands, and the probability was that the other man had deliberately planted the note on Sanders, wishing to get it off his hands, and banking on the fact that it would pass unnoticed should Sanders use it for the purpose for which it had been paid him. If it had been given him for his travelling expenses, a busy railway station was the one place, of all others, where a "wanted" note might be expected to slip through unobserved.

The report on Ling's movements which he found on his desk next morning did not serve to lighten his gloom. According to Ling's errand-boy, Albert Tombs, the newsagent had left his shop at six-thirty-five on the night of the murder. The boy was able to fix the time approximately, as it was his custom to run home at six for his supper and return to the shop at six-thirty, so as to be on hand for the evening delivery. He admitted that he was occasionally a few minutes late, but it appeared that Ling, though on the whole a considerate employer, was apt to deal firmly with unpunctuality, and it was doubtful whether Tombs was more than five minutes out in his estimate of the time. Ling had left the shop about five minutes after the boy's return, taking with him a batch of evening papers which he proposed to leave at their respective destinations on his way home. It was apparently his custom to do this every evening, leaving the boy in charge of the shop until his return about seven-thirty. There was no further trace of his movements until his arrival at his own rooms in Selby Street at a few minutes after seven, when he had spoken to a Mrs. Dugmore, who lodged in the same house with him; but the papers had been delivered to the customers as usual that night, and there was no reason to suspect that he had departed in any way from his usual procedure. Mrs. Dugmore had heard him leave the house somewhere about seven-fifteen, and, according to the errand-boy's report, he was back at his shop at seven-thirty.

Fenn did not overlook the fact that Ling might have been the person Stephens had heard enter Sir Adam Braid's flat when he was waiting in the passage. It was well within the bounds of possibility that he had done so, and come out with sufficient time in hand to leave his papers as usual and reach his lodgings by a few minutes after seven; but, taking into account the evidence of the voices that had been heard in the flat, it would appear that Sir Adam was alive at least as late as six-fifty-five, when Ling must have been already half-way between Shorncliffe Street and his lodgings in Selby Street. Fenn had already ascertained that, of all the inhabitants of Romney Chambers, only Adams, the caretaker, was in the habit of taking an evening paper, so that there was nothing to account for the presence of the newsagent on the upper floors of the building at that hour, should he have gone there.

It seemed to Fenn that his best chance now lay with Goldstein, and Goldstein was a forlorn hope, at best, if, as was probably the case, he was merely mixed up with Johnson's depredations. That these had taken place after the murder Fenn would have had very little doubt had it not been for Stephens' story of the open door.

It began to look as though, even should he succeed in bringing Sanders's death home to Goldstein, he would still be very little nearer to the solution of the Braid case.

CHAPTER XVI

Two nights later Gilroy was fitting his latchkey into the lock of his door when he became aware of a sound on the stairs behind him that brought all his professional instincts to the fore. He paused and listened. Judging by the noise alone, somebody's bronchial tubes were in a bad way, and he was not surprised when Smith made his appearance round the turn of the staircase. For some time past Gilroy had heard him coughing in the flat overhead and had drawn his own conclusions.

He watched him as he paused on the landing to regain his breath. The man looked, and obviously felt, ill, but his dry humour had not deserted him and he grinned as he caught Gilroy's eye.

"A bit of a pull when the machinery isn't working properly," he observed huskily.

Gilroy smiled.

"It's not the best weather for bronchitis," he said. "You ought to be careful."

Smith glanced sideways at him.

"If you can't be good, be careful, eh?" he answered meaningly. "I don't let it worry me, doctor. It's an old friend, had it since I was a boy, on and off, and it hasn't downed me yet. There's more bark than bite about it, and that's the truth."

"All the same, you might give it a chance. Your doctor can relieve it a bit, you know. Hasn't he given you anything for it?"

"Haven't got a doctor. I've had too much of them in the past, I suppose, with all due apologies to you!"

"I don't blame you," said Gilroy, laughing. "I can give you a prescription that will relieve that cough though, if you feel disposed to trust me. Don't tell me you're not dosing yourself with some poisonous contraption or other you've seen advertised." Smith looked distinctly sheepish.

"You've got me there," he admitted. "The truth is, the wife worries if I bark at night."

There was a likeable quality about the man, and it was not merely curiosity that made Gilroy push open his door and invite him in.

"Have a drink, anyway," he said. "And I'll see whether I can't foist a prescription on you as well. Properly speaking, I don't practise now, so you won't feel you're taking advantage of me."

He led the way into his sitting-room and made up the fire. Then he poured out a stiff drink and placed it at Smith's elbow. The man looked as though he needed it.

"You're better without these, you know," said Gilroy, as he pushed the cigarettes towards him.

Smith took one.

"I'm not your patient yet," he observed, with a smile that somehow, in spite of its irony, robbed the words of all malice.

As Gilroy held a match to his cigarette, he looked up at him.

"You're keeping bad company, doctor," he said. "I don't know what Mr. Fenn would say to this."

Gilroy's eyes twinkled.

"He'd probably congratulate me on getting in touch with the only person in this building capable of discussing the Braid case intelligently," he answered.

"Meaning that I may tell you more than I'd tell him," observed Smith shrewdly. "Nothing doing, doctor. But I will say this, and you can believe it or not as you like, neither the wife nor I had any hand in that business."

"I'm quite willing to believe that," agreed Gilroy readily. "I wish you'd give me your frank opinion of the whole thing, though. I can promise it won't go any further if you do. And you can take it that I didn't ask you in here for any ulterior purpose!"

Smith nodded.

"That's a new word to me," he said. "But I take your meaning. Matter of fact, it's the first time any one in this building's held out the glad hand, so to speak, and I appreciate it. The caretaker doesn't like us, and my wife's got to such a pitch that she'll wait in the street rather than meet either of those old pussies downstairs in the hall. She says Miss Webb looks down her nose at her and she don't like it."

"I shouldn't let Miss Webb's attitude worry you," laughed Gilroy. "She's harmless enough, even when her tongue's wagging."

"And it does wag! She was seeing a friend out when I came up yesterday and I caught Miss Braid's name. 'That sweet young thing,' she called her, but it didn't prevent her from speaking her mind about her."

Gilroy stiffened.

"She'll find herself in trouble, if she's not careful," he said. "There is such a thing as libel."

"I shouldn't say that that troubled Miss Webb much. Libel's a thing she must have been flirting with, as you might say, all her life. And I bet she's got away with it, too. She's not the only one, though, who's slinging mud at Miss Braid, and, if what they say is true, she's pretty well for it, unless Mr. Fenn's got something up his sleeve."

"There's more in the whole business than meets the eye," said Gilroy evasively. "But if they say anything to you, you can contradict any rumour that Miss Braid is implicated in any way. She's got nothing to do with it."

He flattered himself that he had kept the rising anger out of his voice, but there was a gleam in Smith's sardonic eye that made him uncomfortable.

"Oh, quite," he agreed. "I'm not trying to fasten anything on to her. Besides, I'm in the opposite camp, so to speak, though I don't hold with violence and never did. According to the wife, she doesn't look the kind of young lady to stick a knife into any one, and I'm willing to take her word for it. All the same, there's more than a bit of gossip going round, and I thought I'd warn you."

He put down his glass and rose.

"Thanks for the drink," he said. "I'll do the same for you one evening, if you feel inclined to come up and look at a little gas contraption I'm interested in. It's the only thing of its kind on the market."

"I didn't know you went in for that sort of thing," commented Gilroy tactlessly.

His mind was on the gossip about Jill Braid and he spoke without reflection.

The sardonic lines on Smith's face deepened.

"Oh, we all have our little hobbies," he said. "Can't work all the time, you know."

Gilroy pulled himself together.

"I should be glad to come up," he assured him. "Meanwhile, if you'll wait a moment—"

He took a sheet of paper and scribbled a prescription.

"Get that made up," he said. "And, if I catch sight of your wife, I shall tell her to make you take it. And keep away from fogs and damp as much as you can."

Smith nodded good-humouredly as he took it.

"I'll drink it," he said, "if only to oblige you. But as for coddling myself, don't I know all about that! You lay up for a week, and then one morning, when you're all warm and cosy in your little bed, blessed if it isn't the old bronchitis again! Thanks, all the same."

He hesitated a moment, then—

"One good turn deserves another," he added abruptly. "You may see me again within the next day or two."

And with that he departed, leaving Gilroy considerably puzzled as to his meaning.

He was as good as his word, however. The next night he turned up again, and Gilroy, as he performed the sacred rites of hospitality, found himself wondering, with some misgiving, whether his neighbour was going to make a habit of dropping in on his evening's work. It was soon apparent, however, that

Smith had come with a definite object in view. It revealed itself before he had been five minutes in the flat.

"To go back to Sir Adam Braid's murder," he began. "You asked me last night for my frank opinion on it. As I told you then, you can hardly expect to find me on the side of law and order. But that doesn't mean that I enjoy watching the police barking up the wrong tree any more than you do. I nearly said something to you last night, and if I'd been the only person concerned, I'd have done so." He paused, and Gilroy took him up eagerly.

"You mean that you have got some knowledge of what happened that night?" he asked.

Smith held up a thin hand.

"Now, don't go off the deep end. What I'm going to say may be so much waste of breath for all the good it will do you. If you're in Mr. Fenn's confidence, as I take you to be, you know a lot more about this business than I do. But, before this goes any further, I want your word for it that you won't pass on anything I tell you to the police without my permission. And by the police, I mean Mr. Fenn. That's understood?"

Gilroy hesitated.

"You're asking a good deal," he said at last. "If you can clear Miss Braid, you can hardly expect me to keep your information to myself."

"I can't clear her, but you're free to act on anything I may tell you, provided you hold your tongue on certain points. But I want your word for it that nothing goes through to Mr. Fenn without the permission of the parties, or rather the party, involved. Without that I don't open my lips."

"I'll undertake to hold my tongue," agreed Gilroy reluctantly, "provided that you do your best to get the required permission from this third person, should it be necessary. Will that do?"

Smith nodded.

"Good enough," he conceded. "After I left you last night I talked the matter over with the wife, and we agreed that there was something you ought to know, and that there was no harm in passing the word to you, provided it went no further. Now I'll just go over what I imagine happened that night. If I'm wrong at any point you can stop me. I'm going by what came out at the inquest and things I've picked up since. We'll begin with Johnson. He went out as usual round about six-thirty and didn't come back again till after seven, by which time the old man was dead. Then there's this chap Stephens. He came in directly after Johnson had left, and, I understand, swears he was out of the house by six-forty. Barring the people who were already in the house, that's the lot, I take it?"

"So far as we know, yes," answered Gilroy guardedly.

"Then you don't know *everything*," said Smith complacently. "Now listen to little Willie. There was another person in this house that night. He was seen to go in, and what's more, he was seen to go out!"

Gilroy sprang to his feet.

"Good God, man, do you realize—"

Again Smith held up a restraining hand.

"Now, what did I tell you? Don't run away with the idea that I'm going to tell you the name and address of the murderer, because I don't know it, and if I did I probably shouldn't spill it to you. Get this into your head. I don't know who the fellow was. I don't even know whether he was old or young or what he looked like. That's the truth. I'm not kidding you. But I do know there was another man here on the night the old man was murdered, and I give you that for what it's worth."

"But why on earth didn't you come forward with this before?"

"For an uncommonly good reason, if you'll bring yourself to listen. You may or may not know that we had a friend staying with us upstairs after Sir Adam Braid's death. She was 'wanted,' as a matter of fact, and we naturally weren't publishing the fact that she was there. Well, Mr. Fenn jumped to it, and the result was that her visit came to an end a bit more suddenly than we'd intended. Now I want you to understand that she'd got no more to do with the killing than we had. We none of us knew of the thing till next morning, and we shouldn't have known then if that old she-Webb hadn't gone bleating all over the shop. But the point is that when Mr. Fenn hopped in on our little party I didn't exactly take him to my bosom, so to speak, and I may have misled him as to one or two facts. One was as to the length of time Gertie Anderson had been in our flat. I may have led him to believe that she had only arrived two nights before. I don't mind telling you that she had been with us for a week, but I've got your word for it that you won't pass the information on, remember."

Gilroy began to think he had been very neatly trapped.

"I'll keep my word," he said dryly. "But I put it to you that it's not very fair to tie my hands like this."

"It's the fairness to Gertie, not you, I'm worrying about. You see, I know she had nothing to do with it. She was waiting out there in the street when Braid was killed, and she never set foot inside the flats till half-past seven. If you ask me how I know, I'll tell you. I brought her in myself."

"What proof have you that she didn't enter the flats of her own accord earlier in the evening?" countered Gilroy.

"None. But I know, from what she told the wife, that she was in the street, as she said, or she couldn't have known the things she did know. Mind you, the wife only let on about what she'd told her after she'd left our flat, and the day Mr. Fenn called on us I hadn't got the story. I misled him a bit then, for reasons of my own, I'll admit, through not wanting him to know that my wife was alone in the flat when the old man was killed. To tell you the truth, Gertie hadn't told me what she'd seen, and I wasn't so sure in my own mind then that she'd been in the street all the time as she said. And I wasn't going to have my wife mixed up in anything of that sort. So I let Mr. Fenn think I'd got back by an earlier train, and that Gertie hadn't come to us till two days before he spotted her."

"I still don't see what makes you so certain that she was speaking the truth," objected Gilroy.

Smith bent forward impressively.

"Because the things she told my wife on the night of the murder were things she couldn't possibly have known then, unless she'd seen them with her own eyes. This is what she said: There was no light in our front rooms when she got here. Otherwise she'd have gone straight up. My wife was in the kitchen at the back, as she told Mr. Fenn, and Gertie thought the flat was empty and waited in the street to catch one of us on the way home. In the end, she waylaid me and we went in together. While she was waiting she saw three people come into the flats, two men and a woman. Three, mind you! The two men she saw come out again, but the woman, who must have been Miss Braid, didn't come out. Now, at the time she told the wife all this, no one knew about Miss Braid or Stephens, and, to this day, no one knows about the second man. That's how I know she was speaking the truth, apart from the fact that she wouldn't go out of her way to lie to my wife."

"Couldn't she describe the second man?"

"No such luck. She was too far off. When the first man, whom I take to be Stephens, arrived, she was sheltering in a doorway opposite, and she saw him pretty clearly. Then she moved up the street, and, though she saw the second man go in and then saw the two of them come out, she was too far off even to be sure which of them was Stephens. But she says the second man went in within five minutes of the other, and one of them came out almost at once and seemed in a hell of a hurry. It was ten minutes or more before the other man came out, and he was taking it easily. It was after that that the woman turned in, just after the church clock had struck seven. Is that any help to you?"

"None," said Gilroy hopelessly. "We've got proof that Miss Braid could not have reached the flats before seven, and this simply confirms it. But this story about the third man does shed some light on things."

"Well, you can take it from me that he was there, if Gertie says so. And now you see where I stand, doctor. If you can pass the glad news on to Mr. Fenn, without giving us away, you can do it. But Gertie must be kept out of it. I've got your word for that. And there's another thing I can tell you, though I know Mr. Fenn doesn't see it as I do. That noise my wife heard at a quarter to seven was the old man being done in. She told me about it after Mr. Fenn's visit, and she's repeated it since, and I'm as sure of it as I stand here."

"There's nothing else you know that you haven't told me?" asked Gilroy, with a sudden suspicion.

"Not a thing!" asserted Smith, with such conviction that Gilroy was inclined to believe that, for once, he was speaking the truth. "But that's what I think, and I stick to it. She was right about the time, too, whatever Mr. Fenn may say."

After he had gone Gilroy was left to face the problem of how to convey to Fenn the information he had just received without giving away Smith or his compromising visitor. He was disposed to take the man's word for it that she had no connection with the murder, and he recognized how disastrous it would be for one with her record if it were known that she was actually in the vicinity of the flats when it took place. He decided to sleep on it, and began to prepare for bed, first making a careful note of the times at which, according to Smith, the two men had entered the building.

He had hardly begun to undress when his bell rang, and he went to the door, to find the person he was least prepared to meet standing there.

"Good Lord, Fenn!" he exclaimed.

"I won't keep you out of your bed," said Fenn, as he stepped into the passage. "I only dropped in for a moment on my way back to Putney. We've had a nasty set-back. The Southampton police have telephoned to say that Stephens' witness, Macnab, has been picked up in the street with a hole in his head. He's in hospital now, and it's a question whether his skull's fractured or not. Anyway, he's not likely to be able to speak for some time yet. Whoever did it evidently left him for dead."

"Macnab! But why should any one want to put him out of the way?"

"I can't tell you, but, if you ask me who did it, I'm ready to make a shrewd guess that it was a gentleman of the name of Goldstein, and when we know why he did it we shall have got the missing link in this confounded case."

CHAPTER XVII

THE NEWS OF the attack on Macnab left Gilroy hovering between relief and disappointment. It seemed to him not unlikely that the steward's assailant was the mysterious second man Smith's friend, Gertie, had seen entering the building on the night of the murder, though why he had been at such pains to silence Stephens' witness it was difficult to imagine. At best, Macnab could do no more than clear Stephens, and in view of the fact that, according to the wireless message, the man was returning to London for the express purpose of corroborating Stephens' statement, whoever attacked him must have known that he would gain little by putting him out of action. That there was some deeper motive behind the assault on Macnab seemed pretty evident, and it looked very much as though there might be a direct connection between it and the Braid case. And it was all to the advantage of Jill, assuming she were innocent, that anything should occur that pointed, however vaguely, to some solution of the mystery. The assault on Macnab, while it delayed the progress of the case in the eyes of Fenn, also definitely postponed any action with regard to Jill Braid, a fact for which Gilroy was proportionately grateful. So long as Stephens was under suspicion, Fenn would no doubt be able to hold his hand.

Gilroy slept badly, and was sick and tired of his own thoughts when he sat down to breakfast next morning. His ancient charwoman, Mrs. Cotswold, whose loquacity he had suffered without protest since Fenn's suggestion that it might prove useful, chose this particular morning, of all others, on which to let her tongue run freely, and she pottered about the room while he ate, chattering unceasingly. By the time he had reached his second cup of tea she had reverted to Sir Adam Braid's murder, which was still her favourite topic of conversation.

"To think that only a month ago the poor old gentleman was a-sittin' eatin' of 'is breakfast, same as you. And 'im now dead and buried! It do bring it 'ome to one. Another month and you and me may be gone, too, sir!" she declaimed unctuously.

Sustained by this exhilarating thought Gilroy attacked his egg, emitting an inarticulate sound that Mrs. Cotswold no doubt took to mean encouragement, for she continued in the same strain.

"Well, they say that to dream of death means a weddin'! And it's a funny thing, if you ask me, that a weddin' should 'a come of it, after all. Looks as if there was some truth in them old sayin's. If the old gentleman 'ad lived, I suppose that there Johnson'd 'ave been a free man to-day. And glad of it, I shouldn't wonder! Much good marriage 'as done 'im!"

Gilroy looked up from his plate.

"What's the matter with Johnson?" he asked.

"If you ask me, sir, 'e's got the same disease as Cotswold, though Cotswold ain't got the same cause for it. For I *'ave* been a good wife to Cotswold, though I say it as shouldn't. Johnson's up at 'The Nag's 'Ead' every night now, and 'e don't leave afore 'e's chucked out, and then it's as much as 'e can do ter get 'ome. At least, that's what Cotswold tells me, and 'e ought ter know," she finished bitterly.

"Drinking, is he? He never seemed to me a drinking man."

"Nor 'e wasn't. I'll lay that 'ussy's leadin' 'im a dance. A rare temper she'll 'ave, if she takes after 'er mother. There's some as could tell you a thing or two about 'er, if they chose!"

"A bad lot, was she?"

"Well, if you ask me no questions, you won't get no lies, and I ain't sayin' anythin', mind you. But *I* never see 'er marriage lines, and it's my belief she 'adn't any to show. She was married to 'er first, all right, poor feller. I can remember *'im* bein' fished out of the river as well as if it was yesterday. A lighterman, 'e was. Got 'imself run down by a tug one dark night, and that was the end of 'im. And 'e 'adn't been dead three weeks afore she went off with the other. Been goin' on with 'im a fair scandal, too, she 'ad, while 'er 'usband was alive."

Gilroy's interest had evaporated. He had drawn his own conclusions as to Mrs. Johnson at Brighton, and Mrs. Cotswold's gossip about her mother only served to confirm them.

"I don't know nothin' and I'm not sayin' nothin'," she went on, flicking aimlessly at Gilroy's writing-table with a duster. "Of course, she always let on as she was married to that there Ling, but, as I say, I never saw 'er marriage lines and I never met any one else as did."

Gilroy's cup clattered on the saucer.

"What's that about Ling?" he asked sharply.

"It was Ling as she went off with. Didn't you know that, sir? That's what I was sayin'. With 'er first 'ardly cold in 'is grave—"

Gilroy broke in ruthlessly on the recital.

"Look here," he demanded. "Who was Mrs. Johnson before she married?"

Mrs. Cotswold stared at him in hurt surprise.

"Ruby Ling," she answered. "'Aven't I just said so? I expect you wasn't listenin', sir."

Gilroy hastened to conciliate her. He did not want the fount of eloquence to dry now.

"I'm sorry, I'm afraid I wasn't. So Johnson's wife is Ling's daughter, is she? I never realized that."

"*And* the livin' spit of 'er mother! Mr. Ling's a sober, 'ard-workin' feller, and always 'as been. Ruby's mother 'ad more luck than she deserved when she got 'im. A good father 'e's been to Ruby by all accounts—"

She prattled on, but Gilroy once more was not listening. He was trying to fit in the information he had just received with the facts as he knew them. When he remembered the spate of gossip he had endured from Mrs. Cotswold on the subject of Johnson and his marriage, he could have kicked himself for not having inquired into the parentage of the man's wife.

He made a dash for the nearest public telephone, got on to Fenn, and, within half an hour, was in his office at the Yard.

"Ling's daughter, is she?" was Fenn's comment. "This is full of possibilities."

"It certainly opens out quite a new field of conjecture," said Gilroy. "Johnson owed Ling money, and goodness knows what hold the man may have had over him and how he used it. If Johnson left that door unlatched for somebody, it may very well have been for Ling."

"And it's Ling who has been issuing those notes, and Ling's daughter who was wearing Sir Adam's ring. It looks as if things were beginning to drift in a definite direction at last."

"Johnson got spliced uncommonly quickly after Sir Adam's death, and, from all accounts, it doesn't look as if it had been a love match. It certainly didn't seem like one when we ran into them at Brighton."

Fenn leaned back in his chair and thrust his hands deep into his pockets.

"And the fellow's got as good an alibi as Johnson's if, as we have every reason to suppose, Sir Adam was alive at seven o'clock," he said gloomily.

"Unless Mrs. Smith was right and the cry she heard really did come from Sir Adam. The murder may have been committed then."

"With all the evidence we've got to the contrary, I should doubt it. Besides which, nothing that comes from the Smiths can be looked upon as very reliable. Their account of their own movements that night is incredibly contradictory," Fenn reminded him.

"All the same, I'm very much inclined to call on Mrs. Smith and see just whether I can move her as to the time at which she says she heard the noise. Have you any objection to my having a shot in that direction?"

"None whatever. You may get more out of them than I did. They won't tell more than they're obliged to the police."

Gilroy, with Smith's information weighing heavily on his mind, could endorse this only too heartily. He decided to lead the conversation as far as possible away from the Smiths before revealing what he had learned.

"Johnson's wife's got a pretty poor family record behind her on her mother's side, if Mrs. Cotswold's to be believed," he said, blandly trailing his red herring. "She spoke well of Ling, but she hadn't a good word to say of the woman."

Fenn nodded.

"Mrs. Johnson's a fine strapping girl, and quite capable of inflicting the wound that killed the old man, if that's what you're leading up to," he admitted. "But, honestly, I find it a little difficult to fit her in with the known facts. Of course, it's not impossible that she may have had an interview with Sir Adam which ended in a quarrel between them; but an uneducated woman, especially one of Mrs. Johnson's type, gives herself away pretty thoroughly when she loses her temper, and you must remember that Webb, though he couldn't distinguish the words that were being said, listened for some time to the voices, and his impression certainly was that the woman belonged to Sir Adam's own class. I'm pretty sure that, at the bottom of his heart, he believes she was Miss Braid, but being a kind-hearted little chap, he isn't going to say so. If it had been Mrs. Johnson he heard, he wouldn't be under any such delusion."

"All the same, if Johnson did leave the door open for any one, why not for the woman he was going to marry?"

"I'm not saying she's beyond suspicion, but I admit that I share Jill Braid's conviction that she knows nothing of Johnson's peccadilloes. She was genuinely taken aback when she realized that he was in trouble, though she rallied pretty quickly and showed extraordinary presence of mind over that business of the ring. She's got a head on her shoulders all right."

Gilroy nodded absent-mindedly. The moment had come in which to pass on what he had learned from Smith, and he was searching in vain for an opening.

"There's one bit of information I've stumbled on," he said, conscious that he was making an uncommonly awkward plunge, "that I think you ought to have. The trouble is that I've promised not to give away the name of my informant."

Fenn turned on him sharply, and, for a moment, Gilroy thought he was going to give trouble. Then he caught the twinkle in Fenn's eyes.

"I couldn't help it," he said hastily. "I couldn't possibly have got the information in any other way, and it's worth having."

"I've been expecting something of the sort," was Fenn's comment. "That's where you blessed amateurs have the pull over us. We can't lend ourselves to that sort of thing. At least, not officially. If you're confident that you're justified in withholding the name of your informant, I suppose I must let it go at that. Fire away."

"It appears that there was an extra person in the flats on the night of the murder. He was seen both to go in and come out."

Fenn did not waste his time in questioning the information.

"What time did he leave?" he asked sharply.

"That's exactly what my informant does not know," admitted Gilroy. "Whoever saw him was standing too far off to identify him, and can only say that two men went in and two left, sometime between half past six and just before seven. There's no clue as to which of them left first."

"But they both left before seven? That doesn't help Jill Braid much, if Sir Adam were alive at seven. If her evidence didn't fit in so well with the accounts of Webb and Stephens I should be inclined to think she was the victim of her own imagination. As it is, the thing's a deadlock. Get on to the Smiths, if you like, and see what you can do. They're shy birds, but, from what you've told me just now, it looks as if you might get round them."

Gilroy cast a quick glance at his face, but it was inscrutable, and, for the life of him, he could not make out whether or not there was a hidden meaning in his last words. They were ambiguous enough, however, to cause him to heave a sigh of relief when he found himself on the other side of the door of Fenn's office.

He went straight back to Romney Chambers, intent on rounding up Mrs. Smith. But there was no answer to his ring, and the flat seemed to be deserted. Looking out of his own sitting-room window, half an hour later, he was both amused and annoyed to see a careworn individual, wielding a big reflex camera with a top-heavy lens, assiduously photographing various aspects of Romney Chambers. He had press photographer written all over him, and Gilroy retired hastily from view, conscious that, however much the Webbs would no doubt enjoy this sort of thing, he might have considerable difficulty in dodging the reporters, once it became known that he had been called in to view Sir Adam's body.

The photographer was a conscientious worker. On leaving Romney Chambers he did not put his camera away, but strolled down the street, pausing at the corner, outside Ling's shop, to take a last photograph. This done, he turned into the shop, bought a packet of cigarettes, and adroitly led the conversation to the recent murder.

Ling was ready enough to tell what little he knew.

"We can use that, you know," said the pressman appreciatively, as he put away his note-book. "An independent opinion like yours is always interesting, and we always try to get as much local colour as we can. Now, if I might have a snap? Standing in front of the shop, by the doorway here, would be best. I'll send you a copy."

For a moment Ling looked dubious. Now that the interview was over he was no doubt wondering, as many before him have wondered, how much he had been led into saying, and how foolish it would look in print. In the end, however, he yielded to the blandishments of the photographer, and consented to step out on to the pavement and pose in front of the camera.

"It's a good many years since I've been took," he said, with a chuckle. "It'll be a funny thing if I see my own face lyin' on the counter one mornin'!"

"You're lucky in your weather," was the photographer's cheerful comment. "If it had been like yesterday, I should have been hard put to it to get you at all. Now, one more, if you don't mind, from the side here. That's right. Much obliged to you. You'll hear from us in a day or two. Good-morning."

He packed his camera into the case and went on his way.

Three days later Ling received two excellent and highly glazed portraits of himself. There was nothing on the envelope which contained them to indicate which of the big daily papers had so highly honoured him, and he searched in vain through his stock, day after day, for the illustrated article he had understood was shortly to appear, and eventually concluded that it was being kept back until the case was actually in the courts.

CHAPTER XVIII

THE MORNING AFTER Ling's interview with the press photographer found Fenn in the train on his way to Southampton.
A message had come through, the night before, to say that
Macnab had recovered consciousness and was in a condition
to make a statement, and the detective was determined to lose
no time in hearing what he had to say.

For the first time since the death of Sir Adam Braid he was
feeling hopeful, for he shared Gilroy's conviction that, once
they knew the motive of the attempt to put Macnab out of the
way, they would find themselves on the track of the murderer.

It was a relief to hear, when he reached the hospital, that
the man was improving steadily and was, mentally, none the
worse for his adventure. Fenn realized how much he had been
counting on this interview, and wondered ruefully whether
he had not been allowing his imagination to get the better of
his judgment.

He found the ship's steward lying at the end of a long ward,
a screen on one side of the bed to keep the light from the window from his eyes. His face was almost as white as the bandage
round his head, and he looked weak and shaken, but his eyes
were clear and reassuringly intelligent.

Fenn began by taking his account of his and Stephens'
movements on the night of the murder. As he had expected, it
tallied, word for word, with the statement Stephens had made.
He admitted that Stephens was carrying a waterproof over his
arm and that he seemed anxious to move on all the time they
were chatting together. This was what had led to his suggestion that Stephens should walk with him to the station and
talk over old times on the way. He denied emphatically that
Stephens' hands or clothes were stained in any way, and declared that he could not have missed seeing it if they had been.

"You take my word for it, inspector," he concluded, "he
ain't got nothing to do with the murder. I didn't serve all that

time with him for nothing. He'd never bring himself to do a thing like that."

"If the murder was committed at the time we think," answered Fenn, "you've cleared him all right. Now we'll get on to your business. Any idea who hit you?"

"None!" was the prompt answer. "But I'd like to get my hands on him! I was on my way back to my lodgings, as innocent as you please, never suspecting nothing, when he got me, plump on the back of my head, and I didn't know nothing more till I came to myself in this bed. I might have had a glass more than usual, but I wasn't what you could call the worse. If I hadn't been so unsuspecting they'd never have got me like that."

"You hadn't had words with any one that evening?"

"Not a soul! I reckon whoever did it was out for what he could get. And he must have been disturbed, because he didn't get nothing."

"So you're none the worse except for a crack on the head. Ever come across a man called Goldstein?"

Macnab stared at him.

"Never heard the name before. Anyway, I'm not partial to Jews, and I take it he'd be one."

"He is," answered Fenn.

He produced an envelope from his pocket and took out a photograph.

"Ever seen that face before?" he asked.

Macnab examined it with obvious distaste.

"No, and I don't want to," he said decisively.

Fenn retrieved it.

"That settles Goldstein, then," he said. "Though the chances are that he wouldn't have appeared himself, even if he had had anything to do with it. Now, what about these?"

He produced the two photographs of Ling that the pseudo press photographer had taken the day before. As he placed them on the bed he watched his man narrowly. He had sent his photographer down to Ling's shop as a matter of routine, and at the last moment, just as he was leaving his office, had slipped the prints into his pocket on a sudden impulse.

Macnab was staring at them in obvious perplexity.

"I've seen that chap somewhere," he said slowly, "but, for the life of me, I couldn't say where. Not so long ago, either."

The photographer had included the doorway of Ling's shop and a row of news-boards, propped up against the wall. The sight of them seemed to stimulate Macnab's memory.

"I know that place," he exclaimed suddenly. "It's that paper shop close to where I met old Stephens. And that's the chap that keeps it. Don't know what he calls himself, though."

"How did you come to see him?" asked Fenn.

"I dropped into the shop to buy a paper and just passed the time of day with him. That's all I know about him. Seemed a pleasant enough chap, from what I remember."

"What time was that?"

"Shortly before I met Stephens. Five minutes or so, I should say."

Fenn consulted his notebook.

"According to Stephens, he met you about six-thirty-eight. Say you spoke to this man in his shop at six-thirty-three, would that be right?"

"Near enough, I should imagine."

"That tallies with his own account of his movements. He says he left his shop at about six-thirty-five. That would be after you'd gone?"

"That's right. I didn't say more than a couple of words to him. Then I strolled out and down the street. If I hadn't stopped to light my pipe I should have missed Stephens. And if he says he left his shop, he's speaking the truth. He passed me and I said 'good-evening' to him, just before I ran into Stephens. Stephens must have seen him too. Didn't he say nothing?"

"He never mentioned him, but there's no reason why he should have noticed him. I don't suppose he'd have made any impression on you if it wasn't for the fact that you'd just seen him in the shop." Macnab looked sceptical.

"I should think he'd have remembered him. Why, he must have passed him on the stairs."

"What stairs?"

The question came like a pistol shot.

"Why, the staircase of the place Stephens came out of. I saw him go through the door and up them."

Fenn drew his chair closer.

"Let's get this right," he said. "You stopped to light your pipe and this man passed you. What happened then? Try to be as exact as possible."

"I recognized him and wished him 'good-evening,' as I said. So far as I can remember he didn't answer. Then he turned into the building, the same one Stephens came out of. That's the last I saw of him."

"How long was it before Stephens came out?"

"Not more than a minute, I should say, but it's some time ago, you must remember. I wouldn't like to be exact. But it couldn't have been long. That's why I thought Stephens would have met him on the stairs."

Fenn leaned back in his chair with a sigh. Several things were becoming clear to him.

"He didn't see him," he said quietly. "But he heard him go into the flat. This clears the air with a vengeance. You say you spoke to him. That means that he knew he'd been recognized. No wonder he tried to stop your mouth!"

"You don't mean that it was that chap from the paper shop as bashed me on the head?" demanded Macnab, in aggrieved bewilderment.

"Unless I'm very far out the actual bashing was arranged, if not carried out, by the unpleasing gentleman whose portrait I showed you just now," answered Fenn. "But there's no doubt now who his employer was. You've helped me to the best day's work I've done for a long time, and I'm grateful. I'm afraid we may have to ask you to come up to London as soon as you're on your feet again, though."

"I'll come, if I can do old Stephens a good turn," Macnab assured him. "We've been through some funny times together, him and me, and I ain't forgotten it."

It was late in the afternoon when Fenn got back to London. He dropped into the Yard to see to one or two important arrangements, then went straight to Gilroy's flat. He found him at home.

"Have you tackled Mrs. Smith?" was his first question.

Gilroy shook his head.

"She was out when I called," he said. "But I'd meant to have another shot to-night. You look as nearly rattled as I've ever seen you. What's happened?"

Fenn grinned.

"What a thing it is to be a doctor," he gibed. "Rattled is not the word, though. Listen to this!"

As briefly as possible he told Gilroy what had happened.

"There's your second man for you," he said, when he had finished. "And that's the person Stephens heard go into the flat when he was hiding in the passage. Our only stumbling-block now is the time of the murder. Ling reached his lodgings at five minutes past seven, and, to do that, he must have left this building before seven. In which case, whose were the voices Jill Braid heard at seven in her grandfather's flat?"

"It's like some rotten chorus to a comic song," said Gilroy disgustedly. "Whatever happens we always get back to that. 'Whose were the voices, tum-ti-tum-ti-tum!'"

"Very funny," was Fenn's unappreciative rejoinder. "But I suppose you realize that it's a serious matter for Jill Braid. It seems to me that we shall have to accept Mrs. Smith's theory as to the time of the murder."

"It isn't Mrs. Smith's. I don't fancy she's got the smallest belief in it. It's Smith who is so keen on the idea."

"And Smith's no fool," said Fenn. "But what I don't like to contemplate is the play the counsel for the defence will make with those people who were overheard talking in the flat. Once he gets Webb and Stephens and Jill Braid into the box, it won't be a bit like a comic song, I can assure you! And there's another thing. It's only going on the assumption that Sir Adam was one of the people who were speaking that we've cleared Stephens, and what clears Stephens, clears Ling, though I admit it's by a narrower margin. It's quite sufficient for the defence, though. I wish Mrs. Smith's evidence was a bit more conclusive!"

"Are you going to tackle her, or shall I have another shot to-night?" asked Gilroy. "I think she's more likely to talk to me."

"I'll leave her to you, for the present," said Fenn. "I've got to get back to the Yard. We've got Ling under observation, and we can lay our hands on him when we want him. I'm still living in hopes that Goldstein may show up. If he's hard pressed and goes to Ling, we can close down on both of them." Gilroy saw Fenn to the door, and then went straight upstairs to the Smiths' flat. This time he found them both at home, and the man, at any rate, seemed genuinely pleased to see him.

He tackled Mrs. Smith as to what she had overheard on the night of the murder, but could get no more from her than the account she had given Fenn. As to the time, she was immovable.

"And you're sure you heard no one talking in Sir Adam's flat?" asked Gilroy.

"Certain. But unless they were talking in the bedroom side of the house I shouldn't have heard them. You must remember I had the bedroom window open or I shouldn't have heard what I did. All the windows in the front were shut, and there's your flat in between this and Sir Adam's."

"I wish to heaven I'd been at home," said Gilroy. "It might have made all the difference. Though, as a matter of fact, if I'm working, as I generally am at that time, I hear very little of what's going on outside. I've noticed your wireless occasionally. I remember setting my watch by Big Ben one night last summer when all the windows were open. But, as a rule, I'm too absorbed to notice what's going on upstairs."

"It wasn't our wireless you heard," said Smith. "We haven't got one. It must have been the old gentleman's. We used to get it sometimes upstairs, when all the windows were open."

Gilroy stared at him.

"I could have sworn it came from your flat," he said, in astonishment. "It just shows how deceptive sound is. But, as I say, it takes a pretty loud noise to take my mind off my work, so you can comfort yourselves with the thought that I'm not the kind of inconvenient neighbour who makes a fuss because the tenant overhead takes his boots off at one o'clock in the morning!"

He stayed for a time chatting, and then, realizing that his visit had been fruitless, went back to his flat.

After writing a couple of letters he strolled down Shorncliffe Street and across King's Road into Chelsea to the small restaurant where he sometimes dined. As he ate he turned over his visit to the Smiths in his mind.

He had reached the coffee stage when an idea struck him that held him spell-bound, the cup halfway to his mouth, for the space of about five minutes. Then, as though suddenly released, he sprang to his feet and made for the kitchen at the back of the restaurant.

"Can I telephone?" he demanded breathlessly.

He was taken into a passage off the kitchen, and a few minutes later was talking to Fenn.

"I say," he exclaimed, "can I have the key of Sir Adam's flat?"

There was a grunt from the other end of the wire.

"I don't know that you can," said Fenn's voice. "What do you want it for?"

"I'd rather not say until I've made a little experiment. When are you leaving?"

"This office, do you mean? Almost immediately."

"Can you leave the key with me on your way back to Putney?"

Gilroy's voice was urgent.

"I can, I suppose. Do you want to get to work to-night?"

"I'll explain when I see you," said Gilroy, and rang off before the other could expostulate.

He paid his bill and hurried back to the flat, and when Fenn arrived, rather irate and considerably mystified, he was waiting for him.

"Look here," he said, as he took the key and thrust it into his pocket, "I want you to give me a free hand in this. If you don't hear from me, will you meet me at the flat downstairs at three o'clock tomorrow afternoon? I shall know then whether I'm on the right tack or not."

Fenn glanced at his face and gave in.

"Do you know," he observed thoughtfully, "I believe that this is the first time I've ever seen you humanly excited. There's one thing to be said for the Braid murder, it's shaken the dry rot out of your system. You can have the key and do your damnedest with it, but if I don't see you to-morrow, you'll bring it back to the Yard yourself. I'm getting too old to climb in and out of the Putney bus after a hard day's work. Good-night and good luck to you."

"Don't forget! Three o'clock to-morrow afternoon!" shouted Gilroy after him.

Shortly afterwards Gilroy left the flat, intent on gathering material for his experiment. He found it more difficult than he had anticipated and it was past midnight when he returned, with a bulky parcel under his arm, having at last run what he was looking for to earth.

But, though weary, he seemed well satisfied with his evening's work.

CHAPTER XIX

IT WAS SHORTLY after nine o'clock next morning when Gilroy let himself out of Sir Adam Braid's flat. As he closed the door behind him, his face alight with triumph and satisfaction, he was aware of hasty footsteps mounting the stairs from the hall below.

His heart sank as he recognized Miss Webb. She was breasting the stairs with a celerity surprising in one so plump, and her rather protruding blue eyes positively bulged with excitement. Gilroy told himself bitterly that she looked like nothing so much as a fat Pekinese, aquiver at the sight of food. She almost fell upon him in her enthusiasm.

"I was just coming up to your flat, Dr. Gilroy!" she exclaimed breathlessly. "But I see you've already noticed it."

Gilroy mastered his exasperation with an effort.

"I'm afraid I'm responsible," he said, with his pleasantest smile. "I'm so sorry if I alarmed you."

"Well, I wasn't frightened exactly, but being Sir Adam's flat, if you understand me, after what happened—"

"I know, I ought to have been more careful. I promise not to startle you again."

He made a decisive move towards his own flat, but she did not intend to let him off so easily. Before he could escape she was by his side.

"I know you won't mind my asking," she exclaimed eagerly. "But, as a friend of Mr. Compton's, you're bound to know."

"Mr. Compton?" he interrupted, genuinely puzzled. The name conveyed nothing to him.

"Sir Adam's lawyer. You must have got the key from him. You see, there are only two keys to all these doors, and I know that the police have one, and when I asked Adams if he had the other, he said the lawyer had got it."

In her absorption she was almost thinking aloud, and Gilroy listened, amazed at the unerring logic born of curiosity.

"I see," he said. "But I'm afraid I haven't the pleasure of Mr. Compton's acquaintance."

For a moment she looked really baffled, then her face cleared.

"Of course, he would naturally have handed it to Miss Braid by now. Then that means she really has inherited her grandfather's money! That was what I wanted to ask you. I'm not being inquisitive, really, but both my brother and myself are so interested in Miss Braid, and we've been hoping all along that it would come to her."

"There again, I'm afraid I can't help you," answered Gilroy smoothly. "It wasn't Miss Braid who lent me the key."

With which parting shot he ran swiftly upstairs and into his own flat.

Miss Webb descended very much more slowly than she had come, her brows knit in meditation.

Gilroy waited until he heard the sound of her front door closing, and then hurried out of the building. This time his quest took him to Southampton Street, whence he returned, well satisfied, in time to put in half a morning's work before lunch.

Punctually at three o'clock Fenn knocked at his door.

"Well," he said, with a rather sardonic smile, "you've brought me down here in the middle of a heavy day's work. What of it?"

Gilroy declined to be impressed by his manner.

"You wait, my friend," was his answer. "You'll sing to another tune in a minute. Go on in, I'll be back in a second."

He disappeared downstairs, while Fenn strolled down the passage to Gilroy's sitting-room. He had put down his hat and was shrugging himself out of his greatcoat, when he paused suddenly, his attention arrested, his chin thrust forward, his eyes bright with interest.

It was thus that Gilroy found him when he returned, and his face lit up with mischief at the sight.

He tucked his arm through Fenn's.

"Come on," he said, as he led him out of the flat and down the stairs to the landing outside Sir Adam Braid's door.

Fenn said not a word. He was listening intently.

Gilroy released his arm.

"Now," he said, "put yourself in the place of little Webb on the night of the murder and tell me what you make of it."

From behind the closed door of Sir Adam's flat came the sound of a man's voice. It was impossible to distinguish the words that were being said, but the voice flowed on uninterruptedly.

"Good lord," said Fenn at last. "Sounds like a foreigner."

"It is," was Gilroy's quiet answer. "It's a gentleman called Signor Galli."

He handed Fenn the current number of the *Radio Times*, and pointed to an item on the programme: "Elementary Italian Lesson," by Signor Galli.

"Sir Adam used headphones," snapped Fenn, recovering himself. "This is a loud speaker."

"Sir Adam was using headphones when Johnson left him on the night he was killed," answered Gilroy; "but he had a loud speaker. I've heard it myself in the summer, when the windows were open; but, like a fool, I never put two and two together until Smith said something last night that put me on the track."

He opened the door of the flat and led the way into the study.

"Do you remember that potty little wireless that the Webbs gave Johnson?" he asked, as he switched off the set. "There was a loud speaker standing on the table beside it when we paid that visit to his rooms, and I was amused at the idea of his trying to run it on a crystal set. I'm willing to bet that that was Sir Adam's loud speaker, and that the fellow had pinched it from this flat after the murder. I thought then that it was much too expensive for his pocket. I raked London last night for one of the same make and size. It was too late to buy one and I had no end of a job running this to earth, but I was determined to make a thorough job of it while I was about it. I found this, at last, at the Children's Hospital."

He picked up another copy of the wireless paper from off the table.

"This about clinches it, I think," he went on, handing it to Fenn. "Look at the programme for November the sixth."

Fenn ran his eye down the page till he arrived at the item scheduled to take place at six-forty-five. With a gasp of comprehension, he read it.

THE ELOPEMENT
A Comedy by Roland Ney. In One Act.

> Arabella Fanshaw.
> Sir Robert Fanshaw, her father.
> Richard Armstrong, a young gallant.
> Toby Giles, an innkeeper.
> Larry, a postilion.

Gilroy pointed to a sentence he had underlined in pencil in the short synopsis of the play that followed.

"In the course of a stormy interview with her father, Arabella avows her intention to remain true to Richard."

"I think we may take it for granted that that was what little Webb heard through the keyhole," he said, with a chuckle. "And the men's voices overheard by the others are easily accounted for. The play must have lasted till well past seven o'clock, as the next item, an organ recital, isn't timed to begin till seven-thirty."

Fenn had already fished out his notebook, though he could have recited the times his various suspects had entered and left the building by heart.

"Johnson stated that he left Sir Adam with the earphones on listening-in," he began slowly.

"He was probably listening to the B.B.C. Orchestra playing Schubert's Unfinished Symphony. It's down for six-ten on the programme and was probably still going on at six-thirty. Very likely he used the headphones for good music, partly because he was slightly deaf, and partly owing to the greater purity of the tone. A lot of people do this. Then, after Johnson had gone, he turned on the loud speaker for the play, in which he wasn't so interested."

Fenn consulted his book again.

"Then, assuming that the cry Mrs. Smith heard came from Sir Adam and that the murder took place at six-forty-five, Stephens was already clear of the flat and Jill Braid had not yet arrived. We've got evidence of the time of her departure from the hairdresser who did her hair, and it is physically impossible for her to have reached this building before the time she said. Smith was in the train on his way to London. We've found a porter, by the way, who knows him well by sight, and who saw him get out at St. Pancras at six-fifty. He took the money off that American all right, and it was just his luck that the man should have been too drunk to identify him. That leaves only Ling unaccounted for. Macnab spoke to him and saw him enter this building just before Stephens came out, and he must be the second man your witness saw leave, shortly before Miss Braid entered the flats. If the attack on Sir Adam took place at a quarter to seven, Ling was the only one of the lot who was on the premises at the time."

Gilroy nodded.

"Ling it is, unless he can prove he was delivering his papers just then. And Johnson left the door unlatched for him. No wonder he's been scared stiff ever since the murder! I wonder which of them switched off the loud speaker."

"We shan't have much trouble in getting that out of Johnson, I'm thinking. I'll take a chance and rope them both in to-night. I can hold Johnson for the theft of the loud speaker, if for nothing else, until we've got a bit more to go on. That's an expensive set. I wonder whether the name of the firm that sold it to Sir Adam is on it."

Gilroy bent over the set.

"Here it is, bless 'em," he said, "on a neat little ivory label. Carrick and Venner, Victoria Street. And the chances are that he bought the loud speaker from the same people."

Fenn made a note of the name and also of the make of the loud speaker.

"You're sure that's the one you saw in Johnson's rooms?" he asked.

"Positive. It's lucky that I'd played about with wireless myself, or I shouldn't have noticed it."

"Right. I'll settle that little question on my way back to the Yard. Want to come along?"

But Gilroy shook his head.

"Haven't got time," he said. "I'm busy."

Fenn glanced at him with suspicion in his eye.

"I can't have you queering my pitch at this stage of the game. What's your business?" he demanded.

Gilroy, who had uncoupled the loud speaker and tucked it under his arm, was already on his way to the door.

"I'm going to return this to the kids at the hospital, and then I'm going to dig out Jill Braid and take her out to tea. Any objection?" he vouchsafed, over his shoulder, as he disappeared without waiting for an answer.

"And less than a month ago that was one of the oldest young men in London!" announced Fenn to the empty air.

It did not take many minutes for the salesman at Carrick and Venner's to look up and verify the sale of the loud speaker to Sir Adam Braid. It was, as Gilroy had predicted, identical with the one they had seen in Johnson's rooms.

After a short interview with the area superintendent in charge of the case, Fenn set out, armed with the necessary warrants, in company with a couple of plain-clothes men, to bring in Johnson and Ling.

CHAPTER XX

FENN HAD little trouble with Johnson. At first he was inclined to be sullen and aggrieved, but once he realized that this time the police meant business, he lost his head completely, and, for a second, Fenn surprised blind panic in his eyes. His relief when it dawned upon him that the charge was one of theft was obvious, and he made no bones about admitting that he had taken the loud speaker. He declared that, knowing it was unlikely to be missed, the temptation was too great for him. He had the effrontery to ask to see Jill Braid.

"If I could explain to her, I know she'd understand," he whined. "She isn't one to be hard about a thing like that."

"Meaning because she let you down lightly over the ring," was Fenn's grim answer. "You won't get round her a second time, Johnson. I don't suppose this was all you helped yourself to."

Johnson wrung his hands together.

"I give you my word, that was all!" he protested frenziedly. "I never touched another thing. You can search the place. It was when I was alone there, after me and Mr. Webb found the old gentleman. It was being upset and all made me do it. I'm not a thief!"

"It doesn't make much difference what you call yourself," said Fenn unkindly. "There was no loud speaker in the study when we got there. Where was it?"

"In the wardrobe in my bedroom. I knew no one was likely to miss it. I didn't mean to take it, really, even then."

Fenn gave him a keen glance.

"Oddly enough, I'm disposed to believe you. You were pretty well knocked out when you discovered the murder, weren't you, Johnson?"

The man gulped, and his face whitened at the mere recollection of that night.

"I wasn't myself, sir," he pleaded.

"Seeing that you were so upset, it seems funny that, at such a moment, you should have thought at all about the loud speaker. What put it into your head?"

"It was hearing it. I'd forgotten all about the wireless set, and when I heard a man speaking in the study, I got the fright of my life. Then I thought it was some one—"

He pulled himself up just in time.

"You thought it was some one you had reason to suspect might be in the flat," finished Fenn gently. "Some one you had left the door on the latch for when you went out!"

"I didn't!" protested Johnson violently. "And there wasn't no one in the flat. Miss Braid'll tell you I went all over it while she was there."

His face was ghastly now.

"Seeing the state you were in, I'll wager it was a pretty cursory inspection. Did you look behind the curtains in the study, for instance?"

Johnson's voice was almost inaudible as he answered.

"No. But there wasn't no one there. The flat was empty."

"But you didn't think so when you heard a man's voice in the study. You expected to find somebody there. Who was it?"

"I knew before I went in that it was the wireless," asserted Johnson sullenly. "Seeing the state I was in, I was ready to believe anything."

"What did you do when you went into the study?"

"I turned the wireless off. It didn't seem right for music and things to be going on just then."

Fenn took a step closer to the man, who recoiled instinctively.

"What made you hide the loud speaker?" he asked sternly.

Johnson's eyes flickered. He tried to answer, failed, moistened his dry lips, and at last found his tongue.

"What I said. It was a sudden temptation," he muttered.

"Had Mr. Webb spoken to you about the woman's voice he had heard when he was waiting outside the door?"

"He may have mentioned it when we were going up the stairs."

"In fact, he did tell you. Did you realize that it was probably the wireless that he heard?"

"Not at first, I didn't. After I'd turned it off, I thought it might be."

"You were puzzled when he told you he'd heard a woman in the flat, weren't you?"

"I didn't understand it. I didn't know of any woman that was likely to be there."

"I put it to you that you did know of a man? If it had been a man's voice, you wouldn't have been surprised?"

"Sir Adam did have gentlemen in to see him sometimes."

"There was no one you expected to find in the flat just then? No one you would be prepared to shield, if you had found him there?"

Johnson shook his head. He seemed beyond speech.

"Then what was your object in hiding the loud speaker, if not to lead people into thinking there was a woman in the flat?"

"It didn't make any difference to me what they thought," muttered Johnson.

"Then why didn't you tell the police that it was the wireless Mr. Webb had heard?"

"It wasn't any affair of mine. I hadn't anything to do with the murder."

"But you admit that you turned off the loud speaker and concealed it, and at the first opportunity got it out of the flat?"

"I've told you I took it. I'm sorry now."

"I fancy you'll have reason to be even more sorry later. You can take him, Parker," said Fenn grimly.

He was feeling anything but grim, however. He had got all he wanted out of Johnson for the present, and as soon as the man heard of Ling's arrest, there would be little difficulty in getting more. He was not of the type to prove a satisfactory accomplice.

Fenn realized that the arrest of Ling might be a very different proposition, and he set about his task warily. He found the man he had set to shadow the newsagent waiting for him in Shorncliffe Street.

"He's in the shop now, sir," he informed him. "He was telephoning when I passed just now."

Fenn quickened his steps. Mrs. Johnson had been nowhere to be seen when he took her husband, but it did not follow that the news of his arrest had not reached her. There was a possibility that she might have telephoned to her father.

He could see the door of the shop, and, as he watched it, a woman crossed the road and turned in.

"That's not the daughter," he said quickly. "She's not tall enough."

"More likely to be a customer," answered the detective. "Archer is at the corner. He'll have sized her up."

"You're sure there's only the one exit?"

"Certain. It's just a lock-up shop, with no window at the back and no basement."

"I'll go in alone, then. You stay with the others and see that no one leaves. If there's trouble you can take a hand."

But when he entered the little shop, Ling was nowhere to be seen. A woman was standing at the counter, with her back to him. As he passed through the shop he saw her half turn in his direction, but he wasted no time on her. A glance at her back had told him that she was not Mrs. Johnson.

The tiny room at the back of the shop was empty. As the detective had said, it contained no window or door. The floor was littered with packing-paper and cartons of cigarettes and stationery. Almost blocking the doorway stood a couple of tall packing-cases, one on the top of the other, the only object in the room large enough for a man to hide behind.

"You there, Ling?" asked Fenn quietly.

There was not a sound from behind the obstruction, nor could he detect any movement. As he had foreseen, Ling was not going to surrender easily.

He called again, but once more there was no response.

With a rapidity and lightness that would have done credit to a boxer, he skirted the packing-cases—and only just saved himself in time!

He had almost tripped over the head of a ladder, protruding from the mouth of an open trap-door.

He hesitated for a moment, then, returning to the door leading into the shop, gave a low whistle.

He was joined immediately by Parker, the man who had been shadowing Ling. He gave a gasp of surprise at the sight of the trap.

"You were wrong about there being no cellar," said Fenn. "I'm going down. Give me time to get to the bottom of the ladder, then follow."

He bent over the trap.

"Ling," he called. "You're wanted."

There was no answer, but this time his quick ears detected a movement below. His man was there, sure enough. He peered down, but the cellar was in darkness, save for a patch of grey light, at the foot of the ladder, that filtered through from the trap above.

"Got a torch?" he whispered.

Parker took one from his pocket and handed it to him.

Fenn did not light it. He knew better than to expose himself as a target to the man below. Holding it ready in his hand, he began to descend the ladder.

He had not gone down four steps when it was jerked suddenly from under him and he found himself on his back, sprawling, half on the ladder and half on the floor of the cellar. He recovered himself in a second, but a boot caught him full in the stomach, winding him, and as he lay gasping he could see the trap above him blocked by a struggling black bulk, heaving its way through the narrow opening. Ling had made the leap for the trap, caught the edge, and managed to get his elbows on to the floor above.

Fenn scrambled painfully to his feet. For the moment he was incapable of any effort, but he knew, from the sounds overhead, that Parker had got his man and was being hard put to it to hold him. Then the sound of running footsteps told him that the men outside the shop were hurrying to the rescue.

He got the ladder back into position and then mounted it.

As he emerged through the trap, the little group of struggling men sorted itself, and Ling was revealed, a savage and unkempt figure, singularly unlike the respectable and competent tradesman who had been so ready to collect witnesses against Stephens after the murder of Sir Adam Braid.

He stood gasping in the grip of two of the detectives, and Fenn, watching the rise and fall of the man's great chest, realized, for the first time, the gorilla-like strength that lay concealed in the stocky, thickset figure. There was something apelike, too, in the naked ferocity of the small, deep-set eyes that gleamed from under the heavy brows.

Fenn surveyed him quietly.

"You're doing yourself no good, you know, by resisting the police," he said, in his even voice. "Will you come quietly, or must we take you?"

Ling neither moved nor spoke.

"Very well, then," went on Fenn, taking a pair of handcuffs from his pocket, "we'll have to put the darbies on you. You've only yourself to blame."

For a second Ling's features were convulsed with fury, then he mastered himself. When he spoke, it was in his usual measured tones, and Fenn found himself marvelling at the man's powers of self-control.

"What's the charge?" he asked.

"You are charged with the murder of Sir Adam Braid on the evening of November the sixth," answered Fenn. "Now, what about it? Are you coming quietly or not?"

He was watching his man closely, but Ling had not flinched at the ominous words.

"I'll come quietly," he said. His voice was expressionless, and his eyes never wavered from Fenn's face. "But I've something to tell you that may make you change your mind."

"If you've got anything to tell me, I'm ready to listen," replied Fenn. "But I warn you that anything you may say may be used against you."

"I never set foot in Sir Adam Braid's flat that night," said Ling earnestly. "I delivered Mr. Adams's paper to him as usual, and then, when I was goin' out, I heard a noise upstairs. There was somethin' had made me suspicious."

He paused.

"Well?" snapped Fenn impatiently.

In spite of himself, he was impressed by the man's manner.

Ling took a step forward, and the two men on either side of him relaxed their grip instinctively.

"I went up that first flight of stairs," Ling went on impressively.

The thing happened in a second. Fenn, who was watching the man's eyes, saw them shift and got his warning. But it was too late to act.

Ling's foot lashed out sideways and caught the shin of one of the men who was holding him. In his agony the detective released his grip of his captive's arm, and before Fenn or the man on Ling's right realized what was happening, Ling's left fist had landed on the point of the remaining detective's jaw.

That respite was all he needed. In a flash he had wrenched himself free and hurled himself through the doorway into the shop. In another second he would have been in the street, had not a totally unexpected obstacle blocked his way.

The woman Fenn had noticed when he entered the shop had remained, forgotten and unheeded, in the background.

Unnoticed by any one, she had approached the back room, and, when Ling made his last wild bid for freedom, was standing blocking the narrow doorway. Ling, unable to stop himself, cannoned full into her in his flight, knocking her backwards and hurtling over her prostrate body. Unable to save himself, he crashed to the ground, catching his head on the edge of the counter as he fell.

Fenn was the first through the doorway. He found Ling, insensible and bleeding from a wound on his forehead, on the ground.

Painfully raising herself to a sitting position in the centre of the shop, was a plump, dishevelled, middle-aged lady.

Fenn bent and snapped the handcuffs on to the wrists of the unconscious man. He was taking no further risks with Ling. Then he went to the assistance of the lady.

The breath had almost been knocked out of her body, but she could still speak, and she gazed up at him with eyes that even pain could not rob of their eager brightness.

"Do you know, I always did feel that there was something not quite nice about that man Ling!" announced Miss Webb, as, helped by the speechless Fenn, she rose with considerable difficulty to her feet.

CHAPTER XXI

GILROY AND JILL BRAID lingered so long over their tea that all the tables in their vicinity were not only deserted, but had been ostentatiously cleared even of their tablecloths, before they realized that they had long ago become the objects of detestation in the eyes of every waiter in the room.

Their departure, in consequence, was both hurried and undignified, and they arrived in the street slightly flustered, but still wrapped in that roseate and protective haze that envelops all men at least once in a lifetime.

Not many days before, Gilroy had asked Jill a question which she had declined to answer until she was definitely cleared of all suspicion, but Gilroy, though the least vain of mortals, had little doubt as to what her verdict would be. Therefore he walked on air. But he would have been an even happier man if he could have been sure that Fenn was carrying out his plans for the arrest of Ling satisfactorily.

It was significant that Gilroy had said nothing to Jill Braid about these recent developments, the truth being that he was uncomfortably aware of the fact that the evidence against the man was of the slightest, and that, in spite of Macnab's evidence, they would have considerable difficulty in bringing the murder home to him. Fenn, he knew, was counting on Johnson's chicken-heartedness. With his father-in-law under arrest, there was every reason to hope that, in the endeavour to save his own skin, Johnson would confess to his own part in the affair; but, unless his evidence was very damning, Fenn might find himself hard put to it to justify his arrest of Ling. And, most disconcerting of all, there remained the fact that, if Ling was in the flats when Sir Adam was killed, Jill Braid was there also, unless they could prove Smith's theory of the actual time of the murder to be correct. In the face of this, Gilroy had judged it better not to raise a hope that might, in the end, prove to be false.

He saw Jill home, and went on to his own flat in a queer mood that hovered between exaltation and depression. In his letter-box he found a note from Fenn that sent his spirits once more soaring.

"We've done the trick," it ran. "Pulled in Ling this evening, and got enough evidence to convince the most hard-boiled jury. Let Jill Braid know, and bring her to 'The Goose' at one o'clock tomorrow."

Ten minutes later Gilroy was hammering at the door of Jill Braid's flat.

"The Goose" is one of the few chop-houses left in London where each table is divided from its neighbour by a wooden partition, and where it is still possible to eat in comparative privacy. Gilroy and Jill Braid found Fenn waiting for them, and one glance at his face was sufficient to convince them that his letter had not erred on the side of optimism. He was literally beaming, and when the colossal lunch he had ordered arrived, he attacked it with the gusto of a man who has done his job and is well satisfied with it.

"I took a chance when I took Ling," he admitted, in answer to Jill's first eager question. "But, by Jove, I was justified. He'd got that cellar of his so well hidden that he'd hardly taken the trouble to conceal the things. There was neither window nor door to the place, and no indication, except the trap-door into the shop, that the place had any basement. He seems to have kept a couple of packing-cases over the trap, and, unless a regular search had been made of the shop, no one would have stumbled on it. It was his certainty that no one would come on it that proved his undoing, for he'd had time and to spare in which to destroy the stuff. There was the old hat-box that you were so interested in, Robert, among other things, with the lining cut to bits. He must have had some idea that Sir Adam had hidden his money there, as, according to Johnson, he was bitterly disappointed in the amount the hat-box contained. Johnson went to pieces altogether when he heard of Ling's arrest and spilled everything, but we haven't got a word out of Ling and I don't suppose we ever shall. He's no fool, and as hard as nails into the bargain, but he doesn't stand a chance. Apart from Johnson's confession, which is enough to hang him, we found a raincoat with the sleeves cut away below the elbow and part of the front missing. He didn't do his work thoroughly enough, though, and there's a bloodstain on the lining that he overlooked. It's typical of the man's coolness that he did actually deliver the rest of his papers that night, probably with the coat carried over his arm. We found the bulk of the notes rolled up in a bit of sacking and stuffed into the straw in an old packing-case. The jewellery was there too. It's a clear case. You can go to sleep with a quiet mind to-night, my dear," he finished, turning to Jill, his eyes alight with affection and sympathy.

She had ceased to eat, and was leaning back against the partition, her face white and tired now that the strain was over, but her only sensation was one of sheer happiness and unutterable relief.

"You'll have to look after that young woman of yours, Robert," remarked Fenn quietly. "She'll need a firm hand for the next week or so."

The faces of both his guests became suffused with a rich scarlet.

"This is as good a time as any to drink your health," he went on, raising his glass as he spoke. "If you don't think beer's good enough, I can't help it."

Then as he looked at them, his expression changed.

"You may not believe it," he said gruffly, "but this is one of the happiest moments of my life. Bless you both. When did you fix it up?"

"Last night," answered Gilroy. "Jill wouldn't listen to me before. What did you expect?"

"It wasn't so much what I expected as what I hoped," retorted Fenn. "It's a comfort to feel that some good's come out of this wicked business."

"What will happen to Johnson?" asked Jill. "He's a disgusting little coward, to say the least of it, but I can't help feeling sorry for him, in a way."

Fenn nodded.

"He never had a chance at Ling's hands. He's an accessory and he'll have to take what's coming to him, but he was merely a tool from the beginning. It was betting that was his undoing. He's cutting a pretty poor figure now, though, and I believe he'd give away his own mother if he thought it would help him. I shouldn't waste too much sympathy on him, if I were you."

"He admits now that he left the door open, I suppose?" said Gilroy.

Fenn nodded.

"He left it unlatched, by arrangement, for Ling. It was Johnson who told Ling about Sir Adam's habit of hiding his money away in the hat-box, and Ling terrified him into letting him into the flat. I believe Johnson's speaking the truth when he says that he did his best to dissuade Ling. In the end he refused to take any hand in the affair, beyond leaving the door open, and went off to 'The Nag's Head,' frightened out of his wits that Ling would bungle it and his share in it come out. That Ling would use violence never seems to have occurred to him, and it's no wonder he went to pieces when he discovered what had happened. His life hasn't been worth living since, and I believe it's almost a relief to him now that the whole thing's come out. Ling chose a rotten accomplice!"

"I suppose he knows what happened while he was away?"

"Ling told him everything afterwards. He had to. Johnson knew too much already. They were counting, of course, on Sir Adam's absorption in the wireless, and it was sheer bad luck for them that he should have elected to take off the earphones and turn on the loud speaker just after Ling entered the flat. If he had kept the earphones on he would probably never have heard Ling, and the tragedy would never have happened."

He glanced at Jill.

"We needn't go into what occurred," he said briefly. "It's enough that Sir Adam heard a noise in the bedroom and went in to investigate, and Ling, presumably, lost his head. He was in the flat when Webb rang the bell, and got away immediately after Webb went downstairs."

"Leaving the wireless still on," put in Gilroy.

"Yes. It was the wireless that Webb and Stephens and Jill heard, and Smith, as it now turns out, was right when he insisted that his wife had established the time of the murder. Ling handed over part of the money he took to Johnson, and it was he, of course, who sent Ike Sanders to Brighton with the letter warning Johnson not to circulate any more of the notes. If it hadn't been for that slip of mine, when I told Ling to his face that I was tracing the numbers, Sanders would be alive to-day."

"Do you suppose that Ling killed Sanders?" asked Gilroy.

Fenn shook his head.

"I think Mrs. Sanders is right and that Ling put Eddie Goldstein on the job. We haven't been able to trace the connection, but Ling had no doubt run into Goldstein at some period of his career. His business would bring him in touch with gentlemen of Goldstein's persuasion, though the small bookies and the race gangs don't usually run in double harness. He was a shrewd customer, Ling, and he may have had some hold over Goldstein. Anyway, he was just the man for his purpose, and he undoubtedly used him again to get Macnab out of the way."

"Does Johnson know anything about that business?"

"He says that Ling told him that Macnab spoke to him outside Romney Chambers and that he nearly chucked the whole thing in consequence. Then he remembered that Macnab, when he was in the shop, had told him he was just sailing for America, and he decided to risk it. He was right there, for if he had simply done what he was out to do and robbed the flat, it's unlikely that the affair would ever have come to Macnab's ears. It was sheer bad luck for him that Macnab was Stephens' witness."

"How on earth did he know that Macnab had been recalled?" asked Gilroy. "It was not in the papers."

Fenn turned to him with a rueful smile.

"That's where I made my second howler," he admitted. "My dear chap, I told him myself when I answered the telephone message from the Yard in his shop, under his very nose. You were there! He was a quick worker, I'll say that for him. He must have got on to Goldstein at once, and I've no doubt that that was the job Goldstein offered to Sanders, and that Sanders, thanks to his wife, refused. I've a strong suspicion that Goldstein, for once, was driven to do his own dirty work, and I'm going to get him for the assault on Macnab, though it's an open question whether we ever manage to bring the murder of Sanders home to him."

"There's been no news of him, I suppose?"

"None. He's covered his tracks well this time, but he's bound to come into the open sooner or later, and he hasn't got a dog's chance when he does." He dismissed Goldstein from his mind and beamed on Jill.

"That's that," he concluded. "Now I'm going to enjoy my good food, and I advise you to put the whole thing out of your head for the present. I got your grandfather's solicitor on the telephone this morning, by the way, and put him wise to what has happened. He wants to see you, and, if I were you, I'd trot round and see what it feels like to have a comfortable balance at the bank. Meanwhile, I'm going to commandeer your young man for the afternoon, if he's nothing better to do."

"After I've seen Jill to Lincoln's Inn, I'm at your service," said Gilroy, pink, but determined.

Fenn grinned.

"I was young once," he reminded him. "Meet me at three, outside Ling's shop. I want to go over the ground again there, and there's no reason why you shouldn't make yourself useful."

"Why not ask Miss Webb to join the party?" suggested Gilroy, with a twinkle in his eye.

"I suppose the whole of Chelsea knows that she was in at the death by now," groaned Fenn. "Good lord, what a woman!"

"I don't know how many other people she may have told," answered Gilroy, with a chuckle, "but, when one meets a perfectly respectable spinster lady on the stairs with a really beautiful black eye, it's difficult to contain one's curiosity. I must say she showed none of the reticence that is generally connected with that particular form of injury!"

Gilroy kept his appointment with Fenn punctually, and together they entered the shop and climbed down the ladder into the cellar.

"You may as well take a glance at Ling's little retreat," said Fenn, "though our real objective is the house where he lodged. I want to have a good look through his papers and see whether, by any chance, he rented a third room somewhere. There's something here that wants explaining, and I've got a suspicion that I know what it means."

He indicated a package, done up in newspaper, that lay on the top of one of the packing-cases. The string was already unfastened, and Gilroy unfolded the paper and looked inside.

A goodly pile of sandwiches and a couple of bottles of beer met his astonished gaze.

"Seems to have been a far-seeing sort of beggar," he remarked. "But these wouldn't have lasted him long, if he was contemplating lying low down here."

"He wasn't," said Fenn decisively. "This place was no good to him, for the simple reason that he couldn't mask the trapdoor once he was inside. No, I've got my own theory as to the destination of that parcel, and I'm counting on the fact that the person for whom it was intended is getting a bit hungry by now."

Gilroy's eyes met his.

"Goldstein?" he queried.

"Goldstein it is, unless I'm very much mistaken, and the question is, where was Ling harbouring him? That's why I think he may have another room somewhere. It's not unusual for these people to have an extra shed or a lumber room for their clients to bring the betting slips to. If the house he lodged in had a backyard with an old shed in it, I'd be willing to bet on that, but it hasn't. He must have had a place outside somewhere."

They went round to Ling's lodgings, and Fenn questioned his landlady once more, but it was soon evident that she knew very little of her lodger's affairs. Then they spent an unprofitable hour going through a pile of old bills and invoices connected with the man's legitimate business. Beyond these, they could find nothing.

At last Fenn stood up and stretched himself.

"Nothing doing," he said, with a sigh. "We shall have to wait till our man comes into the open, and if he was dependent on Ling for food, we shan't wait long. A nasty, dusty job this, and if you ask me to your flat for a wash and a cup of tea, I shan't say no. Or have you got another engagement?" he added, with a wicked gleam in his eye.

But Gilroy was proof by now against his insinuations.

"My only engagement is going shopping after she has done with her lawyer," he said imperturbably. "So my time is my own."

They strolled back to Romney Chambers. As they went in Gilroy nearly fell over a man who was on his knees just inside the half-closed front door.

"Hallo, Adams!" he exclaimed. "What are you up to?"

The porter looked up from the pail of water over which he was bending.

"Looks as if some one or other had been dossin' behind this door and had been a bit careless with 'is supper," he said, with a grin. "I've always said as it ought to be locked at night, but the tenants won't be bothered with the extra key. If I hadn't happened to push to the door, I should never 'ave seen this."

He pointed to the pool of liquid he had been about to wipe up.

"Some one's been wastin' good stuff!" he commented.

Gilroy bent over it, and as he did so, was aware of a familiar aroma.

He straightened himself, and his eyes met Fenn's.

"Good lord, it's beer!" he exclaimed.

CHAPTER XXII

FENN TURNED to the porter.

"Have you ever found anything before, behind this door?" he asked sharply.

Adams shook his head.

"Never," he said. "And what any one wanted to stand a bottle of beer there for is more than I can see."

"Supposing some one did put, say, a parcel there, would you be likely to see it?"

Adams hesitated.

"I should see it when I was scrubbing out the hall; but, the rest of the week, the door stands open, night and day, and it's almost flush with the wall. If there was something there I might miss it for a day or two."

Fenn guessed that the man was not in the habit of sweeping out the hall as often as he might, and did not care to admit it. He pursued his inquiries tactfully.

"Which is your day for scrubbing the hall?" he asked.

"Monday. It's been done once a week regular ever since I've been 'ere."

"Four days ago," said Fenn thoughtfully. "You stick to Monday, I suppose?"

Adams nodded.

"Monday's always been my day, and Monday I do it," he answered emphatically.

"Have you looked behind that door since Monday last?"

"Not to my knowledge," answered the man, with a note of defiance in his voice. "There's very little dust blows in here, and there's never been any complaints about the hall, so far as I knows."

"I'm not blaming you," said Fenn. "What I'm trying to get at is whether any one, knowing you did the hall on a certain day, would know also that a parcel could be left here for a day or two with impunity."

"I suppose it might," admitted Adams grudgingly.

He threw his rag into the pail and got on to his feet.

"I suppose neither of you gentlemen knows who's got the key to Sir Adam's boxroom?" he asked, as he turned to go. "Would it be the old gentleman's lawyer?"

Fenn stared at him.

"What's this about a boxroom?" he asked.

Gilroy explained.

"There's a row of small boxrooms up on the roof which are let out to the tenants at a small rental. You get to them through a door at the top of the main staircase. They're numbered, and each tenant has the key to his own room."

"How many keys did Sir Adam have?" asked Fenn of the porter.

"He'd have one, unless he had another made," answered Adams. "It used to hang on a hook in the kitchen, with the key of the coal cellar. I've seen it many a time when I've been up to see about washers for the taps and that."

"What made you ask about it?" demanded Fenn.

A slow grin crept over Adams's face.

"There's an idea goin' round that there's a ghost or somethin' in Sir Adam's boxroom," he answered. "One of the tenants was up in the room next door to it a couple of days ago and heard somethin'. The truth is, they're all a bit jumpy after what's happened. Still, I thought it wouldn't do no harm to have a look."

Fenn smiled.

"I'll see about it, as I'm here," he said carelessly. "Don't you worry. It's probably only a rat or something of that sort."

Adams's grin widened.

"According to what I can make out, it's a sneeze that was heard," he volunteered. "And, I must say, I've never heard tell of a rat sneezin'!"

The three men laughed.

"Some one's got plenty of imagination," was all Fenn said, as he made his way up the stairs.

"It would be the simplest thing in the world for any one hiding in the boxroom to come down at night and fetch food from behind the front door," said Gilroy, as soon as they were out of range of the porter's ears. "And Ling used to come into the building every evening with Adams's paper. He could drop his parcel behind the door then."

"If there's anything in that theory, it's pretty evident where Sir Adam's key is," answered Fenn. "In the lock of the box-room door, inside! However, we'll soon make sure of that."

He paused outside Sir Adam's flat, and, taking a key from his pocket, let himself in.

The key of the cellar was hanging, as Adams had said, on a hook on the kitchen dresser, but the box-room key was no-where to be seen.

"I'm not tackling Goldstein single-handed, I don't mind telling you," said Fenn thoughtfully. "But I don't want to take any risks of his getting the wind up in the meanwhile. Have you got a room up there?"

"Yes. And it's at the end of the row. I've got to pass Sir Adam's to get to it. Do you want me to have a look?"

Fenn hesitated.

"Any windows to these boxrooms?" he asked.

"There's none to mine, but I'm not quite sure about the others. I should think not. They're so small, little more than sheds, that you get enough light from the door when it's open."

"What about ventilation?"

Gilroy laughed.

"The door's so rotten that, as far as mine's concerned, I should think there's more draught than ventilation!"

"Plenty of slits a man might put his eye to, eh?"

"Very likely. I've never tried."

"Then we'd better not risk anything. You go up. Take your key with you, and, if you can, get through the door at the top of the stairs without making a noise. You may manage to see something before you have to declare yourself. After that, make the dickens of a row and go openly to your own box-room. Fetch something out, and, if possible, try to see if there's a key in the lock of Sir Adam's room as you go by. That's all we can do for the moment. But don't do anything to rouse his suspicions."

Gilroy nodded and ran upstairs.

Fenn followed him more slowly and waited outside the door of his flat till he heard the sound of footsteps returning.

One look at Gilroy's face was enough.

"There's some one there," he whispered, as he let Fenn into his flat. "Come inside. I've got a feeling that the fellow followed me."

He stood listening for a moment just inside the front door, but there was no sound from above. Then he led the way into the sitting-room.

"My luck was in," he said. "The door at the top of the stairs was open when I got there, and as it happens I'm wearing rubber-soled shoes. I'd hardly got my head round the corner when I saw that the door of the third boxroom was open— wide open. I crept back down the stairs and then turned and went up again, whistling and making as much racket as I could. I went slowly, so as to give the fellow time to shut his door. And he had, too, by the time I got up there. I went straight to my room and got out an old suitcase, and, on my way back, I had a squint at the door I'd seen open. It was Sir Adam's right enough, and it was not only shut, but locked. I couldn't see if there was a key inside or not, but as it wasn't outside, and as somebody had locked that door within the last few minutes, we can take it for granted that it was there."

Fenn made for the door.

"That's good enough for me," he said. "I'll be back in ten minutes with a couple of men from the station here."

He was as good as his word, and Gilroy found his heart beating a little faster as he followed the three men up the stairs to the roof.

Fenn spoke over his shoulder.

"The doors open outwards, I suppose?" he said.

Gilroy nodded.

"Stand at the top of the stairs, here," went on Fenn, "and head him off if he breaks in this direction."

Gilroy, from his post by the door, watched one of the detectives take a short jemmy from his pocket. He and Fenn stationed themselves on each side of the boxroom door, while the third man stood in readiness behind Fenn.

Then the man with the jemmy inserted it in the crack of the flimsy door, just below the lock. There was a sound of splintering wood as the door burst open, and Gilroy instinctively braced himself for action.

But there was complete silence from within the little room.

Fenn, keeping well within the cover of the wall, called to the occupant to come out, and it was as well he had not exposed himself, for the last word had hardly left his lips when there was an explosion that sounded terrific in the confined space of the little room, and a bullet sang past his head.

"Resisting the police isn't going to make things easier for you," he said, his voice, despite its ominous note of authority, steady and unperturbed.

The only answer was a second shot from within, but the man was wasting his ammunition. From where he stood he could not hope to reach either of the detectives, and he must have realized the impossibility of covering them both, should he attempt to come out.

"Better come quietly," said Fenn mildly. "We can afford to wait."

Gilroy was conscious of the sound of hurrying footsteps on the stairs, and turned to see Adams's agitated face peering over his shoulder.

"Gawd, then there was some one up there!" he breathed incredulously.

A third shot rang out, and he disappeared with the abruptness of a rabbit into its hole.

Then, in a second, the man was out.

As he dashed through the door he fired point-blank at Fenn, at the same time thrusting his fist into the face of the other detective. He got home on the detective's mouth, and Fenn, who had ducked as his assailant fired, grabbed at him, lost his balance, and let the man get past him. The third detective seized his wrist and the revolver clattered to the ground. Then Fenn closed with him.

Gilroy ran forward, but by the time he reached the group of struggling men the fight was over, and Fenn had his prisoner securely handcuffed.

He was not a beautiful object as he stood glaring at his captors. Unshaven, with the grime of several days on his sallow face, his mean mouth spluttering curses, and his dark eyes, the one almost unfailing beauty of the man, ablaze with venom, he looked what he was, a brute, whose only tools were violence and intimidation.

He said nothing when Fenn charged him, but as they were leading him away he glanced from his manacled hands to the detective.

"So Ling's done the dirty on me at last!"

He literally spat out the words.

"You can tell him from me to mind himself when he comes out!" he finished.

"He won't come out," was Fenn's answer, and he saw the man shrink at the words.

Fenn watched him through the door and down the stairs. Then he turned to Gilroy.

"There's the end of the Braid case," he said, with a note of deep satisfaction in his voice. "And as neat a clean-up as I could wish."

"I take my hat off to Ling," was Gilroy's comment. "To have hidden him here, of all places!"

"And yet, like most strokes of genius, the thing was simplicity itself," Fenn reminded him. "Johnson had the key of the boxroom, and, until Sir Adam's affairs were settled up, it was unlikely that anybody would go there. And no one would have gone there if Adams, here, hadn't happened to be cleaning up that beer as we came in, and if Goldstein hadn't chosen to sneeze at the wrong moment."

A sudden suspicion assailed him.

"Who was the tenant who spotted the fact that there was some one in the boxroom?" he demanded, turning to Adams.

But even before the porter spoke both Fenn and Gilroy knew instinctively what the answer would be.

"Miss Webb, sir. She happened to be up there getting something out of a trunk."

In silence more expressive than words, Fenn left him and made his way down the stairs.

When he reached the hall he quickened his steps, but as he passed the ground-floor flat he was aware that the door was open, and that Miss Webb, a quivering interrogation mark, was standing on the threshold.

THE END

Made in the USA
Middletown, DE
17 February 2021